THE
MALLEVILLE
CONSPIRACY

BY H.L. ROETHLE

TypeWrite Press

Table Of Contents

Dedicated to my dear mum, without whom this wouldn't be possible.

Chapter One

THE ELECTRONIC DISPLAY BOARD in the London City Airport flashed from red to green, indicating the arrival of the eleven-forty-five from Wales. A tall, spindly man disengaged himself from the people clustered around the board, and began walking down the corridor towards the boarding platform. Dressed as a security guard, no one took any particular notice of him. About five paces from the platform door, he stopped and casually adjusted his belt. His finger pressed a tiny button on what looked like a mobile phone attached to it, causing a red light to blink and flash. An answering light came from one of the windows of the newly-landed airplane. Both lights went out instantly.

"Vansant, is everything set according to plan?" The small hearing device hidden in his right ear transmitted the words with perfect clarity.

"Yes," he muttered.

"Good. Now, remember – get the briefcases to the luggage terminal in a leisurely fashion, and whatever you do, don't act dodgy."

"Yes, sir."

"Only fifteen minutes or so, now. Got it?"

"Yes, sir." Opening the door, Vansant headed out onto the tarmac. The cold night air enveloped him, causing him to shiver involuntarily.

"Hiyah, Vansant!" called an airport worker. He was waiting to get inside the plane to start unloading all the luggage. "I see you're ready for *The* Cargo." He wagged his eyebrows significantly. The Cargo, as it was referred to, consisted of two large briefcases, loaded with cash and precious gems owned by a rich businessman on his way to a gem convention. "I'll get it out to you in *un momento!*"

"Alright, I'll be waiting." Vansant shifted nervously from one foot to the other, cursed himself for looking stupid, and tried to act confident as he followed the worker towards the plane.

Vansant had been working at the airport for over a month now, and was well-known to many of the employees, despite the size of the airport. With a faked set of credentials, he had passed as a trusted security guard, capable of handling precious cargo. Nobody suspected him, and as far as he could see, Icabod's plan was working perfectly.

~

A flurry of activity swept through the plane which moments before had been filled with the silence of sleep. Though it hadn't been a long flight, the lateness of it had caused most people to nod off. As the passengers began filing out, three men got up from their seats and made quick eye contact with each other. They had seated themselves several rows apart to ensure no one knew they were companions.

Standing near the cockpit, Icabod muttered, "Vansant's getting the bags." The others heard him through their ear pieces. He was the one who had spoken to Vansant only seconds earlier.

"Oh, good," whispered Otto in the far back, wiping his hair off his greasy forehead with his fat, stubby fingers.

"And Quentin's ready too," continued Icabod. His curly black hair and powerful physic were in utter contrast to Otto. One glance of his piercing black eyes was enough to intimidate anybody.

"*Ex-ce-*len-*té!*" Alvar almost sang with excitement.

"Shut up!" hissed Icabod, who was clearly the leader. The small, muscular Spaniard dropped his head in submission.

Icabod mentally ran over the finer points of his plan. Or rather, his brother's plan. Once Vansant had The Cargo, all Icabod had to do was head for the luggage terminal, where he would steal it, jump into a waiting car, and get away as rich as Croesus. Of course, the stealing part had to look convincing in order to clear Vansant. Otherwise, he could never use Vansant as an inside man again – he'd have a record, and would very possibly end up in jail. The charade had to be pulled off perfectly; but Icabod was up to the challenge.

This heist was so very important. Though an isolated event, it would provide funding for the master plan, one that was six years in the making. He grinned maliciously to himself. There wasn't a person in Britain, besides his cronies, who had any inkling about what was going to happen.

~

Near the back of the plane, eighteen-year-old Flynn yawned, stretched, grabbed a small carry-on, and tried to smooth out some of the wrinkles in his much-loved burgundy Cambridge sweatshirt as he slipped into the line of exiting passengers. Trying his best to comb his jet-black hair with his fingers, he noticed Icabod's angry expression and the way Alvar's head dropped in response.

Although his brain was still a bit befuddled from sleep, he found this exchange rather unusual. The two were ten feet apart, with no means to communicate with each other, yet their body language indicated otherwise. He narrowed his green eyes and studied the two, making a mental note to keep his eye on them. He was so engrossed in observing the men, he noticed little else around him.

"Ye a-lookin' fer soom'un, laddie?" asked an old Scottish woman as he accidentally bumped into her.

"N-no, not really," he stammered. "I'm awfully sorry I nearly ran you over."

"Donnae mention it, laddie. Whe'e ae ye froom?"

"Wales." Flynn smothered another yawn.

"That's nice! I'm a-goin' tae live wi' m'dear lassie in Da'tfoord." The old woman continued chatting pleasantly in her thick accent. Flynn nodded absently, responding occasionally with one-syllable sentences, being too much absorbed in attempting to satisfy his curiosity. He was trying to make sense of what he had just seen, and finally came to the conclusion that the two men had hidden communication devices. But why the secrecy? He rose up on tip-toes and craned his neck, trying to get a better look at the men through the shifting mass of passengers.

~

Otto was directly behind Flynn, and watched him curiously. After a moment or two, he whispered, "Ic!" over their communication system.

"What?" Icabod snapped through stiff lips.

"The kid with the black hair talking to that old woman is acting strange. He's in front of me. I think he was watching you and Alvar."

Icabod's black eyes narrowed. He looked around suddenly as though his name had been called, managed to catch sight of the boy's face, shrugged his shoulders, and kept walking as though nothing had happened. "Keep an eye on him, Otto," he hissed. "If he gets in the way, we'll deal with it, but don't get distracted. And I don't need a colorful commentary on every odd passenger, clear?"

"Yeah." Otto tried to concentrate on nothing but Flynn, but his stomach growled, and his thoughts started drifting towards pizza and hamburgers.

Through the airplane windows, the three men watched as Vansant took possession of two small briefcases and returned to the building. The men made their way into the airport as quickly as they could without arousing suspicion...

~

Saying goodbye to the old woman, Flynn tailed the men at a distance, his curiosity heightened when they began to walk close together. Back on the airplane, his only thought had been of meeting up with his Uncle Ian and Aunt Leslie who he hadn't seen since Christmas. As close as he and his uncle were, Flynn hadn't been to his flat in over two years, due simply to life circumstances. But now, all thoughts of family were driven from his mind. By nature, he was very observant, and he had a feeling that, not only were the men in league with one another, they were up to no good…

~

Vansant headed for the luggage terminal near the exit doors. His brow was bathed in sweat as he mentally braced himself for what was coming…

~

A nervous-looking young man with close-cropped brown hair and eyes similar in color watched as the belt of the carousel in the luggage terminal began moving. After watching the luggage pass by for a few minutes, he darted forward, hastily grabbing three bags and two small suitcases. He then headed for the exit doors as fast as he could – which wasn't really fast at all considering the amount of luggage he was handling…

~

Flynn's Uncle Ian Tazer, along with his wife, Leslie, and friend, Alexander Pierson, started down the escalator into the terminal. They were debating the best route home, Alex being completely convinced that his way was shorter and faster. Ian was in disagreement, and Leslie remained neutral as she always did when the two had such "rows." Her mind wandered a little, and she wondered vaguely if she had prepared enough food for Flynn. He had always had a voracious appetite, and she knew it would be heightened by his travels. She smiled at the thought of seeing him once more, and let her eyes rove over the crowd in the hopes of spotting him first…

~

As he made his way through the airport, Icabod couldn't shake the feeling that he was being followed. He didn't want to own that maybe Otto had been right about something for once, but the only person who remained consistently in his peripheral vision was the kid from the back of the plane.

Realizing that the boy wasn't going away any time soon, Icabod frowned deeply and radioed Alvar, who had split off with Otto a few moments before. "Alvar, do you see that black-haired kid in the old Cambridge sweatshirt comin' down that escalator? He's too snoopy – get rid of him!"

"Sí, boss," murmured the Spaniard. Slipping behind a wall next to the luggage terminal, he leaned nonchalantly against it, as though waiting for someone…

~

Vansant and Flynn entered the terminal at the exact same time, and Icabod headed straight for Vansant. With one swift blow, he knocked him out cold, snatched up the two briefcases, and sprinted towards the exit doors.

"Hey! You there! Stop!" shouted Flynn as he took off after Icabod.

Alvar stuck his foot out, and Flynn tripped over it. Grabbing a gun from a hidden nook in the wall, Alvar fired recklessly at Flynn, gave him a vicious kick to the head, and dashed for the exit. Otto ran after him. They leapt into a waiting SUV, its doors wide open, as security guards streamed after them. The thieves slammed the car doors, the driver hit the accelerator, and they raced out of the airport, vanishing into the night.

~

The airport was in an uproar: people screaming, yelling, and running around haphazardly, security guards swarming every inch of space, and alarms blaring like crazy. At the sound of the gunshot, the conversation between Ian and Alex was abruptly cut off.

Leslie clutched Ian's arm, fear welling up inside of her. A hundred questions whirled through her brain: was that really a gunshot? Where had it come from? Why was there only one shot? Who was hurt? And most importantly...where was Flynn?

"Ian, what's going on?" she cried.

"I'm not sure," he said as he quickly scanned the crowd, taking note of everything. He saw a man lying flat on his back in the middle of the room and security guards racing after several men dressed in black who were running for the exists. "It looks to me like a robbery," he said aloud. He tried to find the gunman, but to no avail. Neither the guards nor the men in black had visible weapons. Ruling out a terrorist attack, he concluded the shot had been a single incident. Why, he couldn't say, but it didn't appear as though anyone else was in danger of getting shot. He was just about to reassure his wife when he noticed a figure dressed in a burgundy sweatshirt sprawled on the floor on the opposite side of the terminal. The word, "Flynn!" escaped under his breath, and his eyes widened. The sweatshirt had been his own, and he had worn it everywhere for as long as he could remember. His nephew had adored it when he was little, and thus Ian had gifted it to him a few years ago.

Alex tapped him on the shoulder, rousing him out of his reverie. "Hey, what's with the face? You look like a ghost."

"Flynn? Did you see him? Where is he?" Panic seeped into Leslie's tone. She tightened her grip on his arm. "Ian, talk to me."

By now, they had reached the bottom of the escalator. "Follow me." Ian grabbed her hand and took off running in the direction of his nephew, skidding down on his knees next to him.

Leslie gasped in horror. "No, oh no," she moaned.

Ian noticed the blood was isolated to Flynn's right arm, and the sweatshirt was ripped across the top of the sleeve, indicating the bullet had only grazed him. Relief washed over him. "Les, don't panic. He'll be fine. It only grazed his arm. Give me your scarf." Leslie instantly unwound it from around her neck and handed it to him. He carefully began to wrap it around Flynn's arm to stop the bleeding.

"He's not bleeding out, is he?" asked Alex.

Noticing the terrified look on Leslie's face Ian quickly said, "No, he's not." He glared at Alex, his face clearly indicating that such a comment was not helping. "Ring Doc Liam and see how fast he can get over here. I don't want him taken off by some random paramedics."

Alex nodded and unpocketed his mobile phone. "Sure." He dialed the number and tapped his foot as he waited for their doctor friend to pick up. "Hullo, Liam? Yeah, this is rather an emergency. ...No, nothing life-threatening. Ian's nephew had a bullet whiz across his arm. Looks like he was knocked out too. ...Yeah, he used Leslie's scarf. ...Really? ...Great!" Alex gave him directions on where they were in the airport and then hung up. "Said he was on his way home from the hospital, and he'd be here in about fifteen minutes."

Leslie barely heard what he said, so focused was she on Flynn. "Oh, I hope he'll be alright!" Her eyes were wide with anxiety as she brushed the boy's hair off his face and softly murmured a prayer.

"He will be, m'love. Don't you worry." Ian squeezed her hand reassuringly.

Flynn slowly opened his eyes and looked about in a bit of a daze, struggling to remember what had happened. His arm hurt, his head throbbed, but he didn't know why. The last thing he remembered was running after the man who'd stolen the black briefcases. That's when he noticed Ian. "Uncle? Am I glad to see you," and he tried to sit up.

"Hey, take it easy. Just lie still. You hit your head pretty hard." As Ian spoke, Leslie took off her sweater, rolled it up, and placed it under Flynn's head.

"Well, this certainly is a fine way to greet us," she said, smiling at him. "However, I could've gone without all the theatrics."

"That makes two of us," Flynn replied. "Only...I don't really remember what happened."

"I didn't see everything, but it appears you were caught in the middle of a robbery," Ian explained.

"My arm," Flynn started.

"A bullet grazed it. It's nothing serious," Ian quickly said. "I rang my friend, Doc Liam, and he'll be here in a few minutes. He'll have you right as rain, and then we'll head for home."

He was interrupted as five security guards forced their way through the curious crowd that had gathered. Ian glanced up at them, mildly surprised that it had taken them this long. Once they had ascertained that Flynn was all right, three of them began dispersing the people, while the remaining two began to question Ian. Ian explained that Flynn was his nephew whom he was picking up at the airport. The guards began to pester him as to whether Flynn was involved with the robbery in any way, and implied that they would need to take him into their custody for further questioning. Ian simply took out his wallet and showed the guards his badge.

"Scotland Yard," he said. "I appreciate your service, but as far as Flynn is concerned, I'll be taking it from here. This one is personal." They were obviously disappointed to be taken off this part of the case, but understood the circumstances.

As the guards were leaving, Alex straightened up and shaded his eyes. "Is that Liam? Yeah, it is." He answered his own question and waved his arms to get the doctor's attention.

Liam spotted him and quickly made his way through the crowd. He knelt down next to Ian, opened his medical bag, and removed his stethoscope. As he did, he said, "Hey Flynn, I'm Doc Liam, a friend of your uncle's. I'm just going to take a look see, and then fix you up so your uncle can take you home, okay?" After examining Flynn and bandaging his arm he told Ian, "He looks fine to me. I don't see any signs of a concussion, but I'll check on him tomorrow. Just let him sleep as long as he wants and give me a bell when he's up."

"Thanks, Liam." Ian shook his hand and smiled gratefully.

"Don't mention it. I'll see you tomorrow."

As Liam took his leave, Ian looked down at his nephew and said, "Let's see if you can stand, shall we?" He carefully helped Flynn to his feet. Flynn winced and held onto his uncle's arm. "Are you alright?"

"Yeah, just a little dizzy, and my head still hurts. But I can walk, really." He tried to let go, but Ian held his arm fast.

"Lean on me. Alex, would you bring the car around to this entrance?" Ian fished his keys out of his pocket and tossed them to his friend.

"Sure thing!" Alex dashed off.

"I'll get the rest of your luggage, dear." Leslie handed his carry-on to Ian. "What else did you have?"

"Just a small green suitcase. You know, the one I've always had. Nothing else." Flynn looked ruefully at his arm as his uncle led him away. "I can't believe I've ruined your sweatshirt." He stared at the jagged tear in the burgundy fabric.

"It wasn't your fault, my dear nephew. And don't you worry; your aunt is very handy with a needle and thread. She'll have it looking like new when you get up tomorrow."

"She must really be good with that needle. This thing has never looked new," Flynn retorted.

Ian laughed. "I see you haven't lost your sense of humor! And by the way, it's not my sweatshirt anymore, but yours."

"Will she be able to get the blood out?" Flynn asked anxiously.

"Of course. Leslie can get bloodstains out of just about anything." Ian settled him on a bench just outside the exit doors to wait for Alex. Leslie joined them a few minutes later.

"Are you hungry?" she asked Flynn.

"No, not really. I'm just knackered." Closing his eyes, he leaned his head back until it rested against the cold cement of the wall.

"The food won't go to waste, love, I can promise you," Ian said as she sat on Flynn's other side. "Alex will make sure of that, don't you worry."

Leslie smiled. "You have a point there."

Alex pulled up in Ian's Mazda CX-9 just as Flynn was dozing off. Ian helped his nephew into the back seat, and as they drove off, Flynn fell asleep almost instantly. Once they arrived at his uncle's house, Ian helped him up two flights of stairs to his room.

A thought began forming in the back of his mind. Stairs? Was he really going up stairs? His uncle didn't have any stairs. At least, not inside the flat itself. So where were they? He gave up the thought, however, as they reached his room. His headache was worse, he could barely keep himself awake, and his brain refused to work. Leslie gave him some Tylenol, took his sweatshirt, and put him to bed. Flynn managed to mumble goodnight before slipping off into the land of dreams.

~~

Chapter Two

THE SUN ROSE IN A VAST ARRAY of reds, pinks, yellows, and oranges as it cast its rays on a large, three story, old Victorian-style home in the heart of London. The sun tried to enter every window of the house that it could, but there was still one room whose curtains stopped its entry. For hours, the sun was denied entrance, until it was high in the sky.

Flynn groggily opened his eyes. The first thing he noticed was that his headache was gone, and the second, that he was in a room he had never seen before. He tried to sit up to examine his surroundings when a sharp pain shot up his right arm. As he glanced down at it, the events from the previous night came flooding back. The strange men, the robbery, the gunshot, his aunt and uncle… He vaguely remembered arriving at their flat except…he'd never seen this room in his life.

It was a cozy sort of room. A large rug lay in the center on top of the hardwood floor. To his right was a nightstand and wardrobe, and across from him was a beautifully carved vanity. The wall to his left had a window seat, made up with cushions and pillows. It was flanked by a bookshelf on the left and a tiny desk on the right. It lacked decorations to be sure, but that was something easily fixed. Throwing the blankets off, he walked over to the window and opened the curtains, finally allowing the golden sunlight to enter in. He scrunched his eyes up at the sudden light.

Gazing out at the street below, his mouth fell open. All the houses on the street were several stories high, with meticulous hedges and spotlessly clean cars in the driveways. He could see a small flower garden at the front of the house he was in, and knew in an instant that his aunt had planted it. Leslie loved azaleas and planted as many different colors as she could find.

Flynn was exceedingly puzzled. He was quite used to his uncle's comfortable flat out near Windsor, and never had he heard him express a desire to move. A gentle tap on his door interrupted his thoughts, and he called out, "Yeah?"

"It's me, may I come in?" his uncle called out.

"Of course!" Flynn turned from the window to greet him.

Ian smiled and gave him a quick hug. "Well, it's good to see you up and about! Did you sleep well?"

"Very. I didn't wake up until a few minutes ago. How late did I sleep? Or rather, what time is it?" Flynn looked around for a clock.

"Half-past eleven, my dear chap. You had a pretty rough night, so we let you sleep as long as you wanted. How are you feeling?"

"Much better. My head doesn't hurt, but my arm's a little sore."

"Do you remember what happened last night?" Ian asked, eyeing him.

"Yes, I do. I was —oh! My sweatshirt, it's not ruined, is it?" He cut himself off and gave Ian an anxious look.

Ian shook his head with a smile. "No, it's not. Your Aunt Leslie cleaned the bloodstains out and sewed it up this morning. The stitch marks aren't too obvious on the arm, and now you have quite a story to go along with them. I want to hear all about it, but first you should get something to eat. Are you hungry?"

"Yes, but," Flynn hesitated.

"What is it?"

"Where am I? I mean," he added in a rush, "it looks like Aunt Leslie's flower garden down there, and you brought me here, and I'm guessing this is my room but...whatever happened to your flat?"

"Yes, this is your room; we sold the flat a while ago," Ian began.

"But, why? And when? And why didn't you tell me?"

Ian held up his hand. "When you go down those stairs, you will probably see a lot of things that will confuse you. However, it's best if I explain it all at once instead of piecemeal. So, hold your questions until later."

"Oh dear. You make it sound like I'm going to bombard you or something," Flynn said apprehensively.

Ian laughed. "I'll have Leslie make you a cup of tea. Anything specific you want to eat?"

"Can't I just go downstairs with you?"

"No, I'd rather you stay here and rest until Liam arrives. Once he checks you out, then you're quite free to roam the house as you please. Now, what do you want?"

"A full English breakfast sounds great, but that's probably a bit much to make," Flynn said sheepishly. "So...how about an omelet?"

"Flavor of tea?"

"Earl Grey, please." Flynn suddenly laughed. "I feel like I'm ordering room service!"

"I'll be right back. Just make yourself comfortable. Oh, and the bathroom is down the hall. You'll find a towel and your personal items on the counter. Leslie laid them out for you this morning." Ian turned and left.

Seating himself at the window seat, Flynn leaned back and idly watched the birds and random passerbys. The previous night had been a whirlwind, and he hadn't had time to think about it much. He wondered how long it would be before he could explore his uncle's new house and get answers to his fast-multiplying questions.

~

By early afternoon, Flynn felt like a genuine human being. Doc Liam had pronounced him okay, (save for his arm, of course,) he'd had a hot cup of tea, taken a steaming shower, and his beloved sweatshirt was mended, clean, and dry. He opened the door of his room to head downstairs and found himself engulfed in a bear hug by Ian's nine-year-old son, Sean.

"Hullo, Cuz!" He grabbed Flynn by the waist. "Mum made cookies for you. She said you got shot at the airport! What did the bullet feel like? Dad's gotten shot before. Though your bullet just grazed you, Mum said. Do you have the bullet? Can I see it? Does it hurt much? Why'dtcha get shot, anyways? *You ain't a criminal!*"

Flynn tousled the little boy's hair. "Hi, Sean. I was in the wrong place at the wrong time. I tried to stop a couple of guys from stealing some luggage, but they tripped me and shot at me. And I'm sorry to say, I don't have the bullet."

Sean's eyes bugged. "You tried to stop a heist? That's ace, Cuz! I wanna do that one day! But I don't wanna get shot. That doesn't sound like fun. You hungry? I think it's almost lunch time; c'mon!" Sean dragged him down two flights of stairs. Flynn wasn't able to get a good look at the beautiful, wooden stairwells, and he finally stopped Sean short when they reached the bottom. "What? Don't you want lunch?" Sean asked.

Flynn didn't reply right away. He was struck dumb with astonishment. Instead of the modern furnishings he was used to in his uncle's flat, nineteenth-century furniture and decorations met his gaze. The floors were all old, hardwood, and there was crown molding on every wall. It was like stepping back in time. Gilded chandeliers lit the rooms, and furniture that must have been at least a hundred years old decorated every corner.

"It's…it's…" he stammered. "It's beautiful!"

"I know, isn't it though? So much prettier than our old flat. But c'mon, you can look at that later!" Sean tugged on his hand and led him into the kitchen.

Leslie was busy heating something up in the oven, but looked up as they entered. "Hello, Flynn. Sean, dear, will you lay the table please? Thank you." She turned back to Flynn with a smile and gave him a quick hug. "How are you feeling?"

"Jolly well, I daresay. My arm is a little sore, but that's all. Thank you for fixing my sweatshirt."

"Oh, it was easy. No thanks necessary." She set the timer on the oven and then motioned to a couple of barstools where a blond-haired man in his mid-thirties was sitting. Flynn tried not to stare at the fresh, two-inch, dark red scar that ran straight from the corner of his right eye and up over his temple. "Flynn, you remember our friend, Hawk Nigel?"

"Yes, I do indeed. Pleasure to see you again." Flynn held out his hand.

Hawk shook it firmly. "You as well. You've grown a mite taller since I saw you last." His dark blue eyes ran up and down Flynn as he spoke. "It's been what, two years now?"

"It was at that rugby tournament, right? Oxford vs. Cambridge, I think it was."

Hawk gave a short laugh. "Indeed. And may I remind you Oxford won the day quite soundly?"

"We had a bad day," Ian interjected defensively, poking his head in the doorway. "And the refs didn't help much, either."

"Oh, don't you always have a ready excuse?" Hawk retorted.

Alex slipped by Ian, watched Leslie to make sure her back was turned, and started to eat the fresh cookies that lay on a cooling rack. "You guys and your rugby...who cares?" he said as he finished one and started on a second. "Like, seriously, grown men fighting over a ball? It's worse than football!"

Flynn stared at him. "How can you not like football? I mean, I knew you weren't a sports fan but..."

Alex licked one of his fingers that was covered in melted chocolate and grabbed a third cookie. *Stop eating those!* Hawk mouthed at him. Alex stuck out his tongue and ignored him. "Football is pointless. A bunch of guys running around and kicking a ball into a net. For hours. Only they rarely ever get it *in* the net." He rolled his eyes. "Rugby, at least, isn't so horribly boring. Still pointless though."

Hawk and Ian were about to argue with him, when Leslie turned around and gasped. "Alexander, those are not to eat!"

Alex backed up, his half-eaten, fourth cookie in hand, and gave her a looked of bewilderment. "Not to eat? What are they for then? Decoration? That's *torture!* Not to mention an absolute waste of good sugar and chocolate chips."

"Alex, they're not to eat *now*. They're for *later*."

"Well, I reckon it's later! Later, you see, could be a few seconds, minutes, hours, days, or even *years*. Since you didn't specify...yep! It's later." Alex grinned as he popped the other half of his cookie into his mouth and reached for another.

"I told you to stop eating 'em, mate," muttered Hawk.

Leslie marched over to the stove, ripped the wet hand towel off the handle, and turned to face Alex who was calmly downing a fifth. "Mister, if you touch those cookies again..." she left her sentence unfinished for added effect.

Alex's smile of pleasure vanished. "O-*kay*. Uh, I surrender!" He lifted his hands in the air. "I have a great — repeat, *great* — respect for that wet towel of yours. Really, I *surrender!*" he added as Leslie didn't lower the towel. He backed off, bumping into Ian.

"I think you've learned a very valuable lesson, Alex — never touch food in the kitchen without asking the cook first. Hey, do *not* thump me on the back until you've washed those hands!" Ian quickly backed off.

"Aye, Mummy-dear," Alex piped in a high voice as he left the room.

Ian shook his head, smiling. "What's on the menu, m'dear?"

Leslie returned the towel to the stove as she answered. "Cornish pasties and roast beef sandwiches. The pasties are about done, just need a few more minutes."

"It sounds and smells delicious," Ian said as he opened one of the upper cabinets and removed some plates. Sean bounced into the kitchen and took them, promising not to drop them.

Flynn was bursting with curiosity. At first, he had assumed Hawk and Alex were just guests, but now he wasn't so sure. They acted as though they, too, lived in the same house. Grant it, the place certainly was big enough for them, but it didn't make sense to him. He wanted to ask his uncle about it, but grudgingly saw the wisdom in waiting for a time when there would be nothing to interrupt the narrative.

His eyes strayed to Hawk's injury. "Can I ask you something?"

"Sure. What is it?"

"How did you get *that*?" Flynn made a simple slashing motion at his own temple.

Hawk threw a quick glance at Ian before replying, which didn't escape Flynn's notice. "I got that and this," and he held up his left hand, revealing a jagged red scar across the top, "courtesy of your uncle's botched plan to arrest someone."

"My plans are never botched. You just need to work on your reflexes," Ian retorted.

"There's nothing wrong with my reflexes!" Hawk protested.

"Okay, you two," Leslie interrupted. "You can squabble over that later. Come and eat before the food gets cold."

"Yes, Ma'am," Hawk drawled.

"It was nice to see Liam looking so well," Leslie said once they were all seated in the dining room and had prayed for their meal. "I think he and Gwen needed that cruise."

"What cruise?" Alex asked, wiping his glasses on his shirt. There was a particularly stubborn smudge that just wouldn't go away.

"You know, the one they took for their tenth anniversary," she explained. "They just got back last week."

"Oh. I wasn't aware they went anywhere." Scowling at his lenses, Alex rubbed them vigorously with a wet napkin. "I've never been on a cruise before. It sounds boring except for the food; my brother said it's included in the bill, and you can get as much as you want whenever you want. And you don't get slapped by a wet towel for eating hot cookies instead of cold." He flashed Leslie an impish grin. "Hey, Ian, if you decide you're going to do that for your anniversary, can I be chaperon?"

Ian looked at him askance. "Are you serious? Chaperons are needed for unmarried couples, okay? Not anniversaries."

Alex waved a hand dismissively. "Details, details." Grabbing another sandwich he continued, "Seriously, have you made any plans yet? I mean, I need to be in the know. Do I get the house all to myself, or am I watching the munchkins?"

Flynn chuckled. "I don't think I count as a munchkin."

"Oh, whatever, you get my point. It's more a question of, am I binge watching *Lord of the Rings* or *Lost In Space*?"

"I like *Lost In Space!*" Sean piped up. "Do Lukas and me—"

"Lukas and I," Leslie corrected,

"Yeah, do we get to watch it all, Dad, please?" He cast large, pleading eyes at Ian.

"I'm not sure. Let's talk about it later, shall we?" Ian said quickly.

Throughout the conversation, Flynn noticed the uneasiness between his aunt and uncle, and wasn't surprised when Ian cut the discussion short. He had also observed that Hawk had fallen strangely silent, and had an odd expression on his face, almost as if he were trying to wipe all emotion from it. It was all very peculiar.

He was startled out of his thoughts as he heard Hawk ask Leslie, "Where are you going?"

"I was going to bring Lukas up a bowl of soup," she replied. "It ought to be hot by now."

"Oh, you don't have to do that. Just finish your lunch." Hawk got up and left.

Flynn stared blankly. He knew Lukas was Hawk's son, but why was he here, and why did he need a bowl of soup brought to him?

"You remember my mate, Lukas, right?" Sean asked him.

"Yeah."

"Well, he's sick, so I was reading to him upstairs before lunch," the boy continued, barely giving Flynn time to answer. "Have you ever read Grimm's Fairy Tales? They're scary. Sometimes. Some are just weird. I like *The Brave Little Tailor*, but I don't like his wife. She wasn't nice at all! I mean, who cares if you're actually a hero or not?"

"I...don't remember that story." Flynn racked his brain, trying to think of the plotline.

Sean's eyes bugged. "You don't remember *The Brave Little Tailor*? He was so dench! He killed flies, but the giants thought it was men, and he beat the giants, so the king hired him and he had to capture a unicorn and boar to get out of the army, kind of like the Labors of Hercules, and he married the princess, who found out he was just a tailor and tried to kill him, but he got rid of her and ruled happily ever after." The boy took a deep breath after this hurried recital.

Flynn stared at him, still confused. "Nope, still don't remember it."

"Didn't you ever read the book?" Alex asked, wiping horseradish sauce off his fingers with his napkin.

"No. I've read bits and pieces of it, but most of them were creepy." Flynn shrugged.

"Eh, it's a classic. Every classic has its creepy side, as well as its good side. I've got a big ol' copy with huge illustrations you—"

"Oh yes, you have to read Uncle Alex's book! It's so amazing!" Sean cried.

"Sean, you just interrupted Alex," Leslie reproved gently.

"Oh. Sorry Uncle Alex," Sean said, lowering his head.

"Never mind about it, little guy. As I was saying, Flynn, you can read it any time you like. My room is in the basement, so just you come down and get it whenever you like." Alex gave Leslie imploring eyes. "Now can I have a cookie?"

"Yes, Alex. In fact, bring in a plate for all of us, will you?"

"With pleasure!" Alex was up and gone before she had even finished her sentence.

~

"Alright, so please, tell me *everything*!" Flynn sat down on the sofa next to his uncle and waited for an explanation. The house had gone fairly quiet. Leslie was writing a grocery list and finishing up another batch of cookies in the kitchen, Alex was doing something in the basement, Sean was outside jumping in mud puddles, and Hawk was reading to Lukas upstairs. It was an unusually chilly day, and thus a fire blazed merrily on the old, stone hearth. The large living room was just as comfortable as it could be, and it had begun to rain, which made everything seem cozier. At the same time, however, the unusual circumstances left Flynn with a vague feeling of unease. He had been expecting to move into the familiar, small flat with his uncle, aunt, and cousin with little ceremony. Instead, he had been caught in the middle of a heist, shot at, and now found himself in a huge house that appeared to be home to a whole bunch of other people. It was bewildering, to say the least.

"Why don't you tell me what happened to you, first," Ian said. "Explaining everything could take a while."

Flynn sighed. "Very well." He quickly recounted how he'd noticed the two men on the plane somehow communicating, how he'd felt a sense of apprehension about it, how he'd tailed them, and then was tripped and shot at. "Have you been able to suss out who they were and what they stole?"

"No, I don't know who they were exactly, but I have a few suspicions. As to what they stole, that's been all over the news. The briefcases were carrying about a million's worth in diamonds and rubies, and one-hundred-thousand pounds in cash."

Flynn's mouth dropped open. "Who in the world would just be carrying around all those valuables so carelessly?"

"A rich businessman who assumed he had everything under control," Ian said with a shrug. "He was headed for a gem convention, and the thieves figured out his security measures. I'm waiting now to hear from an Inspector friend of mine for further details. The stolen SUV was found and is being processed for prints or other evidence, and that's all I know at the moment."

"Well, I've answered your question. Now it's your turn to answer mine." Flynn grabbed a couch pillow and leaned back against it comfortably. "This house is gorgeous, to be sure, but I don't understand why you moved. Didn't you like the flat? And what about Alex and Hawk? They seemed right at home. Are you all living together or something?"

Ian hesitated briefly. "Yes and no. It's not as complicated as it seems, really. Your aunt has always dreamed of living in a Victorian house, and not only was this one listed at a good price, it cuts my commute time to work. We do all live in the same house, but the arrangements keep things separate, too. Alex's landlord had raised the rent and he was looking for a place to move into. Since we had an entirely unused basement, it just seemed natural to rent it to him. As for Hawk, well, after the incident with his wife, he and Lukas began to spend a lot more time over here." Ian stopped. "Did I ever tell you what happened to her? No? For some reason I thought I had... Carliss disappeared about a year and a half ago. We tried everything we could to find her, but..." Ian's voice trailed off and he shook his head. "We found her car and her purse, but that was all. She vanished without a trace, and we have no idea who took her, or why, or if she's even still alive."

"That's awful!" Flynn was aghast.

"Yes," sighed Ian.

"And that explains why you all were acting so weird when Alex brought up your anniversary."

Ian nodded. "Anyways, they were over here so much, Leslie said it made more sense for them to move in to the empty rooms upstairs. It just…sort of happened, I guess, and before we knew it, we were a full house."

"That all makes sense," Flynn said, giving his uncle a searching look, "but somehow I get the feeling there's a little more to it than that. People don't 'just happen' to live with you."

"Nope, that's it. It really did happen just like I told you," Ian replied nonchalantly.

Flynn crossed his arms over his chest. "Uncle, one thing I've noticed over the years is when you're not being one-hundred-percent truthful, you look to the left, and your right eyebrow goes down. So spill it. What aren't you telling me?"

"Nothing," Ian said evasively. "Everything I've told you is true."

"Uncle. I'm not a naive ten year old!" Flynn was getting exasperated. "You're hiding something, and I'm not going to stop asking questions until I get answers."

Ian huffed. "You're far too observant and stubborn for your own good."

"I guess it runs in the family," Flynn shot back.

Ian grinned slightly. "Touché." He sighed and shifted his position. "Okay, everything I told you is true. Your aunt has always wanted to live in a Victorian house, but the reason we moved is beyond that. You know I work for the Scotland Yard.

Well, Hawk and Alex do, too. We spend a lot of time together on assignments and cases, and the living arrangements just sort of happened," he finished lamely.

Flynn scowled. "This conversation is about as bad as that time you tried to get Sean to tell you how he ended up with a strange kitten in the kitchen, both of them covered in mud. Why do I have to drag everything out of you? I'm not a child! Please, just level with me. What is so frightening or dangerous or, or...ridiculous that you can't tell me?" he sputtered. Ian looked away, but said nothing. "It has to do with your work, doesn't it?" Flynn persisted. Ian remained silent. "And it's dangerous, or something, and you don't want me involved, is that it?" Still, there was no response. Flynn lowered his voice and said in his best imitation of Luke Skywalker, "Uncle, your thoughts betray you. I can feel the conflict in you."

Ian rolled his eyes. "Oh, knock it off. You can't read the thoughts inside my head."

"I don't have to. They're written all over your face." Flynn smirked.

Ian frowned. "You know too much as it is. Don't give any more thought to it, okay? Yes, it's dangerous, and no, I don't want you involved. I want you to enjoy a completely normal life, go to university, and live with us as long as you like. Understand?"

"My life is not going to be normal if you're hiding things from me," Flynn snapped. "I don't care how bloody dangerous it is! We're family, and if I'm living under the same roof, I have a right to know."

Ian sat quietly for a while, trying to come to terms with the whole situation. Part of him desired to shield Flynn from the dangerous lifestyle he and his friends had chosen. They had all made a conscious decision to accept this job, but Flynn hadn't. He was being thrown into it, and Ian had wished to keep him in the dark; although he wanted Flynn to lead a "normal life", he realized now that it was an impossibility.

He knew Flynn wasn't your average eighteen-year-old. Whether he was born that way, or life circumstances had molded him that way, the boy was sharp, and he could always tell if there was more than met the eye. Ian had discussed with his superior officer the inevitability of Flynn figuring out about his secret life, and they had decided that when he did, Ian would tell him the truth. Ian knew Flynn had wanted to follow in his footsteps and become a Scotland Yard Detective, but there was a chance the boy wouldn't be keen on the secret agent part. If such was the case, Ian would vouch for his nephew's secrecy. His superior wasn't entirely pleased with this arrangement, but he trusted Ian's judgement on the matter.

Telling Flynn about his secret line of work wasn't what gave Ian pause. It was the timing. He hadn't counted on him figuring it out on the very first day of his arrival, and he hadn't thoroughly worked out in his mind yet how he would tell him.

"Very well," he said finally. "I admit, I'm hiding a lot from you. It's not because I don't trust you; I want to protect you.

What the guys and I do, well, it's not your average Scotland Yard job. It's dangerous. Unpredictable. I felt that not telling you was the best way to keep you safe. Somehow, I thought you could still live here and not get mixed up in our crazy world, at least, not for a while. At your age, you're supposed to be going to university, hanging out and having fun with kids your age, not loaded down with all the dangerous situations we deal with."

Flynn spread his hands. "Uncle, you know me. I've never hung out and wasted time with random, immature acquaintances. That's never appealed to me. Kids at school think life is about football, fun, and parties, but it isn't. Well, except for football, but you get my point. That other stuff just isn't me." He looked pleadingly at his uncle. "My life has been different, and I'm perfectly happy with it. My only dream has been to live with you someday, and do what you do. You know that. Ever since the day you told me you were Scotland Yard, I've dreamed about following in your footsteps.

"Can't you, like, consider this my apprenticeship?" Flynn scrambled for words, desperately hoping his uncle would understand just how much this meant to him. "Sure, the university will teach me the rule book, and give me a slip of paper that says I'm ready for the job, but they'll never teach me the real tricks of the trade. School isn't real life. But here, not only do I finally get to live in a real home with my family, I'll get hands-on training. Please, Uncle Ian, please just tell me, and teach me, won't you?"

Ian sighed and made a little gesture of defeat. "Okay, but first, let me reiterate that what I and the guys do isn't exactly what you'd even be going to school for. This is extremely risky stuff we're talking about here. If you don't want to get involved, and would rather just learn what you originally intended, I can make other living arrangements for you. It's not that I don't want you here," he added hastily seeing Flynn's horrified look, "but...Scotland Yard agents live an already dangerous life, and ours is three times that. Nobody knows who we are, but if our enemies ever figured out our identity, well, let's just say it wouldn't be conducive to our health. That kind of life isn't for everyone, and I certainly don't want to force it on you."

Flynn's eyes widened. "Uncle, are you kidding me? You couldn't keep me away if you tried! I don't care how dangerous it is. I knew being Scotland Yard involved some risks; so what if they're ramped up a bit? I'm not leaving you, Uncle. Like I said, I've only ever wanted to live with you and become like you. Come what may, I'm in this with you."

He looked at his uncle very seriously. "My life isn't my own, you know. It's God's, and I've asked Him to direct it and guide it as He wills. I don't think it was an accident that I got thrown into your way of life like I did. Besides, remember what you once told me? We are invincible, until God calls us home. So it doesn't ultimately matter if I have the safest job or the most dangerous, does it?" It was more of a statement than a question.

Ian smiled wryly. "Well, I can't exactly argue with that, so you win." He took a deep breath and scowled in thought. "To return to your original *demand* to tell you everything, I shall do my best, but I'm warning you, it's a bit of a long story. Some of what I'm about to say you might know from the *Times*, but bear with me. You probably remember, about three years ago, the counterfeit money that swamped the UK?"

"Oh yes. You replaced my fifty-pound note that was bad."

"Ah, yes, that's right. So I did." Ian paused momentarily as the incident passed through his mind. "No one could find out who was making the money, or where it was coming from. At the same time, several schools and other public buildings were being torched or blown up around London and the surrounding suburbs. Each time this happened, the word 'Saboteurs' was found spray painted on the pile of rubble. Once again, no one could find out who was a part of that gang. And if that wasn't bad enough, the Mallevilles started to rear their heads, pulling off some difficult heists and leaving several murdered innocents in their wake."

Flynn shivered involuntarily. "The Mallevilles are evil incarnate," he interjected.

Ian gave a short laugh. "That's a good way of putting it, though I will say the press has, either intentionally or unintentionally, attributed many crimes to them that they had nothing to do with. The Mallevilles had their fingers in both the counterfeiters and Saboteurs, but we didn't know that at first. Scotland Yard was hard pressed to get evidence linking any specific people to the crimes, since these gangs were extremely professional. Any slip-ups that were made they quickly put to rights. Evidence went missing, witnesses ended up dead, it was a nightmare. Numerous agents from many organizations, such as Mi5 and even Mi6, went undercover to try and infiltrate the gangs to discover information. Nothing worked. Hawk, Alex, and I worked those cases tirelessly. We lost a lot of sleep in those days.

"Then some of the undercover agents starting ending up dead, or..." Ian hesitated. "Well, let's just say you wouldn't want to have been in their shoes. No," he added seeing Flynn's shocked expression, "those details weren't put in the papers. Even the families of the agents began to be targeted. It wasn't good. The Saboteurs were emboldened by their success and our failure, so they started to publicize their next targets, as if taunting us to see if we could do anything to prevent it.

"And that is when Alex managed to hack into one of their mobile phones. Don't ask me how he did it. That kind of stuff goes way over my head. From there, he was able to figure out their next real plan of action, and Hawk, I, and our team thwarted the Saboteur's plan to torch Big Ben. However, the guys we caught were so low on the chain of command, they had no useful information to give us." Ian stuffed a pillow behind his back before continuing.

"As you can imagine, even such a small victory as that was all over the news. Our names were kept out of the papers, but they apparently went to the higher-ups. Hawk and I were approached by a superior officer, who offered to let us take the entire Saboteur case. He said it in such a way, Hawk and I could tell it was a test of some sort. Thus, we went way undercover." A light smile crossed his face as the memories came flooding back. "We told no one anything. Only our little team knew something was up, and we pretended we knew nothing. Secrecy was of essence, and we decided to trust no one outside our team. We began to get discouraged, however, because in three weeks, the Saboteurs had just disappeared. But then Alex discovered they were going to blow up London Bridge through some random video game chat site."

"Video game chat site?" Flynn raised an eyebrow. "How in the world did Alex manage to do that? I mean, how would he even know where to look?"

"We knew they had to be communicating with each other in some fashion, and it wasn't mobile phones since they figured out Alex had hacked into one of them earlier," Ian explained. "Hawk did a little digging and discovered they were mild gamers. He procured a list of games they were currently into, and Alex, who knows a lot more about that than I do, set about trying to see if they were communicating through one of those sites. Turns out, they were. And, as you know, the Saboteurs were caught red-handed, the London Bridge sustained no damage beyond a few bullet holes, and the terrorists were put in prison.

"After that success, we were again approached by our superior officer, who brought us before several individuals who are very high-up in the government. They were impressed with how we'd been able to solve a case no one else could, and laid before us a proposition that they had been toying with for a while. The idea was called the Shadow Agents. Basically, it was a group of men who would go undercover, yet remain at their regular jobs as though nothing were out of the ordinary."

"Oh, I get it. Bruce Wayne-style," Flynn interjected.

Ian cracked a smile. "Yeah, I guess you could call me Batman. To the rest of the world, we would look like regular agents. But to our superiors and to those in our circle, we would be so much more than that. It would be our job to take out the big threats that local and even national agencies couldn't handle. However, there was a catch. We would be unofficial, which meant we wouldn't be traceable to any government agency. Yes, we would work for the government, but it'd be off the record. If something were to go really wrong, they couldn't protect us or help us.

"Being a double agent comes with a lot of risks, both known and unknown, and we all knew that. We were given a week to think about it and discuss it with our families. We didn't sleep much that week! But we finally decided that it was the right thing to do. Each one of us is exceptional at what we do. God has given us unique gifts and talents, and together, we make a good team. We had sworn to protect the innocent at all cost, and this was an even bigger opportunity to do so. Thus, we accepted the job, as well as the inevitable dangers that would follow. That was two years ago."

Flynn stared at him. "Seriously? Two years? And you've never told me?"

"It wasn't like I could just broadcast my life publically," Ian replied a little defensively. "You're the only person outside of our team who knows. Not even my mum has a clue. Now, if you keep interrupting me, I'll never get this finished." Flynn gave him a sheepish look and promptly shut his mouth. "Our first assignment was no surprise: identify and catch the counterfeiters. We eventually dubbed them the Challengers, since they were a family-run crime ring whose last name was Challenger. I'm not going to get into the details of the case right now, since it was long and messy, but suffice to say we caught them just before Hawk lost Carliss.

"We also lost two agents to that case. The Challengers were a violent crew, and they didn't go down without a fight. Those agents have not been replaced as of yet. Our team is composed of several other people, besides the ones living here in this house. They are scattered all over the UK, but some live close by, such as Liam, our doctor friend, whom you met last night and this morning. If we are injured in any way while on the job or otherwise, he's the one who puts us back together. His house is just a street or two away from the hospital, and he has special license from the Queen and the Head of the Hospital to use whatever he needs, and, if possible, in his own house. He has a full operating room in his basement, and his wife is a certified nurse who has also been sworn to secrecy. We set it up that way so no one would be able to recognize us and identify us; you understand, of course, the imperative need for secrecy.

"But I'm getting off track. After we caught the Challengers, we were able to trace some of their connections and funds back to the mysterious Mallevilles. The Mallevilles had done nothing spectacular as of yet, beyond their afore mentioned heists and murders. At first, we didn't even know who they were. But as we unraveled the mess of both the Challenger and Saboteur gangs, we discovered traces of them all over the place.

"They are, at their core, a group of power-hungry men who want money and influence. They enjoy terrorizing people, and they love attention. In short, they thirst for infamy, and lots and lots of money. We have been chasing them for over a year and a half, and in that time I have learned much about them. The unfortunate thing is, I'm no closer to catching them than I was at the beginning."

"Do you have names?" Flynn asked.

Ian made a gesture of assent. "I have the names of the main ring, but their gang is at least a hundred strong, and I have yet to figure out all the layers. The leaders of the gang are brothers: Icabod and Damian Malleville. They are cunning, cruel, and consumed with greed. Their co-conspirator is a boyhood friend, Axel Crane. He is vicious, ruthless, and if someone's in his way, there's nothing he won't stoop to in order to get rid of him. Alvar Currito is the son of a Spanish soldier. He's an excellent shot, and is cautious, unlike Axel. Otto Kyler is a recent edition — been with the gang about a year. He's overweight, easy to panic, jumps to conclusions at the snap of a finger, and never passes up an opportunity to eat. I'm not really sure what his level of expertise is, but hey, I'm not the one recruiting criminals. Quentin Lathrop has been with the group for about three years. He's level-headed and cunning, and extremely good at slight-of-hand. As for Emory Vansant," Ian frowned. "We don't have any idea how long he's been connected with the Mallevilles. He's not a steady member, but he appears every now and again. He's a bit of an odd chap; skittish, yet I'd bet you he knows way more than anyone suspects.

"They are a dangerous crew, and are always on the lookout for those who are running from a recent brush with the law. Unfortunately for us, those seem to the only ones we can catch, and the main gang 'conveniently' slips away. But we caught a break a few weeks ago when we managed to capture Axel."

"Was it Scotland Yard, or you and your team?" Flynn asked.

"No, it was me and my team." Ian settled himself more comfortably on the couch as he launched into the narrative. "One of our informants got wind that Axel was going to meet a supplier in a sleazy pub over in the East End. Hawk wasn't so sure the information was reliable, so only he and I went to check it out. We were a little unprepared, to say the least.

"Turned out, the information *was* good, and Axel was totally unawares. It was his surprise that turned the tide in our favor. We worked out a plan where I would approach him and ask if he could spare a cigarette. As he reached for it, Hawk would come up behind him and take him down. As luck would have it, though, a waitress dropped her tray, which drew his attention away from me. He noticed Hawk and before either of us could react, out came his flick knife, giving Hawk those cuts you asked about earlier. Axel put up a nasty fight, but we came out the conquerors. He is currently in a holding cell at Scotland Yard.

He's going to be transferred to Wandsworth Prison later this after—"

Before he could finish his sentence, his mobile phone went off abruptly. He glanced at the number and frowned. "I'm sorry, I have to take this." Seeing Flynn's look of annoyance he added, "It's Grant. He's a Detective Chief Inspector for the Metropolitan Police, and he's also privy to the Shadow Agents. He's probably ringing me about some evidence they found from the airport heist last night." Flynn paid little attention to the conversation that followed. He was still trying to process everything his uncle had told him, and he didn't notice Ian hang up until he heard his aunt's voice.

"Was that Grant? Did they find anything?" Leslie asked from the doorway. She knew Ian had been waiting for the call, and had come into the room when she heard his phone ring.

Ian laid his phone on a side table. "It *was* the Mallevilles, just as I suspected. Grant was able to place Icabod both on the plane and entering the SUV, and Quentin was seen getting their luggage just before they stole the briefcases. I told Grant I'd get in touch with a contact of mine who keeps an eye on the black market. They'll be anxious to cash in the jewels, and we can hopefully use the sale to trace them. Other than that, there's not much we can do."

"Don't worry, m'love. We'll catch them yet."

Ian sighed. "I'm beginning to wonder if we can. I know a ridiculous amount of information about them, but I don't have *them*, and that's all that really matters!"

Leslie gave him a sympathetic look. "It's frustrating, I know, but remember, there's no such thing as a perfect criminal or a perfect crime. Humans make mistakes, and sooner or later, they will mess up in such a way that will allow us to trap them. You guys look like you could use a break," she added. "There are fresh cookies on the counter and milk in the fridge, if you want them. I made some more, since Alex did so much damage to the first batch. I'm taking Sean with me to the supermarket, and I'll see you in an hour or so."

"Alright, bye, love." Ian turned to Flynn and smiled. "I don't know about you, but hot cookies sound mighty good right about now. Why don't we grab a plate and head down to the basement? I want to show you our office."

Flynn rose and followed his uncle into the kitchen. "Ooh, the secret office in the basement! Does that mean I'm officially part of your secret little club now?" he teased.

Ian gave a short laugh as he removed a plate from one of the cabinets. "Very funny, Flynn. However, I would hardly call a top secret group of agents a 'secret little club.'"

"How do we get into the basement?" Flynn asked curiously.

"Behind the staircase," Ian replied. "Follow me."

~~

Chapter Three

THE WIND WAILED MOURNFULLY as it wended its way under the eaves of the old, battered house that sat in a small clearing on the edge of Clump of Trees Wood. The rain was busy making mud puddles in the dirt road, and causing the already-bedraggled house to look completely water-logged. The roof bowed dangerously, and at least half of the windows were broken and boarded up with scrap pieces of wood and metal. The inside of the house wasn't much better. The furniture was old and saggy, the musty smells of cigars, sweat, and mildew permeated the rooms, and everything was coated in a thin layer of grease and grime.

Icabod and Damian Malleville sat across from each other at a small table in what was supposed to be the living room. Several other men were seated in ragged chairs about the room. Alvar Currito was oiling his pistol near the fireplace. Otto Kyler was digging his grubby hands into a bag full of sliced deli meat, and the nervous-looking young man who'd taken care of their luggage, Quentin Lathrop by name, was shuffling a pack of cards over his lap. His hands never stopped moving, and his eyes missed nothing.

Damian softly drummed his strong fingers on the table. "Ic, who did Alvar shoot?" he asked in a low tone.

Icabod shrugged as though it was no big deal. "Just some snoopy kid who stuck his nose where it didn't belong."

Damian, who looked very much like his brother, was frowning. "Shooting was not part of the plan. Draws way too much attention. If you needed to be rid of him, couldn't you have done it in a more discreet way?"

"Not really. Besides, most people were more interested in the gunshot than me grabbing someone else's luggage."

"Is everything a go for Axel's jail-break today?" Alvar asked as he tucked his oilcloth in his pocket.

Icabod leaned back in his seat and crossed one leg over the other. "Yes indeed. Our friendly little rioters are ready for some action, and the Inspectors have been taken care of. All we have to do is get our disguises on and head for the Yard in an hour or two."

"I hope this will work as smoothly as you say it will," Damian muttered.

Icabod was beaming with confidence as he said, "Oh, you worry too much, brother. Relax! This will be fun. I have everything under control."

"That's what I'm afraid of," Damian mumbled under his breath.

Otto crumpled the empty deli bag in his hand. "Isn't it about time you guys got prettied up?"

Quentin glared at him. "Guys don't get pretty, stupid. It's a disguise."

"Enough, you two," Damian snapped. "Otto, get me that bag," and he pointed to a large carpet bag that was filled with make-up, wigs, and masks. "Alvar, get the uniforms out of the closet, and don't get oil on 'em, okay?"

"Like I would do that," Alvar grumbled as he hastened to obey. Damian ignored him and got to work on Icabod's face.

~

Ian led Flynn down the stairs into the basement. The muffled sounds of the *Indiana Jones* theme could be heard coming from their left. "You don't have a movie room down here, do you?" Flynn asked.

"No, no. Alex is rather fond of soundtrack music, and usually blares it pretty loudly when he's alone." Ian turned to the left and rapped on the door before opening it. The music faded into the background, and Alex swiveled in his desk chair to greet them.

"Hey, Ian. Oh, you brought cookies, how nice of you! What's—" he stopped upon seeing Flynn. "Ah, so did he figure it out, or did you just decide to tell him?"

"It's a combination of both," Ian answered, laying the plate down next to his friend.

"Oh come on, it can't be both!"

"Yes, it actually can. He knew something was up, and demanded an explanation." Nodding at Flynn he added, "He's a pretty persistent fellow."

"Dang it." Alex scowled.

"Why does it matter?" Ian raised an eyebrow. Light dawned on him, and he crossed his arms. "Don't tell me you and Hawk placed bets on it."

Alex gave him a sheepish look. "Sort of-ish? I mean, real betting involves money, and we didn't do that. Just...a box of our favorite sweets. Hawk said he'd figure it out, and naturally I bet against him."

Ian massaged the bridge of his nose with two fingers. "You two. What *am* I going to do with you?"

Alex shrugged. "Well, since that's settled..." he spread his arms and grinned at Flynn. "Welcome to our Batcave!"

Flynn chuckled. "It does kind of look like that," he said, trying to take in all the equipment.

A long, unbroken desk ran along three of the walls. Computer screens, laptops, printers, and other interesting digital gadgets, along with a veritable tangle of multi-colored cords, lay on the desk in something of an orderly fashion. It was obvious where Ian's section of the desk was. It was immaculate, with each cord separate from each other, the extra length wound up with a twist-tie. A few notebooks and regular desk items were placed neatly around the base of the computer screen, and three pictures were adhered to the wall just above the screen: one of Leslie, one of Sean, and one of Flynn. No distracting ornamentation could be seen, save for a jar of old-looking change. His computer screen showed a beautiful picture of the wilds of Derbyshire. His was an uncluttered work area, with only the necessities.

Alex's section was the exact opposite. Not only did he have his laptop, he had two large computer screens staring at him, both littered with tons of program icons. One PC screen had the Superman symbol, and the other had the Rebel symbol, while his laptop had a movie still of the *USS Enterprise*. His cords were all bunched up and tangled, and he kept kicking them away from his feet. Sterling silver Batman and the Empire symbols, each on their own black leather strap, hung from the corners of his PC screens. His wall space was covered with small posters, daily reminders, random html codes, and postcards, all stuck to the wall with different colored tacks in no order at all. A large, complex stereo system was hooked up between his space and Hawk's. A pair of blue ear-buds rested on a messy pile of notes and papers. Alex's desk space was littered with pretty much everything imaginable: fandom memorabilia, pencils, extra cords, computer tools, and USB sticks to name just a few.

Hawk's section was not nearly as neat as Ian's, but it lacked the disorganized mess of Alex's. Flynn could instantly tell that he kept things exactly where he wanted them. He didn't keep everything stashed away in his desk drawers like Ian, but he didn't leave everything out like Alex. What he was using at the time was left within his reach. Several large maps hung above his computer screen, as well as a couple pictures: one of Carliss and Lukas, and one of their whole little group in front of some cinema. A pair of orange headphones lay across his keyboard, still plugged into the stereo system. A red "Keep Calm And Carry On" mug was filled with a few pens, pencils, a laser pointer, and a pair of scissors.

His computer screen showed a movie still of *The Black Pearl* riding the ocean waves.

There was a blank computer between Hawk's and Ian's, with only a mouse and pen jar. It was flanked by two printers, modems, and a few other machines. Flynn also noticed some random LEGO pieces scattered in front of the lone console, testament to the little boys' presence. On the wall with the door was a bunch of cabinets, broken only by a small fridge. All this, he took in in an instant. "This is so cool!" he breathed.

"Take a seat!" Alex reached out a leg and tried to kick the lone console's chair in his direction. He missed.

"I confess I'm having a hard time taking this all in," Flynn said, still gazing about him. "I mean, all I expected was to move into your modern little flat and learn some basic Scotland Yard training. Now," he gave a short laugh, "I feel like I'm in some crazy spy movie!"

Ian sat down and leaned back in his seat. "I suppose it is a bit overwhelming. If you have questions, ask away."

"Well...one thing has been sticking in my mind a bit. Just doesn't make sense."

"Fire away, mister. We're all ears," Alex said as he grabbed a cookie and started eating it.

"Okay, so with the Saboteurs, you said you got the whole case, right?"

Alex nodded before Ian could reply. "Sure did. It was both mind-blowing and extremely sobering, getting that much responsibility thrown on us so fast!"

"But, how did you even get the case in its entirety in the first place?" Flynn continued. "I mean, that was a terrorist group at heart, wasn't it? And isn't that what the Mi5 agency takes care of?"

"Oh." Ian frowned. "I didn't explain that aspect of it, did I?"

"Aspect of what?" Flynn asked suspiciously. "Don't tell me you're hiding more stuff from me."

"No, no, I just…agh. It's messy, okay? And I got interrupted by Grant." Ian paused, attempting to piece together in his mind how he ought to say it. "I guess the best way to explain it is, we got the case to ourselves because, technically, we weren't — and aren't — Scotland Yard anymore."

"Wait, what?!" Flynn stared at him in disbelief.

"It's…" Ian struggled to explain. "We're both a part of Scotland Yard, and not. If someone were to look our names up, we'd come up as Scotland Yard Inspectors. But…we don't have a regular job as Metropolitan Police officers anymore. We are actually involved in every intelligence agency in the UK. We have ID cards for everything, including the NCA, Mi5, and SIS. We can take any of the cases within all of the organizations." Ian laid considerable stress on the last sentence, hoping Flynn would understand the gravity of their situation. "Nothing like what we do has ever been done before, which is another reason why this is so secret. Never before has a group of agents been given full access to every government intelligence system. We can go where we need to, do what we want, arrest whom we will, and examine any evidence that suits our fancy. And yet, if something goes

wrong, our names won't be connected to any and all of the
agencies, save the Scotland Yard. Does that make sense?"

Flynn was speechless. He managed to nod, and leaned back in
his seat, stunned. "So...you're like...I don't even know *what* to
compare you to. An all-powerful James Bond?" He rubbed his
forehead. "This hurts my brain."

"I know, it's complicated," Alex said sympathetically. "Just
look at it this way. We're agents of the United Kingdom, not a
specific organization. We work for our country, and while we
must obey the regular laws like every other citizen, we get special
privileges to go places, own things, and do anything we want or
need to, so long as it is related to and necessary for our missions.
That help?" He offered him the cookie plate.

Flynn took one as he said, "Yeah, a little. But, like, who do
you report to?"

Alex shrugged. "Only Ian knows that, and he's not allowed to
tell. If something were to happen to him, the knowledge would
be passed to Hawk. As far as I'm concerned, Ian's the boss. The
gaffer. Top bloke. I take orders from no man but him." He
started on a second cookie, and fished a napkin out of a half-open
drawer.

"Do you get all your missions from your superior officer?"
Flynn asked his uncle.

"No. We've done a few things on the side that we've
discovered on our own, but right now, our assignment from him
is the Mallevilles. And we will not rest until they are caught.

After that, I don't know what's in store, but I'm content to wait and find out."

"Oh, and I was wondering one other thing. Are you all allowed to arm yourselves in any way, or do you have to adhere to the regular Scotland Yard policy of TASERs only?" Flynn asked curiously.

"We have a special license to both own and use any and all firearms," Alex replied, brushing crumbs off his shirt onto his napkin. "And we also each got a license to kill, which simply means we're not held responsible if a situation goes south and a bad guy ends up dead."

"Has that ever happened?"

Ian shook his head. "No. There were a lot of injuries in both the arresting of the Saboteurs and the Challengers, but no deaths. We took intensive training to learn how to incapacitate a target without killing him. We do our best to keep them alive to obtain as much information as we can."

"Yeah, 'cause dead criminals aren't very good at telling you stuff," Alex chimed in. "As Israel Hands said, 'Dead men tell no tales.'" Ian half-glared at him for the flippant remark, and Flynn stifled a snicker. "If I killed a baddie, it would be by accident," Alex continued, unabashed. "I can shoot, yeah, but I'm no crack shot like Hawk. Hawk's our sniper man. He can take someone out without killing them like nobody's business. The guy just can't miss." Alex wadded up his napkin full of crumbs and threw it, aiming for a dustbin near Flynn's chair. "Yes!" he cried triumphantly as it swished in.

"Does that mean I get to learn how to fire a real gun?" Flynn looked excited.

"We don't have to worry about that right now." Ian snapped his fingers and held out his hand to Alex for a cookie.

"But you didn't say no, which means that I will?" Flynn pressed.

"Eventually, yes, but there's a whole lot of other things you need to learn first. And you have to understand, too, that we don't carry them to 'look cool', or to flaunt that fact that we can while the rest of Britain can't," Ian explained. "They're dangerous tools that we only use if we have to."

"Okay, enough with the serious lectures." Alex snitched a third cookie, and held out the plate to Flynn. "Want another?"

~

Icabod and his group filed out of their headquarters and into two waiting vehicles — the fact that they didn't own the cars was no concern of theirs. They were using them anyway. Icabod and Quentin were in a squad car, and Damian, Alvar, and Otto were in a run-down, gray pickup. Both vehicles were headed for one building — the Scotland Yard — but each was taking a different route.

Damian parked in an alley. He and his two conspirators got out of the car and slunk up to the entrance overlooking the street that was home to the Scotland Yard. They watched as Icabod and Quentin pulled up in front of the Yard, sauntered out of the squad car dressed as Inspectors, and entered the building.

"Five minutes," Icabod muttered to himself.

Inside the building, the two were greeted by Detective Chief Inspector Grant. "'Evenin', gentlemen! How d'ya do?"

"Very well, thank you," said Icabod cheerfully.

"Never better!" chirped Quentin.

"I presume you are here to move the prisoner?"

"Yes, of course," replied Icabod.

"Excellent! The sooner he is locked up in prison, the better, so say I, and the whole force with me. We don't usually hold criminals going straight to prison, and I can't say I've enjoyed it very much. The transport van hasn't arrived yet, so how about a cup of tea while you wait?" The two phony policemen accepted the offer. Grant checked their credentials to verify they were, indeed, who they said they were, and soon they were chatting over hot cups of tea. Icabod managed to glance nonchalantly at his watch, noting the exact time his men would start to play their part.

On cue, Damian, Alvar, and Otto began to quarrel violently amongst themselves about nothing important, but it soon became a large ruckus, a crowd gathered, their hired rioters arrived, and a fight broke out in the street.

"Good golly! What is happening?" Grant rose to his feet and hurried to the window.

"It's a riot o'er somethin', sir!" cried an inspector rushing past him and outside to try and calm the crowd.

"The prisoner — it's a diversion! His cronies are going to try something funny!" cried Grant. "Tiernan! Merard!"

Two policemen dashed into the room, the first, tall and thin, the second, short and fat. "Yes, sir?" asked the first.

"We must proceed with our emergency precautions regarding Axel Crane and take him to Wandsworth immediately. We've no time to wait for the transport van. Merard, go with these two to the cell. Tiernan, drive this man's car to the back of the building."

"Yes, sir." Young Tiernan saluted and caught the keys Icabod tossed him.

Merard followed Icabod and Quentin to the small cell where Axel Crane was being held. He looked miserable. His brown hair was greasy and mussed, and his clothes were wrinkled and shabby. He had a pair of thick handcuffs on his wrists. As the officers entered his cell, his gray eyes went from dull orbs to blazing coals.

"No!" he cried, jumping back into the farthest corner of the cell.

"Don't make this harder than it has to be," growled Icabod.

Axel looked furious, but shut his mouth like a trap and rigidly let them take his arms and lead him out of the cell and down the corridors to the back door. Quentin was on Axel's left, Icabod on his right, and Merard took up the rear. Icabod gently and inconspicuously flicked his wrist back and forth, letting the light reflect off of a large ring. Axel betrayed no change, and was as sullen as ever, but his comrades felt him relax slightly in their grip.

When they got to the door, Merard opened it, let them out, and opened the back door of the waiting squad car. Axel was put inside, and Quentin slid in next to him. Icabod locked the back door and took the passenger seat next to Tiernan. He lifted a hand in farewell to Merard as the car pulled away from the curb. Merard returned the gesture and returned to the Yard.

"Whew! I'm glad that went off without a hitch. If our prisoner had escaped…" Tiernan whistled and shook his head. "We'd have been in for it then."

"Indubitably." Icabod leaned back and settled himself comfortably in his seat. Tiernan saw he was not inclined to talk, so refrained from conversation and concentrated fully on the road in front of him.

After about twenty minutes, Icabod said, "Turn off on Falcon Road."

"Why?" asked Tiernan.

"It's a shorter way to the main highway."

"It is?" Tiernan frown deepened, and he started to argue, unsure of these new directions. He knew his London streets pretty well, and couldn't envision how such a road led to the highway. "No offense, sir, but that isn't protocol."

"It is now. Just do it." Tiernan frowned and started to argue, but Icabod raised his voice. "I gave you an order, now do it!

"Alright, alright. No need to get your feathers ruffled." Tiernan wasn't convinced that Icabod knew his streets very well, but he was a superior officer, and Tiernan didn't dare contradict him. After about five minutes, Icabod again directed him to turn.

When questioned, he replied that he was taking a back way, so that no one would tail them to the prison. Tiernan wasn't happy about it, and began feeling uneasy, but Icabod shushed him angrily. Tiernan's patience finally ran out when he was forced to turn down an empty street into Wandsworth Common. No people or cars were around. "Sir, are you sure you know where you're going? This is a recreational place." Tiernan pulled the car forward into the grass, stopped, and was about to turn it around, when Icabod pulled a hidden gun out of his boot and laid it on his lap. "What the dickens are you—" Tiernan stopped upon seeing Icabod's face transformed from a respectable Inspector into a ruthless criminal.

"Belt up and do exactly what I tell you." Icabod raised the gun and deliberately cocked it. "Now, young man, I believe you are in possession of the key for the prisoner's handcuffs. Give it to me."

"No I won't," Tiernan replied firmly. His face was pale, but his brown eyes flashed with anger. "Why do you want it? What are you doing? Have you gone mad, sir?"

"They're freeing me, genius, and I'd like to get these clumsy things off my hands!" hollered Axel from the back.

"You're, you're," sputtered Tiernan, light dawning on his mind, "you're imposters!" He lunged for the radio to signal for help, but Icabod swiftly grabbed one of his hands and then smacked his gun over Tiernan's head with a sickening crack. With a cry of pain, Tiernan slumped over the wheel, blood streaming down his face.

"My dear chaps, you're positive bricks!" cried Axel as Icabod rifled Tiernan's pockets, opened the partition, and threw the key in the back. Quentin unlocked the handcuffs and Axel flung them to the floor.

"Glad to have you back, Axel. Lend me a hand with our hostage, would you?" Icabod pressed a button which unlocked the back doors.

"Who said anything about hostage?" Quentin asked, speaking for the first time.

Icabod glared at him. "Do you realize that once those blokes at the Yard suss out Axel never arrived at Wandsworth, we're going to have every copper in the country looking for this cruiser? He's insurance in case we're caught." Axel didn't wait for the explanation. He leapt out of the car and, after handcuffing Tiernan's hands behind his back, shoved him in the boot.

"Okay, are we sticking with the original plan?" asked Axel as they headed back onto the highway. To avoid any suspicion, Axel was still in the back and Quentin had moved to the driver's seat.

"Of course, Ax," Icabod reassured him. "When this is over, we'll be the richest, most powerful men in the whole United Kingdom."

Though he was excited about the culmination of their plan, which was over six long years in the making, Quentin was considerably anxious about the next few days. They couldn't afford a single slip-up. Everything had to go off without a hitch, or all Damian's planning would be for naught. "Things are going to get pretty crazy," he said out loud.

Axel grinned maliciously. "You said it, covey!"

~

"Hullo, Damian!" Icabod greeted his brother about an hour later as he got out of a car in front of their headquarters. They had ditched the police vehicle in the heart of London.

"I see everything went off without a hitch? Good, good." Damian stood in the doorway. He watched as Axel opened the boot and pulled Tiernan out. Damian's eyes widened. "Who's that?" he asked as they entered the house.

"Sergeant Tiernan, our hostage," replied Quentin.

Damian glowered. "Are you *trying* to ruin my plans?" he snapped at Icabod.

"He was perfect, in the event we were pulled over or something. Besides, how exactly was I going to get rid of him? We only had a limited amount of time before they figured out what happened. He was insurance against getting caught." He waved a hand impatiently. "Maybe we can use him again for something else. Figure it out, and stop questioning me. I have smarts too, anorak." Icabod sneered at him and brushed past him into the house.

Damian clenched his teeth but refrained from making reply. It was just like Icabod to change up the plans with no regard for the consequences. He had always been that way; he was the older brother, and thus didn't have to listen if he didn't feel like it. He was never wrong, (even when he was,) had a ready answer for everything, expected his younger brother to think him out of his scrapes, and was filled with so much pride, Damian could've popped him like a balloon. He was a bully, too, something Damian had learned at a very young age; going against Icabod only caused more problems than it fixed. He was no match for his brother's brute strength, and thus relied on his wits to keep him on top.

Axel brought Tiernan into the living room and dumped him in a corner. Grabbing a coil of rope from a small table near at hand, he roughly bound Tiernan's legs together, and then looped the rest of the rope to an old radiator.

"That'll keep you from wandering off."

Tiernan glared at him. "Who are you people?"

"You happened to have fallen in with the Mallevilles," replied Icabod, a sardonic grin sliding across his face.

"What?" Tiernan gasped in horror and disbelief. "No!"

"I'm afraid it's quite true," Axel sneered as he sat down at a larger table and began shuffling a pack of cards.

Tiernan glared at his captors. "Let—me—go!" he said in a quiet, yet furious voice.

"I'm sorry, but you're our hostage," replied Icabod patronizingly.

Tiernan seethed. "You'll never get away with this, you miserable rat!"

"Aren't you polite." Icabod sauntered over to him, stared at him for a moment, then gave him a sudden kick to the stomach. "That should teach you to mind your manners. Axel, gag him."

Axel, only too happy to obey, grabbed a dirty rag from off the
table, jumped over to Tiernan, ripped his head back, and tied the
gag tightly. Tirenan struggled, but could do absolutely nothing
beyond giving his captors death-glares. Once he had finished
securing the gag, Axel sat back down at the table where he, Alvar,
Otto, and Quentin were beginning to play whist. Icabod returned
to the corner where he and Damian were cleaning their guns, and
the brothers resumed discussing their next plan of action.

~

About the same time, Ian and Alex were showing Flynn a few
of their sophisticated computer programs that they used to track
criminals. Alex had created his own software that allowed him to
track vehicles in the UK. He could also get the name of the
owner and any online files of them – criminal or otherwise.

"How is that even possible?" Flynn was very confused.

"It's a software I designed myself," Alex tried to explain. "I
connected it to the UK tracking satellites, and then worked from
there. It's like using a live version of Google or Apple Maps. See,
there's several ways to do it. Say you know the number plate of a
car. I can type that in, and it will give me the make and model of
the car. I then type that in, and it will narrow down all the
vehicles in the UK that are the exact make and model. If I know
where the vehicle I'm looking for is supposed to be, like London,
then I can narrow the search to only London.

"Another way to do it is to type in the owner, and look up the
make and model under their vehicle registration. Or I can type in
the make, and look up the model, and visa-versa. Once I find the

type of car, it's just a matter of time before I can identify the actual vehicle I want. And if I'm not sure, I can tell my software to track all of the ones in question."

"How...do you even design such a thing?" Flynn rubbed his forehead.

Alex lightly tapped his fingers over the tops of his keyboard. "Uh, that's kind of complicated. I can show you sometime, if you want, though. It's easier to show than to tell. Too many programs and codes and stuff."

"Killing Flynn's brain with all your geekiness, eh?" Hawk opened the door and grinned at his friend.

"Not at all! I am merely explaining the wonders of my tracking software."

Hawk rolled his eyes. He was about to retort, when his eyes fastened on Flynn, and realization dawned. "Hey, does this mean you owe me—"

"Yes, yes, you don't have to rub it in!" Alex waved a hand impatiently.

Hawk kicked at his leg. "I expect that box of chocolate mints right here on my desk by tomorrow," he said as he sat down and tapped a blank area next to his keyboard. "Welcome to the Shadow Agents, Flynn." He unplugged his headphones and carefully wound up the cord before laying them aside.

"Thank you. I'm still rather shocked by it all. It seems so surreal!"

Hawk chuckled. "I know what you mean."

Alex's computer dinged softly, momentarily interrupting the *Inception* soundtrack that was playing in the background. He glanced at the notification that popped up and began to turn back to his friends. "Ah well, looks like Axel has…wait." He blinked and spun back to the screen. "Escaped?!" he shrieked.

Ian stared at him, unable to comprehend what his friend had just said. "What? Are you sure you read that right? Like, 'Tried To Escape', or something like that? I mean, he was being transported to Wandsworth this afternoon."

"No, no, he seriously escaped! The Mallevilles set up a diversion, impersonated officers, and pretended to transfer Axel!" Alex pointed frantically to his screen.

"I can't believe it! You're not jesting, mate, surely?" Hawk got up and leaned over his shoulder. "No, you're not," he muttered as he rapidly scanned the police report. After a minute, he gave a short cry of rage. "How *dare* they mess with Tiernan!"

"Who's that?" asked Flynn, thoroughly bewildered.

"A young inspector I've become rather well acquainted with." Hawk was clearly upset.

"What does it say about Tiernan?" Ian asked.

"He was part of the transport team, and he hasn't been heard from since he left the Yard," Alex replied. "They don't know whether he was in league with the Mallevilles or was unwillingly caught up in their mess."

"Oh, he was unwilling alright, I know him," Hawk snapped.

Ian clenched a fist in anger. He was visibly controlling himself from venting his emotions. After all the trouble they'd gone through to catch Axel and now to lose him. To say Ian was frustrated was an understatement. "I'm going to ring Grant for details," he said rather stiffly. After a quick conversation, Ian hung up and began dialing another number. "They haven't been able to locate the cruiser yet, but they know where Axel was freed; somewhere in Wandsworth Common. Grant will meet us there. I'm going to ring Leslie and tell her we're heading out. Flynn, it looks like you're getting your first introduction to what we do earlier than I thought." He called Leslie, explained the situation, and hung up. Alex hadn't moved. Neither had Flynn. Hawk was pacing the small room relentlessly. Ian sighed heavily, "Alright, gang, I know we're all upset about this," he began.

"Upset? I'm more than upset!" Hawk threw his hands in the air. "It feels like we're banging our heads against a brick wall. We had him, Ian. I had him in my bare hands. And now he's gone. We're no closer than before, and I'm getting fed up with it."

"I know, me too," Ian continued. "But look at it this way. If they're going to pull such a barmy stunt as freeing him in front of the entire Scotland Yard, they're planning something big. The bigger a project is, the more room there is for mistakes. If Tiernan is innocent, we'll get him back, and if he's not, then we'll catch him along with the others. And we *will* catch them. God didn't give us this job so we could fail miserably. Now, let's get a move on. Alex, I want you to grab some snacks. There's no telling how late we'll be out, or if we'll have time to get dinner somewhere. Hawk, it's probably best if only you go armed, as we'll be posing as normal Metropolitan Police officers. Concealed is preferable, but— what am I saying? You know weaponry better than I do."

Hawk got up, but stopped at the door. "Did Leslie say if she was coming back in a few minutes, or should I wait for her? I can't just leave Lukas sleeping upstairs." Alex brushed by him, murmuring something about crisps and chocolate milk as he made a mental list of what food he ought to take.

"Oh, I forgot to mention that, sorry. Yes, she said she was almost home, so we'll go when she gets here," Ian explained. After Hawk left, Ian turned to his nephew. "Most of the time we have to deal with either ridiculous boredom, or extreme frustration. Looks like you're getting a bit of a rough introduction. You ready? You can stay behind if you want to."

"No way! I don't fully understand everything that's going on, but what better way to learn than as we go?" Flynn got up and pushed the desk chair back into place.

"Well, I'm glad to have you along. Ask me whatever you want when we get in the car, and I'll answer you as best I can." Ian shut off the computer screens, stuffed Alex's laptop in a carrying case, and led Flynn out of the basement.

~~

Chapter Four

FLYNN SLIPPED INTO THE PASSENGER seat of
his uncle's dark grey Mazda CX-9. "You didn't get rid
of your BMW, did you?" he asked as he buckled up.

Ian laughed as he opened the sunroof and cracked the
windows. "No, I couldn't part with her. She's in the back of the
garage. I don't use her when I go out in the field."

Flynn glanced briefly in the rear-view mirror as they headed
down the road, and then found his eyes glued to it. "What
is...that isn't..." Turning around, he stared at the back window,
then looked incredulously at his uncle. "Hawk really owns an
MGB?"

Ian raised an eyebrow teasingly. "Suddenly my car isn't so
cool anymore?"

"No, no, just..." Flynn craned his neck for another good
look and shook his head admiringly. "That is one sweet ride.
Jus' sayin'." He turned back around in his seat and was silent for
a moment before asking, "Has he ever let you drive it?"

Ian gave him a single nod. "That he has. It's a smooth ride,
and accelerates beautifully. However, I'm perfectly content with
my BMW. Old cars have a certain charm to them, but they aren't
my style."

"True, I agree, but man! That is the kind of car one dreams of riding in at least once."

"I know Hawk will be more than happy to take you out for a spin. In fact, why don't you switch places with Alex once we leave the crime scene?" Ian suggested.

Flynn's face broke into a wide smile. "This day just keeps getting crazier and crazier!" They rode in silence for a few minutes before Flynn said, "Okay Uncle, you said I could ask as many questions as I wanted so here goes. First, how exactly was it determined that Axel escaped?"

"Around Wandsworth Common, the GPS tracking system for the cruiser was shut off and Axel never reached Wandsworth Prison, where he was supposedly being transferred to. An officer headed out to the last known location that registered on the GPS and found tire tracks in the grass. He called the Yard and reported it, and somebody wrote up the notice that Alex read," Ian explained simply.

"That makes sense," Flynn mused. "Okay, second question: what are we going to do, exactly, when we get there? Search for evidence and stuff, like fingerprints?"

"Indeed," Ian assented. "The Mallevilles probably revealed themselves for who they really were at Wandsworth Common. We'll look at what evidence is to be seen with the naked eye, then let the forensic guys comb the area and process the evidence. They'll send us a concise report in a day or so, but knowing the Mallevilles, they'll leave very little if not any useful evidence behind, and we may not have much to go on."

"Third question: what do we do after that? Look for the cruiser?"

Ian frowned in thought as he turned onto the highway. "Yes, we'll definitely try that. If we do find it, then there's a chance we'll have more to work with than a few tire tracks. See, officers don't usually wear gloves, so for the impersonation to work perfectly, neither could the Mallevilles. Knowing them, they'll wipe the car down pretty good, but there's a good chance they may miss a spot, in which case we could identify them."

"Do you think we'll be able to track where they went, or something? Maybe even recapture Axel?" Flynn asked hopefully.

"No, unfortunately that's wishful thinking. The Mallevilles have a base somewhere either in London, or nearby, and they'd head straight there." Ian sighed and his frown increased. "No, they'll be long gone."

"Hawk seems to think Tiernan is innocent. If he is, why do you suppose they took him with them? I mean, they don't exactly need a hostage, do they?" Flynn rolled his window down a bit, letting the wind whip through his hair. He shifted his gaze to the side mirror momentarily, hoping to catch another glimpse of Hawk's car.

Ian drummed his fingers on the edge of the steering wheel. "I don't honestly know, Flynn. They've never taken hostages before. Then again, they've never murdered an officer of the law either. My guess is, they kept him as insurance in the event they were pulled over before ditching the cruiser. They wouldn't drive it all the way to their base."

Rubbing his forehead, something he generally did when deep in thought, Ian continued, "As to whether they dumped him with the cruiser remains to be seen. It makes more sense for them to do so, but, then again, leaving a possibly unconscious, or bound, officer in a car attracts attention, which is something they can't afford to do. Thus, they very well may have taken him with them and dumped him elsewhere.

"If they do keep him, then it might have something to do with whatever they're planning next. Hostages make good bargaining chips. Maybe that sounds callous, but it's the truth. No one wants innocents to die, and when a hostage's life is on the line, it really ties the hands of the law." Ian sighed again and lapsed into silence. "I just wish we could catch a break for once," he muttered, more to himself than to his nephew.

~

When they arrived at Wandsworth Common, there were at least half-a-dozen squad cars parked at the crime scene. A large section had been taped off, and several officers were milling around. Ian parked his car and pointed out a tall, middle-aged man in a perfectly tailored suit. "That's Detective Chief Inspector Grant." Hawk parked his blue MGB behind Ian's car and he and Alex followed Ian over to Grant. "Hullo, Grant!" Ian called out.

Grant stopped mid-sentence and turned to see who had spoken. He smiled and waved. "Hey, Ian. Good to see you. Who's this?" and he nodded at Flynn.

"This is my nephew, Flynn; you know, the one that was inadvertently brought into this mess at the airport? He has always been interested in my work, and as he intends to follow in my footsteps one day, I took him along for a little hands-on training," Ian explained. A quick look of questioning surprise filled Grant's face as he looked from Ian to Flynn. Ian smiled at his friend and added in a lower tone, "Yes, he's in the know."

Grant stuck out his hand, and Flynn shook it firmly. "Nice to meet you, Flynn. Hullo, Hawk, Alex. Okay, so this is where the GPS tracking was lost. My guess is it was destroyed. As you can see," and he indicated the ground, "the car drove here, and parked over here on the grass, then turned around. We found blood stains on the grass." He motioned in the general direction. "From the information we have, we know there was no violence at the Yard, and no gunshots went off in this vicinity, so we are assuming Tiernan was not involved in the breakout, which means we have a hostage situation on our hands."

Hawk squatted down to get a better look. His face darkened as he noticed the brown stains on the grass and leaves. "They must have knocked him out with some blunt object, a gun maybe," he said, rising. "Did any of the residents around here see anything?"

"We've already knocked on over fifty doors. Nothing. Only two houses saw the cruiser come this way, and then go back out, but nobody saw what went on here at the Common." Grant was cut off as his cell phone rang. "Excuse me a second." He stepped to the side and took the call. "Well, there's some good news," he said as he returned his phone to his belt. "That was Sergeant Edward Finley. He received a tip about what appears to be an abandoned cruiser on Du Cane Road. Since there's nothing more we can do here, beyond letting forensics do their job, why don't we head down and see if it's the cruiser we're looking for?"

"Of course," Ian said.

"Let me calculate the best route," Alex interjected. He was about to say more, when his mouth dropped open.

"What?" Grant asked.

"Do you realize where Du Cane is? It's right across from HMP Wormwood Scrubs. The audacity of those guys! I mean, they could have been caught red-handed, but nooo, they have to taunt us!" He made a face. "They annoy me so much."

"It certainly is a risky move. Their success emboldens them; however, overconfidence can lead to carelessness and mistakes," Grant said with a frown. "I wonder if it's the right cruiser. Well, we have to find out. I know how much you like your little maps, so I'll follow your lead." Grant winked at Ian, who laughed in return.

"Alex, you're riding with me. Hawk, you mind taking Flynn? He's been eyeing that car of yours the entire trip here," Ian said.

"I have not!" Flynn protested weakly, though it was the truth. "I just said it was cool."

Hawk smiled. "Don't mind at all. I'll be right behind you." He flicked his wrist, indicating Flynn should follow him. "And you're right, it is cool."

Flynn could not suppress a grin of excitement as he slid into shotgun next to Hawk. "This is one sweet ride!" he exclaimed as he buckled up.

Hawk's smile widened. "Glad you like it. This was my dream car when I was young." After starting the engine and lowering the volume on the stereo, he backed up into a driveway to let Ian and Grant pass him before pulling out and following close behind.

"How fast have you gone in this thing?" Flynn asked.

"As fast as she can go," Hawk replied.

"No way!"

"It's not ridiculously fast, compared to other sports cars, or even Ian's BMW." He grinned and gestured towards the speedometer. "She barely tops 169km/h[1], but it sure gets the adrenaline going. Carliss was as much of a speed demon as I was, so we would head out to the Bedford Autodrome. We went so regularly, we actually became well acquainted with the owner, and he let us come out on days when the track was closed, so we could have it all to ourselves for as long as we liked. He also has a bunch of cars that he rents if you don't want to totally destroy your own. We'd take this one for the first spin, then use his cars, which he rented to us for pretty cheap. Those sure were good days. There's nothing like riding in a convertible at over 180km/h, top down, stereo blaring..." He got a bit of faraway look in his eyes.

---

[1] About 100 mph.

"That certainly sounds like living!" Flynn agreed. They lapsed into silence for a few minutes, before Flynn asked, "Hawk, how'd you know Tiernan? What's he like?"

There was a pause as Hawk considered this question. "Skyndar Tiernan is a younger officer — twenty-five thereabouts. Started with Scotland Yard a year or so ago. He's about three inches shorter than me, thin, sandy-haired, eyes a brownish-green. Very nice, yet very stubborn, and has a bit of a temper. Has a ridiculous memory, too, like none I've ever seen. He's also a Bible-believing Christian, same as us. I mentioned to Ian about him replacing one of the agents that we lost over the Challengers a while back, but Ian said to wait 'til he was a little older. I was going to get in touch with him on the subject later this year." Hawk stopped and frowned a little.

"You don't think the Mallevilles will kill him, do you?" asked Flynn.

"No. They don't have a reason to. They'll either keep him for their own nefarious purposes, or dump him in a ditch somewhere."

"Supposing they did keep him, do you think we can rescue him, or not? I mean, from what Uncle Ian said, you don't know where their base is yet, but there's always a chance, right?"

"I don't know Flynn, but I pray to God we can." Absent-mindedly, Hawk rolled his fingers on the volume dial and sighed. "We've been searching for their H.Q. ever since we learned of their existence. We've gotten close several times, but they vanished before we could get our hands on them, leaving us with a bunch of dirty laundry, broken bottles, and cigarette butts. Not very much to go on." He stopped as the next song on his custom CD started. "Ever driven in a sports car on the highway, 'Free Bird' playing full blast?"

Flynn shook his head. "I've heard of it — guitar solo right? Nah, Uncle Ian never plays that stuff. Mostly classical. He's driven me to the 'Flight of the Bumblebee,'" he added, as though that were comparable.

Hawk snorted. "Ian and I have always differed when it comes to music. And let me just tell you, the 'Flight of the Bumblebee' does *not* count as proper sports car music, no matter what *he* says."

"Are you sure it's...okay to do that now?" Flynn asked.

Hawk raised an eyebrow. "What do you mean?"

"Well, I don't want to make light of the seriousness of the situation by having a little fun."

Hawk thought for a moment before saying, "I'll be frank with you, Flynn. I use music for just about everything. If I'm upset, stressed, can't sleep, need to concentrate, am in a super good mood, or whatever, I turn something on, either to match my mood or improve it. So no, I don't think it's making light of the situation. But, if you do, then I'll save it." He paused the music, letting Flynn think in silence.

"I guess I've never really thought about it before. I like music, but I don't have it on all the time." He shrugged. "And right now, I honestly don't know what to think. Part of me is still extremely overwhelmed with everything I've learned so far in such a few hours. So, if you want to show me how to really ride in a sports car, go ahead."

Hawk restarted the track, turned it up, and flashed Flynn a smile. "Lean back and enjoy." Flynn wasn't convinced the song was any better than the 'Flight of the Bumblebee', until about a third of the way through. And as the lyrics faded away and Hawk rolled the windows down, Flynn realized he was right. There was no feeling quite like this in the whole world, and his uncle was dead wrong when it came to proper sports car music

~

"This is a rum business alright," Ian said. "I still can't believe they parked the car where they did."

"I know, right? And right outside a pizza shop, too. Feels like they're taunting us, huh?" Alex tapped his fingers lightly over his keyboard.

"Definitely. Hey, how much longer does your computer say we have until we arrive at the ditch site?"

"Ten minutes, thereabouts," he said, glancing down at his screen. "Should take only twenty-three total, but what with traffic and all..." he shrugged. After a few minutes, he frowned at the stereo. "What in blazes are we listening to?" he finally blurted.

"Some baroque CD Leslie gave me. I thought it was nice," Ian said. "You don't like it?"

Alex laughed. "Sure sounds broke to me! Like, what is that, a harpsicord? Bleh-heh! Don't you have anything good in this car of yours?" He opened the CD hatch and began rummaging around. "All classical. I like Hawk's selection way better." He slammed the hatch shut.

"You just like blasting your eardrums with constant noise," Ian jabbed.

"And you like killing yours with all this screechy, broken piano music," Alex retorted.

"A harpsicord is not a piano!" Ian cried indignantly. "And it's not screechy. Your electric guitars are."

"No way! Only people who don't know how to play them screech on them. And I don't listen to that stuff. What I listen to is good, quality music. You, my friend, are stuck in the dark ages."

"Ha, I don't think so! Electric guitars do *not* make music, they make noise."

Alex made sympathetic clucking sounds with his tongue and patted Ian on the shoulder. "You poor, poor person. Your ears are being deprived, you know."

Ian swatted his hand away with a laugh. "So are yours, you annoying little git!"

~

The first thing they noticed as they turned onto Du Cane was the smoke, and they hadn't gone far before they saw the blazing inferno. "That looks hot," Alex observed drily, gazing at the melting metal.

"Thanks for the intelligent observation." Ian scowled and parked his car on the opposite side of the street.

"Anytime." Alex shut his laptop and hopped out.

Grant parked behind him, and joined him on the sidewalk. "Looks like they got here first. I doubt there will be anything left for us to salvage."

"What I want to know is, why didn't they torch it right away?" Hawk said, coming up behind him. "If you ask me, their taunts are getting extremely risky. That fire was started in the last couple of minutes, I'd say." He crossed his arms, an angry look on his face. "I hate these guys," he muttered.

Flynn couldn't believe what he was seeing. He'd heard of torched vehicles, but had never seen one in person. He wanted to get a closer look, but as he got out of the car and began to follow Hawk, he noticed that his shoe was untied. Grumbling inwardly, he bent down to retie it. As he stood there, he thought he heard something. Finishing the knot, he straightened himself and looked around, trying to locate what he'd heard. He shrugged. He probably was just hearing the traffic, or someone inside one of the small shops nearby. He was about to turn back to the car, when he heard it again – the distinct sound of someone running. He tensed, wondering if he should go see who it was. Part of him wondered if he ought to mention something to his uncle, but he quickly shoved that thought aside. This was his chance to show he could help out, and if it proved to be nothing, then he wouldn't have raised an alarm for no reason. Without a second thought, he took off after the sound.

Down the street he went, towards the entrance of a small housing district, and finally caught sight of a man running far ahead of him. The runner looked over his shoulder, and, noticing

Flynn, veered onto Wulfstan Street. The realization that he wasn't just chasing someone who was out for a jog exhilarated Flynn, and he raced after him as fast as he could. He rounded the corner in time to see the man turn onto Braybrook Street.

Flynn tried to catch up, but the runner had a good start, and was already half-way down the street by the time Flynn spotted him again. The runner looked over his shoulder, saw Flynn still in pursuit, and turned off the street into Wormwood Scrubbs Park. Flynn followed him, but when he ran off the road and into the grass, the runner was nowhere in sight. He bent over, panting, then shaded his eyes and scanned the area as best he could. Where was that guy? He walked forward, eyeing the clumps of trees and bushes.

Suddenly, he tensed. Something wasn't right. He could feel danger in every nerve of his body. A stone whistled past his ear. Flynn dropped to his hands and knees and hurried over behind a cluster of small trees. Another stone flew by him, landing in the grass with a *thunk*. This most certainly was not going how he thought it would, and he tried desperately to come up with a plan. Unfortunately, he couldn't.

Back at the car, the group was oblivious to Flynn's disappearance, until Hawk saw him rounding the corner onto Wulfstan. "Whoa, what's gotten into Flynn? Where's he going?" he asked.

"What?" Ian looked up. "Wait, where is he?"

"He just took that street there." Hawk pointed to where he'd last seen him.

Ian was horrified, and Hawk saw a flicker of fear in his eyes. "What is he *thinking*? Come on, Hawk. If he saw someone..." Ian didn't finish his sentence. He dashed after Flynn, Hawk at his heels. Hawk outstripped him, and managed to catch sight of Flynn turning off down Braybrook. He waved to Ian to follow him, and finally stopped on the edge of the park.

"Lost him," he said, trying to control his breathing. He scanned the area, and saw a stone fly out of a clump of bushes and strike a near-by tree.

"Flynn's probably behind those trees," Ian conjectured, pointing as he spoke.

"Yeah, and whoever he was chasing is slinging rocks from those bushes over there." Another stone confirmed their theory. "Whoever it is, he hasn't seen us yet, or he would have aimed in our direction. See if you can't get over to Flynn. I'll sneak up behind our mystery man and take him out." Ian nodded silently, crouched low, and headed for the cover of some nearby underbrush.

Flynn was so engrossed in trying to catch a glimpse of his enemy, he didn't even see Ian until he felt a hand on his shoulder. He jerked and yelped in surprise. "Why, Uncle, what are you—"

"No, what are *you* doing?!" Ian snapped quietly. "No, don't tell me. We'll discuss this later," he added in a louder tone as he heard a cry of anger and the crackle of broken branches.

"You can't do this!" a man's angry voice protested.

"Oh yes I can, Mr. Emory Vansant. I'm Scotland Yard, and there's a warrant out for your arrest," Hawk answered calmly. He then listed off the man's rights as he snapped handcuffs on his wrists and took possession of his slingshot.

Ian was livid when he heard the name of the man Flynn had chased. "You...you..." He closed his eyes and clenched his teeth. Flynn inwardly groaned. It took a lot to make his uncle really angry, and he knew he was in trouble. "When we reach the cars, get in mine and wait for me, understand?" Ian said in as even and measured a tone as he could muster.

"Yes, sir."

Ian turned and followed Hawk back to the cruisers. "This trip could be called something of a success, Chief," Hawk said to Grant as they came up. "We caught Emory Vansant."

Grant looked both surprised and pleased. "Put him in the back of my car, and I'll take him up to the Yard for questioning," he instructed. Once this was done, he continued. "I called the fire department, and a tow truck, and they ought to be here shortly. Do you mind waiting for them while I take Vansant away?"

"Not at all," Ian said. "We'll meet you there as soon as we can for the questioning." After Grant had left, Alex handed out snacks and cold sandwiches. They had hardly finished eating before the trucks arrived, and after waiting for the fire to be put out and giving the tow truck instructions to deliver what was left of the car to forensics, they hurried over to the Yard, Alex hitching a ride with Hawk.

Risking a glance at his uncle, Flynn attempted to break the silence as they rode together. "Uncle, I...I'm sorry. I didn't mean to do anything stupid."

"Sorry doesn't cut it, Flynn," Ian said sharply. "You don't understand the seriousness of our job, do you?"

Flynn winced at his tone. "Yes, I do, I–"

"No, you don't!" Ian contradicted him flatly, gripping his steering wheel tightly as he tried to control his temper. "You don't get it at all. You could have been killed, or badly injured in the least. You ran off, by yourself and unarmed, after an unknown person who happened to be part of the Malleville gang. Thankfully, it was Vansant, who is an eccentric enough fellow to carry a slingshot instead of a gun. If it had been anyone else, you would have been shot, numerous times, and the bullets wouldn't have just grazed your arm this time." Ian glanced at him briefly. "The first rule you need to learn is this: *never* go anywhere by yourself when out in the field, do you understand me?"

"Yes, sir."

"And don't you *ever* run off like that again!"

"Yes, sir. I'm sorry," Flynn said softly. "I just wanted to help."

"Getting yourself killed because you want to show off how capable you think you are is not helping." Ian sighed heavily and looked over at his nephew. Seeing how distraught he looked, he felt the anger drain out of him. "I'm not mad at you, okay? You terrified me. I had no idea what you were running into, and since it was connected to the Mallevilles..." Ian's voice trailed off.

Flynn sighed and shut his eyes. "I'm so sorry, Uncle. I didn't mean to scare you. I only wanted to help. Instead, I made a fool of myself," he said bitterly.

"No, you didn't make yourself a fool, you just acted foolishly."

"That's the same thing."

"No, it's not," Ian disagreed. "Your intentions were good, but you didn't go about them in the best manner. Though you learned a lesson the hard way, it was mild compared to what it could have been, and I hope you have learned it well enough never to do so again." Braking for a stoplight, he looked at Flynn and said, gently, "I love you, Flynn, as my own son, and I don't want to lose you. Please, if we're out on the job, don't leave my side unless I tell you otherwise, alright? I would never forgive myself if..."

"Yes, Uncle. I love you too." Flynn found himself smiling.

"And it's just as much my fault as it is yours. You were thrown into my way of life only hours ago, and I don't have a manual to show you how to navigate. I guess we're both winging it a little. Oh, and don't breathe a word of this to your aunt. It would give her a horrible fright." Ian shook his head, took a deep breath, and let it out slowly. "And mind you, I don't usually keep things from her, but in this instance, I think it's for the best."

Flynn ducked his head sheepishly. "Yeah..." After a minute, he gave his uncle a sly look. "I learned another thing today, you know."

"Really? And just what might that be?" Ian raised an eyebrow.

"You have no idea what proper sports car music is."

Ian groaned. "Don't tell me you actually like that awful cacophony Hawk blares on his stereo!"

"It's not a cacophony, Uncle. I mean, I wouldn't listen to it all the time, but on the highway, in an epic car? Definitely."

"Oh, what do you know!" Ian lightly whapped the back of Flynn's head. "Nothing, that's what I say, nothing at all. You're delusionary, and I see I shall have to take you for a spin in my BMW to prove it to you."

~

When they arrived at the Yard, Ian and Hawk joined Grant in questioning Vansant, but Alex brought Flynn into a generic office off to the side. "They might be awhile," he said, opening his laptop. "And since Vansant's part of the Mallevilles, he might say nothing at all, or just a bunch of nothing. I cannot stand that part of the job, so how about a game of chess?"

"I don't see a chess board," Flynn said, scanning the office.

Alex motioned towards a blank computer screen at the desk. "I can set it up so you play your moves on that screen and I'll play my moves on my laptop. You on?"

Flynn shrugged. "Sure, I guess. But I doubt I'll be able to concentrate much. I mean, what if something important happens? Oughtn't we go watch or something?"

Alex signed into the office computer and pulled up the chess game before spinning his chair around to face Flynn. "I used to think like that, and I both watched and recorded every Malleville questionnaire until I realized it was pointless. The guys we catch either don't know a thing, or don't say anything. It's incredibly boring, or frustrating, or irritating, or all of the above. So, I leave the questioning to Ian and Hawk, and if there's something I need to know, they tell me."

"If you say so." Flynn took a seat and tried to pay attention to the game, but he was far too distracted, and Alex was soon toying with him.

"Haven't you ever played before?" he asked, not believing his good luck.

"Yeah, a couple times, but only against school mates. I've never been beaten this badly, though." Flynn frowned at the screen and moved his Queen.

"Ha ha, you fell for it!" Alex moved his Knight, removing the Queen from the board. He then proceeded to take out Flynn's Knights and Bishops, and was just setting up an elaborate check mate when Hawk opened the door.

"You'll never believe it, mate – Vansant knows their current headquarters!" Hawk's face glowed with excitement.

"You're kidding me. You mean to say I finally skip an interrogation and the guy actually says something useful?" Alex was the picture of disbelief.

"Pretty much. Vansant was an absolute wealth of information, and very willing to share what he could to help.

Grant's ringing SCO19[2], and we are going to meet them outside Edgware for a bust. I'll give you the details on the way home. Come on!" Hawk gestured impatiently. Alex snapped his laptop shut and hurried after his friend. Flynn hastily signed off the office computer and followed them.

Ian was waiting for him beside his Mazda. "Get in, and I'll explain as we drive," he said. "As Hawk probably told you, Vansant knew Icabod's current headquarters." Ian smiled at his nephew triumphantly. "This is a huge break, and I can hardly believe it!"

"Where is it?" Flynn asked excitedly.

"In a run-down house just outside of Clump of Trees Wood in Edgware. We're to meet Grant and SCO19 near Target Woods as soon as we can." Ian poured on a little more speed, stretching the speed limit as far as he dared.

"So, why are we going home?" Flynn was confused.

"Raiding their headquarters is potentially very dangerous," Ian began to explain. "We can't just run in there, unarmed and unprepared. The Mallevilles are known for their cameras and traps, so Alex needs to get some equipment in order to render them useless, and since there is the potential for a fire-fight, we will need to go armed. Once we suit up, we'll head right back out."

"I thought this day was crazy earlier..." Flynn smiled wryly.

---

[2] A branch of the Specialist Firearms Command, the Specialist Crimes and Operations, SCO19 is the armed police unit that aids the Metropolitan Police; often compared to the USA's S.W.A.T.

Ian chuckled. "I told you, it comes in spurts."

"Uncle, why was Vansant so compliant?" Flynn asked suddenly. "I thought most criminals resisted and plead innocent."

"They usually do, but sometimes, if the evidence is overwhelming and they know it, they give up information in order to lighten their sentence. Such was Vansant's case," Ian said. "He gave us his whole story, which was very similar to that of all the others we have caught in the past. Back when they first met, Icabod flattered him into his confidence and then saved him from a speeding car, which was all a set-up to get Vansant indebted to him. Vansant rashly promised to do anything to repay him, and Icabod asked him to help out with some less-than-legal transactions. By the time Vansant wanted out, he was in so deep it wasn't an option. Icabod could blackmail him and get him jailed at any time, so he was forced to continue to do the Malleville's bidding, such as the airport heist, and the car bomb."

Flynn was quiet as he thought about what had happened with Vansant earlier. "Why didn't he just get in his car and drive away when I chased him?"

"He thought he could elude you in the residential area, then double back to his car, thereby letting him escape unnoticed. He didn't plan on you following him so closely."

Once they got home, they found Leslie stirring some soup on the stove. "I kept it nice and hot for you all. You must be starving. How did your first trip out on the field go, Flynn? Did you enjoy it?"

"Yes, very much, Aunt." Flynn was about to say more, but Ian cut him off.

"Thanks, m'dear, but I'm afraid your soup will have to wait." Ian gave her a quick kiss on the cheek. "We caught Emory Vansant, and he told us the location of the Malleville's current headquarters. We're going to have to head right back out."

Leslie's eyes widened. "Are you serious?"

"Quite. And there's a good chance we'll actually catch someone this time. They have no idea we're coming." He eyed the soup with a disappointed air. "Pity, though. It smells delicious."

"Well, you can't just go hungry. While you grab your stuff, let me see what I can put together for the drive." Leslie opened a lower cabinet and began removing some containers. "Flynn's not going, right?"

"I hadn't thought about it," Ian said honestly.

"He shouldn't. It's far too dangerous, and it's only his first day here," Leslie said firmly.

Flynn's face fell. "But Uncle, I *need* to go with you and see what happens. And after what happened earlier, you know there won't be a problem."

Leslie froze. "What happened earlier?" she demanded.

"Oh, nothing," Ian said hastily, shooting a warning look at his nephew. "Just that, if it hadn't been for Flynn, we wouldn't have caught Vansant."

"Yeah, Aunt, I was instrumental in the catch." Flynn grinned as innocently as he could.

Seeing Leslie's horrified expression, Ian said, "That he was, m'dear, but we are pressed for time, so I have to go." He was gone before his wife could protest.

Flynn hurried after his uncle down into the basement. As they entered the office, he heard Alex say to Hawk, "Hand me that tripod, will you? Ta. Man, this is so exciting! Who would've thought we'd be busting the Mallevilles tonight? This is *so* worth losing sleep over!"

"Don't get caught up celebrating just yet. Let's hope they're actually there." Hawk opened one of his desk drawers and drew out a shiny black Berretta 92 FS. He checked the cartridge and made sure the safety was set before pulling a leg strap out of the drawer and strapping it on. "I'll be right back." He started to leave, then leaned back in the doorway. "Make sure you take your gun, mate. If they really are there, you might need it."

Alex made a face. "Fine," he murmured.

"Hey, look on the bright side: you don't have to use it except in an extreme situation." Hawk vanished and headed back upstairs. "And grab my FN five-seven while you're at it."

"I hate possible fire-fight situations," Alex grumbled as he got up.

"I know, but that's part of the job," Ian said. "Grab mine too, would you?" he hollered after him. He glanced over at Flynn, who seemed to be staring into the distance. He waved a hand in front of his nephew's face. "Earth to Flynn. You here?"

Flynn snapped out of it and shook his head. "Yeah, yeah, I'm here. Just thinking."

Ian could guess what it was about, and turned toward his computer. "If I allow you to go with us, you have to promise to stay in the car unless I come for you. And that's only if the guys agree."

"Here." Alex held Ian's handgun to him. It was a shiny black Glock with a smooth handle, and Flynn stared at it in awe.

"Thanks."

"And none fer you, laddie," Alex added in a horrible attempt at a Scottish accent as he noticed Flynn's wide eyes.

"I know. I wouldn't even dream of it until I actually knew what I was doing." He hesitated, then asked, "Should you?"

"Should I what?"

"You know...have one? I mean, the way you all talk, you're making me nervous. I don't want you to accidentally shoot me!"

"You won't if you stay in the car like a good little boy." Alex winked. "Nah, I'm not that bad," he continued in a more serious tone, "but I still avoid the whole shooting-while-in-the-field thing unless I have to." Hearing Hawk's footsteps, he winked broadly, picked up Hawk's FN five-seven, and said in a loud voice, "And like I was saying, the only way to see if it's jammed is to look down the barrel, like so."

"No no no!" Hawk ran in, horrified. "Don't you *ever*—"

They all started laughing. "Got you, ol' chap!" Alex slapped him on the shoulder and handed him the gun. "You can't seriously think I'm *that* dumb, huh?"

Hawk rolled his eyes, took the gun, and inspected it carefully. "With you, I can never tell."

"Ooh, *buuuuurn!*" Ian teased. He shut his computer screen off before turning to face them all. "I'm considering taking Flynn along – he would stay in the car until the coast is clear. Any objections?"

"None here. Nothing can happen as long as he's locked up, right?" Alex shrugged.

Hawk scowled in thought, his gaze shifting from Ian to Flynn. "No, I guess it's fine, as long as you don't run off. You stay in that car, and you don't move until either Ian, Alex, or I come for you, got it? There's a good chance the headquarters won't be empty this time, and we don't need any unnecessary casualties."

"Yes, sir," Flynn said seriously.

Ian stood up. "Very well then, since that's settled, let's pray and head out. Obviously, we're optimistic that we'll catch somebody this time, but there's no telling what could happen. This is a raid like any other, and may God bless our efforts to bring the Mallevilles to justice." Ian prayed for the group's safety and asked for wisdom and guidance. Then, after running a quick stock of equipment and weapons, Ian turned to his nephew and said, "Come on, Flynn, it's time to get suited up." Following Ian out of the office and into a large storage room that went several feet back, Flynn's jaw dropped. The walls were covered in racks full of weapons, ammunition, bulletproof vests, and other items.

"Here, put this on." Ian handed him a vest as he spoke, and then handed one to Hawk before strapping one on himself. Alex had gone upstairs to load his stuff in Ian's Mazda.

"Will I need it if I'm in the car?" Flynn asked.

"You don't know, so you go prepared," Hawk answered. "The chances of you actually getting shot are extremely slim, but we don't take chances."

Ian took hold of another vest for Alex and tossed it to Hawk. "Now come on, we've got to get moving."

~~

Chapter Five

LESLIE WASN'T THRILLED WITH THE idea of Flynn tagging along, but Ian assured her he would be kept out of harm's way. Leslie reluctantly agreed to let him go, but cautioned him to do exactly as his uncle said, and to stay out of trouble. "I've packaged up some cold cuts and cheese for you all on the drive," she said, handing Flynn some plastic containers. "Oh, and here's a bag of cookies. Alex would throw a fit if you forgot them," she added, handing it to him.

"Thanks, Aunt. And don't worry, we'll be fine." He smiled at her and headed out into the garage.

"Later, Les. I'll keep an eye on him." Hawk winked at her before following Flynn.

Leslie pulled Ian into a hug. "Be careful, please," she whispered in his ear.

"Always, m'dear." He kissed her gently. "I have no idea when we'll be home, so don't wait up for us, okay? It could be well after midnight."

"Don't count on it. There's no way I could sleep, knowing you're out in the field, and possibly in danger. I'll be praying for you. Ring me once the raid is over. Promise me?" she pleaded.

"I promise."

Leslie hugged him tightly and gave him another kiss. "God be with you, love, and bring you back safe to me."

As he was getting in the car, Flynn noticed Alex unscrewing the number plates. "What are you doing?"

"I'm playing the piano, what's it look like?" Alex put a new, magnetic plate in place, pulled one of the screws out of his mouth, and laid them on a shelf.

"Obviously you're switching number plates, but why? And is that even legal?" Flynn ignored the man's sarcasm.

"'Course it's legal! And I'm switching them in the event somebody looks them up in the hopes of identifying us. Incognito, remember? There, all set." Alex twirled his screwdriver and dropped it into his satchel. "Hop in, kiddo."

"You forgot to put this on, mate," Hawk said, throwing the vest at Alex.

"Ta, ol' chap!" Alex hastily put it on.

Ian took the wheel, Hawk slid into the passenger seat, and Flynn took the backseat next to Alex and his satchel of equipment. "Uncle, why was the car torched so late?" he asked as they headed out.

"Vansant said Damian rigged up a tiny time bomb, which Icabod installed in the cruiser. Only a wire was damaged somehow, and the device malfunctioned. They didn't know it malfunctioned until Vansant, who was in the area getting some things for another phase of the plan, noticed that the car was still very much intact. He called Damian, who instructed him to fix it and manually trigger the bomb. He had only just finished the job when we showed up."

"I thought he hated fires and bombs and pyrotechnics," Alex said.

"He does, but when you've got Icabod Malleville blackmailing you, you'll do just about anything."

Flynn shook his head. "What a mess!"

"The Mallevilles are the definition of mess. The most organized mess we've ever seen, and I am thoroughly fed up with them," Alex said as he opened his laptop and mapped out the best route to Target Woods. He rattled off the directions to Ian, who quickly memorized them.

"What exactly will we do when we get there?" Flynn asked.

"SCO19 will lead the way," Hawk began. "When we arrive at the house, Alex will monitor it for traps, after which SCO19 will force entry. Hopefully, someone will be there. If so, then there's no telling what will happen. There's the possibility of a fire-fight, explosives, and who knows what else; the Mallevilles are extremely resourceful. However, if they're not there, we'll check the whole place for whatever evidence we can find. One of us will come and get you once either they are apprehended or the coast is clear."

"When you do join us, you must use our code names," Ian said, looking at him briefly over his shoulder. "Our real names must be kept a secret, so do not use them, ever, for any reason. Do you understand?"

"Yes, Uncle. What kind of code names are we talking?"

"Ace ones, and all credit goes to me," Alex said without looking up from his screen.

"No, the names weren't all your idea," Hawk contradicted. "Only the idea of their roots."

"Whatever. Same difference."

"So...what are they?" Flynn interjected before Hawk and Alex really went at it.

"I am Cap, Hawk is Sparrow, and Alex is Tuck, short for Friar Tuck in case you were wondering," Ian replied. "In other words, we are all named for someone fictitious, save for me, though Alex would disagree."

"Totally!" Alex hollered with feigned indignance. "He insists it's short only for Captain, but that is soooo boring. It ought to be short for Captain America. Way cooler."

"Alex, you know I could care less about superheroes," Ian said, glancing at him in his rear-view mirror.

"I know, but the idea is to use a name from fiction, and plain ol' Cap doesn't cut it," Alex argued, finally tearing his eyes from his computer to glare at the mirror. "You really ought to have taken my first suggestion. Excalibur is an epic code name."

"That's the name of a sword, not a person," Ian retorted.

Alex waved his hand in annoyance. "Details, details."

"Alex is picky when it comes to names, in case you hadn't noticed," Hawk jabbed. "My first suggestion for mine was Thranduil, but nooo, that wasn't good enough."

Alex rolled his eyes. "Hawk, seriously, not everyone can say that right! It's a mouthful of mispronunciation just waiting to happen."

"Carliss liked it," Hawk said slyly.

"Oh, don't pull that card with me!" Alex was getting exasperated. "You said you were happy with Sparrow. It's a perfect pun off your own name, and the— oh, why do I have to go through this again? You're Sparrow, not Thranduil, and it ain't gettin' changed, so shush it." Alex poked him in the shoulder for good measure.

"Ignore them. They've argued about code names ever since the beginning," Ian said to Flynn. "Now, do you remember who's who?"

"You're Cap, Hawk is Sparrow, and Alex is Tuck. What am I?" he added.

"Anything you like."

Flynn thought for a moment before bursting out, "Oh, just give me something! There are too many choices."

"Alex, you got any ideas?" Ian called out.

Alex looked up from his laptop and surveyed Flynn for a moment. "D'art," he replied simply, dropping his head back to his screen.

"What? What kind of name is *that*?" Flynn cried.

"You obviously need a healthy dose of books," was the dry response. "Try *The Three Musketeers* for one."

"I *have* read it. You mean you're likening me to...to D'Artagnan?!"

"Yes."

Flynn was silent for a moment as he considered this. "I don't know whether to be insulted or complimented."

Alex shrugged. "You're an inexperienced young person who asks way too many questions and is still learning the ropes, not to mention you're sort of like the fourth musketeer. If you want something else, then I'll call you Pippin – how's that?"

"I'll stick with D'art thank you very much," Flynn replied with a wry smile.

~

Leslie found herself standing all alone in an empty kitchen with a full pot of hot soup that needed to be put away for another day. As she took out a glass container, her mind wandered to Ian and Flynn and the guys. Sometimes, being the wife of a secret agent was just as hard as being the agent himself; maybe even worse, since she was the one left behind, not knowing what was going on. It was at a time like this where she felt helpless, as though she couldn't do anything to be of service. But every time such thoughts crossed her mind, she knew she really could help, just in a different way.

After cleaning up the kitchen, she made her way upstairs and checked on the boys who were sleeping peacefully in their bunkbeds. She gave them another kiss goodnight and then went to her own room. Getting down on her knees, she prayed, long and earnestly, that the guys would succeed in their venture, but ultimately that they would be kept safe. A gun was good insurance against a villain, but only God could keep those she loved truly safe.

~

When they arrived at Target Woods, only Grant was there, waiting in his cruiser. Ian got out and spoke with him before returning to the car. "SCO19 will be here in a few minutes. Once they do, we'll follow them to the headquarters." It didn't take long for the ARV's to arrive. Moving back onto the highway, they had but to drive a little ways before pulling off onto a small lane that was overgrown with bushes, weeds, and tiny saplings. After a minute or two, the road veered off to the right, and the ARV's abruptly stopped.

"Why are we stopping?" Alex asked.

"Vansant said to head left when we got to the fork. However, if you'll take your nose out of your computer, you'd notice that the left path is very overgrown, which, if it is the path, it shouldn't be, unless it's made to look that way." Ian shut the car off and turned in his seat. "Alex, run a scan for traps and cameras." Alex typed steadily away at his laptop, then raised his eyes to Ian's face. "Mind opening the window?" Ian complied and pressed the desired button. Alex balanced his computer on the window ledge and let his software start scanning.

"What is that?" Flynn asked.

"It's a metal sensor. It's looking for electronic devices, or anything they may have rigged up. It's hard to make either of them without metal, so my scanner comes in pretty handy. Okay, so there's no traps that I can see, but there's definitely a camera up in that tree over there." Alex motioned to one on the right as he shut down the software and closed his laptop. "I'm supposing you want me to go turn it off?"

"No," Ian said. "If it's a camera, than they might already know we're here." His gaze flashed to the bushes and vines that blocked their way. "My guess is most of those are fake. We should just go right in. Taking out the camera now would be a waste of time." He radioed Grant, and in a few seconds, the ARV's put on a burst of speed and crashed through the path to the left. The path turned sharply, and they came upon a small, two-story house. The ARV's surrounded the house, and the officers piled out, guns drawn and cocked. Ian parked on the far side of the clearing. As he undid his seatbelt, he turned to Flynn and said, "Don't you leave this car for any reason. I don't care what happens, you stay here. Are we clear?"

"Yes, Uncle. God be with you." Flynn reached out and squeezed Ian's shoulder.

"And with you." Ian locked the doors as he left. Flynn scrambled into the front seat. If he had to stay behind, he wasn't going to sit in the back like a naughty child.

Hawk led the way, and they hurried over behind one of the ARV's, while Inspector Grant went up to the front door with several SCO19 officers. Flynn peered anxiously out the window. Now it was his turn to feel fear. What would happen? What if something went horribly wrong?

Grant rapped boldly on the front door. "Icabod and Damian Malleville, I have a warrant for your arrest! Come on out!" No answer. "Do we have to do this the hard way?" Still nothing. Just dead silence. "Have it your way, then!" Grant stood aside and motioned for the SCO19 officers to bust it down.

"Wait!" Alex called out. "The door might be protected with an electrically charged, TASER-enhanced, photoelectric sensor beam. If you bust the door down, let me scan it before you barge in."

Flynn could hear what he said, but it made absolutely no sense to him. What even was an electrically charged TASER-enhanced, photoelectra-something-or-another anyway? He watched as Grant waved Alex over. SCO19 busted the door, but stepped back as it fell.

Alex was incredibly nervous as he advanced towards the gaping doorway. Not even all of the armed SCO19 officers and his bullet-proof vest could make him feel unexposed. He scanned the entrance with a wrist device, and sure enough, a red beam appeared forty-nine centimeters[1] above the ground. Pulling a small black box and collapsible tripod out of his satchel, he attached them together, pressed a few buttons on the box, then aimed his wrist device at it, revealing two green beams of light emitting from the box. He aimed the beams until they met and replaced the red one. "Coast clear," he said. "Just nobody touch the box." He quickly backed up as SCO19 swarmed the house. Hawk and Ian followed Grant in, but Alex remained behind.

---

[1] About 19 inches.

Flynn grew increasingly nervous as nothing happened. He could see the SCO19 officers as they looked out of the upstairs windows, but there was no shooting. No explosions. No nothing. Was that good or bad? The verse, *Be still and know that I am God,* flashed across his mind and he scowled. It was easy to say, but not easy to do. He knew God was with his uncle, but it was so very hard to just sit here and be still and wait. He half-smiled as he imagined his uncle saying something about putting verses into action, and how patience was a virtue.

Finally, Hawk came out of the house, said something to Alex who went into the house, and then walked over to the car. Even with the vague darkness of dusk, it took only one look at his face to reveal the truth: the Mallevilles had vanished, and they were once more left with an empty headquarters. Hawk motioned for him to come. Flynn unlocked the door and got out, asking as he did so, "There's nothing then? They're gone?"

"Yeah, looks like it." Hawk turned on his heels and headed back for the house, his gait rigid and his jaw tight in suppressed anger.

"But how?" Flynn accidentally stumbled over a rut in the dirt driveway and nearly fell over. He felt his face get hot with embarrassment. What a fine way to make an entrance. He hoped none of the SCO19 officers had noticed his fancy footwork.

"I don't have a bloody idea." Hawk clenched his hands in frustration. "They shouldn't have known we were coming, yet everything inside indicates a hasty departure. It's like they vanished into thin air, and we all know that's not possible. Watch the box," he cautioned as they reached the house.

"What's it for?" Flynn eyed it curiously.

"It's disabling a trap, but don't ask me for the details. I don't understand how it works in the slightest; super complicated."

Inside, SCO19 was checking every closet and door to make sure the place was empty. Alex was walking around in a seemingly aimless manner, stamping his foot every now and again as though testing the floor. Ian was on his knees in the living room, examining some stains on the ragged carpet. Grant stood over him, watching intently, but looked over as Hawk entered with Flynn in tow.

"It's definitely blood," Ian was saying. "Tiernan's, probably."

"Why didn't they stay and taunt us with him?" Flynn asked. "Isn't that what criminals usually do?"

Before his uncle could reply, a loud cry rang out from the kitchen. It was Alex. Ian and Hawk exchanged glances of dismay before rushing in the direction of the kitchen. Grant and several other officers entered from another doorway. They were horrified to find a large hole in the floor.

"What happened?" Ian cried.

"I was backing into the corner to get out of his way, but when I stepped on that uneven tile, the floor just disappeared," an SCO19 officer explained nervously.

"Tuck, you down there?" Peering down into the hole, Hawk tried to catch a glimpse of his friend.

"Yeah. Sorry I screamed, just really wasn't expecting the floor to give out." Alex's voice echoed up to them. "I'm on a platform or something. Ouch," and they heard a slight scuffing sound. "Yeah, I'm okay. I'm bruised, but fine. Somebody give me a light, please?"

Grant flicked on his torch and the beam pierced the inky blackness, revealing Alex standing on a wooden platform about half-way down the hole. "Are those stairs?" he asked, shining the light off to the left.

"I think so." Alex dusted himself off and started down them.

"You be careful!" Hawk called, straining to see. "How far back does it go?"

"Not too far. There's a dead end and....whoa, guys, you gotta see this!"

"How are we supposed to do that?" Ian asked, more to himself than to anyone in particular. "It would be too dangerous to jump down to that platform. I wonder...what if it's actually fold-up stairs?"

Without a word, Hawk got down on his knees, thrust his hands in the hole and started to feel around along the edge. After a minute of probing under the floor, he cried excitedly, "I've got something!" He flicked a tiny switch and, sure enough, the platform began to rise, creating collapsible stairs.

"Well, I'll be..." muttered an officer.

Grant led the way, and Hawk followed. Ian was about to go next, when Flynn tapped his shoulder. "Can I come?"

"I have no idea what's down there, so wait until I call, okay?" Ian went down about half-way before he stopped and looked back up. "It's completely empty. Stick close." Flynn stepped down after him, an SCO19 officer on his heels. The room was small, and opened into a short tunnel. Alex had found a light switch, and several annoyingly bright LED bulbs lit up the whole area. At the end of the tunnel was a smooth wall, and in the center of it was a large indentation of the letter M. Flynn gaped at it.

"This is so weird," Alex said, banging a fist against the wall. "It's like a hatchway or something, but there's no handle or switch or anything!"

Flynn watched as the men tried to make sense of the strange, empty room. After a few minutes, he walked over to his uncle and tapped him on the shoulder again. He knew he couldn't call him "Uncle", but calling him "Cap" sounded disrespectful – at least, coming from him – so he found himself avoiding addressing him at all.

"Yes?" Ian gave him an inquisitive look.

"Do you mind if I look around the house a bit? I mean, unless Tuck can work some magic, that wall isn't going anywhere anytime soon, so..." Flynn looked at him hopefully. He felt the urge to explore some, and found staring at an immovable wall rather tedious.

Ian frowned, opened his mouth to say something, then closed it. He hesitated before saying, "Yes, but let me go with you. I doubt there are any more collapsible floors, but, then again, these are the Mallevilles we're talking about. Besides, I have a call to make. I'll meet you in the living room. Just give me a minute."

Flynn was about to go up, when he heard Alex say, "These guys are like spiders, always hiding in some dark, secret place, weaving their webs of deception and trickery. Super annoying. I was bit by a spider once. It was a diving bell spider, you know, the kind that catches air bubbles and puts them in his web to breathe underwater. Absolutely fascinating. They're poisonous, too, but not deadly or anything like that; just hurt, and gives you a fever."

Ian shivered. "That's enough, please, Tuck." Ian hated spiders passionately, and didn't even like discussing them if it could be helped.

"Oh, sorry, Cap, but they're really quite interesting. Did you know, they even have gills of sorts—"

"Tuck!" Ian said loudly. "*Stop.*" Alex shut his mouth and returned his attention to the wall, though Ian could have sworn he heard him mutter, *Whatever,* under his breath.

Flynn couldn't help but smile as he mounted the stairs and headed for the living room. Once there, he surveyed the dusty floor and dingy furniture until his gaze fastened on what appeared to be an old newspaper sitting in the ashes of the hearth. Picking it up, he examined it closely, wondering if there was anything important on it or if it was just a fire starter. He was about to toss it back when his eye caught a long list of tiny numbers written into the margins of one of the articles. There were two columns, one entitled "L", and the other "R". He knew he had to leave the paper to be collected as evidence, but the numbers fascinated him. He felt in his pockets for a pen, then hastily copied the numbers down on the inside of his arm. He suppressed a smile as he remembered his grandmama's remonstrations about writing on his skin; but if he didn't have paper, what else was a fellow to do? He replaced the paper in the hearth and was just rolling down his sleeve when Ian entered.

They didn't stay much longer. Once forensics arrived, there was little to do beyond stepping back and letting them do their job. The whole group was rather subdued, disappointed at their bust being just that: a bust. Not even the secret door could lift their spirits; what good was it when it didn't open? Flynn momentarily forgot about the numbers written on his arm as he listened to the guys conjecture back and forth about the Malleville's escape.

"Oh, Alex, what exactly does your box do?" he asked when there was a lull in the conversation. "I mean, what even is an electrically charged, TASER-whatever-mah-thingibob?"

"An electrically charged, TASER-enhanced, photoelectric sensor beam?" Alex rolled it off his tongue with ease.

"Yeah, that."

"It's…difficult to explain." Alex screwed up his face and tried to think of the simplest way to put it. "A regular photoelectric beam is used in lots of alarm systems. A beam of light is hooked up to an alarm, and as long as the beam is not broken, the alarm won't sound. The Mallevilles, however, hooked up the no-wire TASER technology to the beam of light, thereby causing whatever or whoever breaks the beam to get hit with a violent shock that will render them unconscious. I figured out how to neutralize it, but that's where it gets kind of complicated." Nodding, Flynn refrained from inquiring further. He had a feeling it would go right over his head.

~

Leslie was curled up on the couch, surrounded by pillows and covered with a thick blanket. She had tried and tried to get through a chapter in her book, but, to her annoyance, she kept dozing off every few paragraphs. She'd read that same page probably ten times, but still had no idea what it said. She decided to try and read the page once more, but after nodding off again, gave it up and laid the book aside.

She didn't know why she was so sleepy. She often stayed up when the guys were out, and rarely dozed when she had a book in hand. But for some reason, for the past week or so, she'd just felt lethargic and drowsy. Her allergies had been bothersome, too, and she felt…well, off. That was the only way to put it. Ian had noticed, but she'd shrugged it off. Maybe she was catching Lukas's cold.

She was disappointed that the raid had been for naught, but relieved that no one had been in any real danger, and that they all would be home safe and sound before the night was up. She didn't realize she'd fallen asleep again until the kitchen door opened and the guys came in and headed for the basement to put away their gear. She tried to get up and go say hello, but her muscles refused to move. A few minutes later, she heard Ian's footsteps and managed to open her eyes.

"Aw, did we wake you?" Ian said softly.

"No, well sort of. I dozed off a bit." Leslie stifled a yawn. "Guess I was more tired than I thought." Getting up off the couch, she stumbled, and Ian steadied her.

"Are you even awake?" he asked, taking her blanket off the couch and throwing it over her shoulders.

Leslie shook her head with a very tired smile. "Not really. I want to hear everything, but tell me in the morning."

"Okay, now off to bed with you." After seeing her to their room, he headed back down to say goodnight to everyone else. Alex was raiding the fridge for a midnight snack, Hawk was refilling his water glass for the night, and Flynn was leaning on the counter, looking like he was about to fall asleep standing up. "Sleep in as long as you like," Ian said. "We've got a lot to discuss, but it's best if we do it with fresh minds. Goodnight, chaps."

~

They all slept late the next morning. The day before had been a long one, filled with so many comings and goings, and their brains were just as tired as their bodies. Leslie had prepared a brunch the night before, so all they had to do was throw it in the oven when they woke up and let it bake while they got ready.

Lukas had improved a little and sat in the dining room. His freckled face broke into a smile as he recognized Flynn. "Hi. I remember you. Sean said you got shot. Did you really, or is he just 'zaggeratin'?"

"No, he's not exaggerating. I did get shot, but it just grazed my arm, see?" The bandage had come off in the shower and Flynn had let the injury air-dry.

Lukas's eyes widened. "Does it hurt? It looks all red and angry."

"A little, I guess," Flynn said with a shrug.

"Let me see." Leslie came up behind him. "Oh! You really ought to get some salve on that. Are you sure it shouldn't be wrapped up?" She held his arm carefully, eyeing the graze apprehensively.

"No...? It just kind of came off when it got wet, and I left it that way."

"Come with me, then." Leslie brought him into the bathroom and took out a bottle of salve and some gauze. After washing her hands, she gently spread the salve on Flynn's arm. The salve was cool and instantly soothed the ache. Leslie wiped the tips of her fingers off on her apron, and then firmly wound a bit of gauze around his arm. "There, feel better?"

Flynn fingered the gauze gently. "Ever so much, Auntie. Thank you. You look tired," he added quickly, giving her a look of concern. "Did you sleep alright?"

"Oh, I slept fine. I just feel a little off. It's probably my allergies acting up, or something. Nothing to worry about though." She gave him a reassuring smile and led the way back to the dining room. The rest of the household had come downstairs, and they were presently engaged in reducing Leslie's brunch to mere crumbs.

"Leslie get you all fixed up, eh?" Alex asked Flynn as he heaped his English muffin with jam. "What's she got you smelling like?"

"I'm sorry?" Flynn regarded him with a bemused expression.

"You know, with all her essential oils and stuff. What did she put on? Lavender, so you smell like nap-time? Or peppermint and cinnamon to smell like Christmas?" Alex threw Leslie a teasing grin. Hawk snickered. They all knew Leslie loved her essential oils and used them for just about anything; and while they did (usually) work, Hawk and Alex loved teasing her about them.

Leslie stared at him for a moment. "I completely forgot. I ought to have put some tea tree oil on it."

Alex let out an exaggerated gasp. "You forgot to put oils on? The poor boy is going to *die* without them!"

"You're such a goose, Alex. Remind me, Flynn, and I'll do it after we finish," Leslie said.

Flynn regarded her with an apprehensive air. "It doesn't smell like perfume or anything, right?" He wrinkled his nose in disgust at the thought. "What does it do, anyway?"

"No no, it's not like perfume at all! They have healing properties, and tea tree oil fights infection," Leslie began to explain.

"Yes, but we're eating, so maybe save that for later," Ian put in hastily.

"Good point," Leslie conceded. "More tea anyone?"

~~

Chapter Six

"IT DOESN'T MAKE ANY SENSE!" Hawk leaned back in his favorite chair, a look of irritation on his face. Except for the little boys, they were all gathered in the living room to hash out everything that had happened the previous day.

"It certainly is peculiar," Leslie agreed, seating herself on a small loveseat.

Ian sat across from Hawk in his own comfortable chair. "It obviously has some significance, we just haven't figured it out yet."

"Would you go over it again?" asked Alex, who was stretched out on the couch, contentedly eating out of a huge bowl filled with vanilla ice-cream, topped with hundreds and thousands. Never mind that it wasn't even noon; to Alex, ice cream was the perfect mind-stimulator.

Ian began the explanation. "We had to do a bit of American math, but the hole is twenty-six feet deep, the tunnel is twenty-six feet long, and the tunnel is twenty-six inches wide. There also happens to be twenty-six steps. Obviously, that number means something."

He frowned and rubbed his forehead as he continued. "At the end of the tunnel is a blank wall, and in the very center of the wall is carved the letter M." Unable to contain his frustration at the unknown, he got up and began pacing in front of the fireplace. "If only we knew how to open that wall. It most certainly was a door of some kind."

"Too bad 'Speak Friend And Enter' didn't work," Alex said sadly, pointing his spoon at Ian. Hawk threw him a *you're-hopeless* look. "What? Of course I tried it! If *I* had a secret wall door, I would totally program it to open with that voice command."

Ian ignored him. "It's obvious the Mallevilles saw us through that camera you found, Alex, and then went down into wherever that door leads. The only question is, how did they open it? It would be easier to blow it up, but unfortunately that's not an option, thanks to the house above and the possible cave it leads into."

"Perhaps you need a key of some sort that is shaped like an 'M'," Leslie suggested.

Hawk hooked a small ottoman with his foot and pulled it towards him. "Maybe, but it would have to be some sort of combination key. Just inserting something into the M-shaped hole is way too easy. All we'd have to do is make one out of wood or metal or something and we'd be in. No, there has to be more to it."

"Yeah, but how would a combination key even work on an M-shaped thing? Combination locks are round," Alex pointed out.

"How am I supposed to know? This whole thing is crazy!" Hawk scowled and shifted his position, resting his head on his hand.

Flynn sat on the floor by his uncle's chair, and as he dropped his head in thought, his eyes fell on his arm. Suddenly remembering the strange numbers he'd written on the inside of his arm, he jumped up and ran to his room. Before going to bed, he had jotted them down on a notepad. He grabbed the paper, took the stairs two at a time, and re-entered the living room. "Could this have anything to do with it?" he asked, holding up the piece of paper.

"What is that?" Alex asked.

"It's a bunch of numbers that were written in the margins of a newspaper in the fireplace at the Malleville's. They piqued my curiosity, but I knew I couldn't take the newspaper with me, so I wrote them on my arm, and then re-copied them on paper last night."

"Flynn, writing on your arm—" Leslie began.

"Yes, Aunt, I *know!*" he hastily cut her off. "Grandmama scolded all the time. But I didn't have any paper handy." Flynn handed it to Ian, and his uncle scanned the numbers closely. Like on the newspaper, Flynn had written them under their prospective columns of "L" and "R."

L.	R.
1 – 26	2 – 52
3 – 1	4 – 50
5 – 3	6 – 48
7 – 11	8 – 36
9 – 13	10 – 34
11 – 17	12 – 32
13 – 19	14 – 28
15 – 21	16 – 24
17 – 29	18 – 22
19 – 31	20 – 16
21 – 37	22 – 8
23 – 41	24 – 6
25 – 45	26 – 26

"This is really strange." Ian's brow furrowed. "There are two sets of twenty-six numbers, and the first and last number is twenty-six. Hawk, pull up a calculator on your phone, would you please?" Once his friend had done so, Ian rattled off the numbers one by one.

Hawk typed them in and hit the equal button. "The answer is six-hundred-seventy-six."

"Oh come on, that's ridiculous!" Alex cried.

"Sorry?" Hawk raised an eyebrow at him. "Am I missing something?"

"The square root of six-seventy-six is twenty-six, duh." He scraped the last bits of ice cream out of his bowl with his spoon rather loudly.

"Sounds like somebody is overly fond of that number," Leslie said as she pulled some yarn out of a bright yellow skein at her side. She was busy knitting a scarf, and was almost half-way finished.

"No kidding." Hawk laid his phone aside. "It's probably a combination lock of some sort with fifty-two numbers that you either twist to the left or the right."

"True, but it's an odd code," Ian said. "That would be difficult to memorize."

"Damian obviously came up with it. Little anorak." Alex stared at his empty bowl sadly. "And that's assuming it's a combination code at all. My my, what a rum business! I'm getting more ice cream. Anyone want some? No? More for me." He rolled off the couch onto his feet and left.

"It would be a lovely coincidence if that is the combination code of whatever opens the wall," Flynn said.

"Yes, it would, but it's of no use to us if we don't have the lock." Ian stood in front of the fireplace, hands held behind his back. They were close; he could feel it. That's what was so infuriating. So close, yet so far.

Hawk broke the silence. "Ian, didn't Axel have a large M-shaped pendant on a gold chain around his neck?"

Ian turned his head slightly. "Yes, yes he did. Are you saying...no. It couldn't be that easy." Pulling out his phone, he scrolled through his contacts and tapped on Grant's number.

"Who are you calling?" Leslie asked.

"Grant, to see if he has a picture of that necklace. Grant? ...Hullo, Ian here. ...Yes, just fine. ... No, I was wondering if you had a picture of that chain and pendant Axel Crane was wearing the day we caught him. ...Thanks. ...Yeah, I'm still here. ...You do? ...Great! You're still holding Vansant, right? ...Well, in a way. ...No, I'm not one-hundred percent sure. ...Of course. I'll be there shortly. ...Bye, Grant." Ian hung up and slipped his phone back in his pocket. "He has a picture of it, and since they're still holding Vansant, we can ask him about it while we're there."

"Ask who about what?" Alex asked, tramping back into the room and flopping down on the couch, his bowl heaped high with more ice cream.

"If you'd been here, listening to the conversation, you would know," Hawk answered dryly.

"Thank you, Your Sarkiness. That was terribly enlightening." Alex swung his legs up onto the couch and leaned back comfortably amidst the pillows.

"Remember that M-shaped chain of Axel's? Grant has a picture of it, and we're going to take a look at it, and question Vansant to see if there is any correlation between it and the door-wall," Ian explained.

"That sounds brilliant, ol' chap. Don't know why I didn't think of that." He took a huge bite of ice cream. Seconds later, his face screwed up in pain and he jerked to a sitting position. "Brain freeze!" he squeaked.

"Lift your tongue to the roof of your mouth. It will go away faster," Leslie instructed. "And don't eat frozen foods so fast. In fact, you oughtn't to be eating that much ice cream before lunch anyway."

Alex shook his head violently, as though hoping to shake the freeze away. "Aw, come on, I burn it as fast as I eat it. Egh, I hate it when my brain goes all cold like that." He rubbed his temple with a free hand.

"You coming?" Hawk asked, shoving the ottoman aside with his foot and rising from his chair.

"Yeah, yeah, just let me grab my laptop."

~

"Well, here it is. It's all yours." Grant, sitting at his office desk, handed Ian a photo of the pendant.

Ian examined it closely. "There aren't any numbers," he said, rather disappointed.

"Maybe they're hidden?" Flynn suggested.

Hawk eyed the photo suspiciously. "I say we ask Vansant."

"I'll bring him to you. Just head on over to one of the questioning rooms." Grant rose and left.

Ian sat down at a small table in the bare little room. Hawk stood behind him, arms crossed in his own peculiar fashion: his right arm laying across his chest, and his left hand hooking his right elbow. Alex and Flynn sat at a table in an adjoining room where they could see and hear what went on.

Once Vansant was seated, Ian held up the photo and got straight to the point. "What is this?"

Vansant's jaw muscles clenched. "It's a necklace."

Ian frowned slightly. "Vansant, I'm not stupid. It's much more than a necklace. We found the door, and we're pretty sure this plays a part. What is it?"

Vansant looked at him warily. "You guys did promise to lighten my sentence whenever I help, right?"

"Yes, we did," Hawk affirmed. "And we will keep that promise. The more you help us, the more we can help you."

Vansant eyed the photo and sighed. "Okay, well, it's...it's a key."

"A key to what?"

Vansant hesitated. "I don't exactly know." His eyes shifted between Ian, Hawk, and the table. "It's for some type of lock, I think, used mostly for illegal goods. I was never much involved in that, and Ic would probably kill me if he knew I knew that much." He jerked to a stop and bit his lip. "It's broken, you know." Ian raised an eyebrow and waited for him to continue. Vansant fidgeted in his seat. "I really shouldn't say any more, you know. Ic doesn't know I know." He looked genuinely frightened, and started to nervously twist his cuffed hands on the table.

"The Mallevilles can't touch you if they're in prison, Vansant," Ian said gently. "Everything you tell us gets us one step closer to locking them away for life."

Vansant stopped fidgeting, thought about what Ian said for a few minutes, then took a deep breath. "Icabod and Damian created a lock system used only in their inner circle. That pendant is the key to the lock. You insert it into the lock, press the right numbers, and you're in. To see the numbers, you have to take the outer casing off the front of the pendant, but it's only released by that," and he reached out to point to where the points of the "M" met in the middle. "There's supposed to be a pin. If you press on the bottom of the two legs, and twist the pin, the casing comes off. But the pin has been snapped off, and now it's just a curiosity."

"Is there any way to obtain one of these without having to capture the Mallevilles?" Hawk asked.

Vansant sighed again and looked away. "It's hearsay, okay? I don't know anything for sure. I wasn't involved deep in the illegal goods part of their transactions. But I stuck around enough to hear things. There's a master key at their black market headquarters. I don't know where that is, but I do remember hearing Axel say — he talks in his sleep — 'H.Q.' and then mumble a rhyme. It went like, uh, like this:

"Down where the surf booms

At around one, one, four;

Underneath; where stone abounds;

That KM from Eh-din-bur-oh.

"It only rhymes if you have a strong accent, I guess, but that doesn't really matter. And that's all I know about it. I was never one for riddles, so I was never able to figure out where it was. Icabod doesn't know I know about the rhyme. Neither does he know I know about the master key. If he did... He can't know I

said anything, please." Vansant looked pleadingly from one to
the other.

"Don't you worry, Vansant. You're safe with us," Grant
reassured him. "Anything else you want to tell us?"

Vansant shook his head. "No. I don't really know any more
that would be useful." After Vansant was returned to his holding
cell, Ian thanked Grant for his time, and promised to let him
know if they could make anything of the riddle.

"Down where the surf booms,

At around one, one, four;

Underneath; where stone abounds;

That KM from Eh-din-bur-oh."

Ian recited the rhyme as he started the car and headed back
home. "What can it mean?" he asked himself aloud in an abstract
tone.

"You're always good at solving riddles," Flynn said. "I'm sure
you can come up with the answer."

Ian was silent as he mulled it over in his mind. "It can't be
too obvious," he muttered. "Yet, at the same time, it can't be too
ambiguous either."

"Why not just take it line by line?" Hawk suggested.

"Alright then, first line: 'Down where the surf booms...' The
coastline, obviously. Second line: 'At around one, one, four...'
Around 1:14 A.M. or P.M.? No clue. Third line: 'Underneath;
where stone abounds...' Uh, come on, think! 'Underneath'
equals...under...underground! Of course! 'Where stone
abounds' equals, well, either a quarry or ruins. Yet again, an old

manor house. Which one? No clue." Flynn started to say something, but Hawk held up his hand for silence. He knew from experience not to interrupt his friend when he was rambling out loud, hot on some train of thought. "Fourth line: 'That KM from Eh-din-bur-oh.' Hmm. 'Eh-din-bur-oh'...what the dickens could that mean? Could it possibly...no...then again, *maybe* it's Edinburgh? Leave that, uh, 'KM'. 'That KM'...'That KM'... *What* 'KM'? What even *is* 'KM'? 'KM'...'KM'..." Ian's voice trailed off. "No...it couldn't be...but, but...Oh! That's it! I'm such a bally idiot...'KM' stands for kilometers. So, the H.Q. is on the coast, near a lot of rocks, underground, and 114 km from Edinburgh!" Ian flashed Hawk a grin of triumph. "You agree with me?"

"Completely, mate."

"Me too!" Alex hollered from the back seat.

"But you've only solved the obvious," Hawk continued. "Where on the coast? What do the rocks, or stones, mean? Of course, it can only be within a 114 km radius from Edinburgh, so Alex could run some sort of search thing on his maps— what?" He stopped, seeing the look on Ian's face.

"The riddle said Eh-din-bur-oh, instead of Edin-bur-rah, which, if you spell it out, would either be E-d-i-n-b-u-r-o-h, or, E-d-i-n-b-u-r-r-o-w," Ian explained. "If you go with the latter, burrow would be a clue."

"Which means it's a place that animals live, but don't forget it's got to be stony, too." They lapsed into silence. "Wait, what about ruins? That's a good hideout for creatures, and it's usually made of some kind of stone. Question is, what ruins?" Hawk crossed his arms and leaned back in his seat.

"Could it be some type of castle?" Flynn asked. "Scotland is riddled with old castle and fortress ruins."

Alex opened his laptop. "A ruined castle that's 114 km from Edinburgh? Let me see what I can find." He started tapping away at his keyboard. "Flynn ol' chap, you hit the nail right on the head! Lindisfarne Castle is exactly 114 km from Edinburgh. What do you say we go check it out, Ian?"

"Definitely. There's no guarantee our first guess is the right one, but there's no harm in trying. I'll get in contact with our agent up there and see if we can't check the place out."

"Hey, that's were Von's dad works!" Flynn sounded excited.

"Who's Von?" Ian asked.

"Don't you remember my school mate, Von?"

"No. I don't recall you ever mentioning a Von. And if his dad works at the castle, why in the world was he going to school in Wales?" Ian regarded him with a bemused expression through the rearview mirror.

"Uhm, he's a she, Uncle. You seriously don't remember Evonne Henley?" Flynn was surprised. "I mean, I've only known her since primary school. Her dad got a job at Lindisfarne Castle half way through the last school year, and so she moved."

"Oh, *Evonne!*" Light finally dawned. "Of course, I'm sorry, the nickname didn't ring a bell. You took her out for the previous year's dance, didn't you?"

Flynn laughed. "Sort of-ish. We did go to the dance together, but only because neither of us had anything better to do. She can't dance to save her life, and neither can I, so we just hung out on the portico, drank way too much fruit punch, and played draughts and dominoes until after midnight."

"None of your other friends teased you about it?" Hawk asked.

"No, we didn't have any other friends. Von and I were sort of the...well, not the outcasts, really. We just didn't 'fit in' anywhere, if you get my drift." Flynn set off the words with air quotes. "There were the popular snobby kids, the nerdy anorak kids, and the kids who were trying to join both of those groups. And then there was Von and me. She couldn't stand the other girls, and I couldn't stand the other guys, so we ended up as friends in, oh, I can't remember, fifth or sixth grade, and have known each other ever since." He shrugged. "We got teased, sure, but that's because we weren't in any of the stupid cliques. I didn't give a rip what the other kids thought, and she didn't either, so after a while the other kids mostly ignored us. Which was fine by me."

Alex shut his laptop and turned his full attention to Flynn. "What's she look like?" he asked, sensing something he could tease him about.

"Uhm, auburn-ish hair, blue eyes, and freckles. Lots of 'em. Her dad's Scottish, but her mum was Welsh, so she's got this interesting little lilting accent. I have a picture of her on my phone." Flynn reached for his pocket. "Drat, I left it in my room. Oh well. Guess I'll show you at home, then."

"So you two were just regular school mates, then?" Hawk drawled. He winked at Ian who ducked his head slightly so Flynn couldn't see his broad smile in the rearview mirror. Alex stifled a snicker.

"Yeah. She made school bearable." He made a face. "I really wish I'd been homeschooled like Sean and Lukas. School was awful, and they taught so much junk, or nothing at all. I just hope university is better, at least as far as the teaching goes."

When they got home, Flynn hurried up to his room, grabbed his phone from off his nightstand, and turned it on. He quickly silenced it as notification after notification started ringing and beeping at him. He swiped through his photos until he came to the right one, and then went back downstairs. He heard his uncle ask Sean, "Where's your mum?"

"Dunno. Upstairs somewhere. She said she had some phone calls to make." Sean tried to scramble up on the counter.

"Hey, what has your mum told you about sitting up there?" Ian cautioned.

"We-ell, she's not here, so she won't care." Sean grinned at him and tried again.

"Excuse me young man, rules are rules, and they are made to be obeyed no matter who's here. Now run upstairs and see if she wants some tea."

Sean was gone in a flash, mumbling to himself, "I still don't see what's wrong with it. Uncle Alex does it."

Hawk opened the fridge and took out a can of root beer. Ian eyed his friend's choice of beverage. "You're drinking soda this early in the morning?"

"Yeah, why not? It sounded good." Hawk filled a glass with ice, poured the root beer in, and sipped the foam off the top. Noticing Flynn's almost wistful expression, he motioned towards the fridge. "You can have one if you like."

"Really? Thanks!" Flynn quickly availed himself of the treat.

Ian shook his head as he filled a kettle with water and set it on the stove. "You two are ridiculous."

"Tea is for breakfast and in the afternoon, not mid-morning," Hawk argued.

"To each his own."

Flynn swiped his phone screen and handed the device to Hawk. "That's Von."

"Hey, I want to see!" Alex had gone into the basement to get his laptop charge cord, and now poked his head back in the kitchen. The picture showed Von standing by a sprawling old oak tree. Her dark auburn hair fell in gentle waves down her back and over her shoulders. She had sky blue-eyes, and a million tiny freckles cascaded over her little snub-nose and across her face and shoulders. As thin as a twig, she was sporting a high-necked tank top and a pair of nice skinny jeans, the bottoms rolled up to her ankles. "She's cute," Alex said, taking the phone from Hawk and then handing it back to Flynn.

Flynn blinked and stared at the picture. "Uhm, yeah, guess I've never really paid attention." He set his phone on standby and slipped it in his pocket.

"You still keep in touch with her?" Ian asked as he removed two mugs from a cabinet and placed a teabag in each.

"No, but it's not like we fell out or anything. I dropped my phone in the school pond a few months ago – you remember – and lost her number. For some reason, I couldn't keep my old number, so I haven't heard from her either." He shrugged and grabbed a soda for himself. "But if we're headed up to Lindisfarne, I can see her then and catch up a bit." He was about to pop open the can, but stopped. "None of you seem very…I don't know…*excited*, about this venture. I mean, isn't what Vansant told us really, really good news?"

"Not exactly. We've had so many tip-offs and insider information that went wrong, or was false, we have to take everything with a huge grain of salt." Hawk winced at the fizziness of his drink.

"We've learned to save the excitement for actual victories." Ian took the kettle off the stove as it began to whistle loudly and filled the mugs up almost to the brim just as Sean skidded into the room.

"Yeah, she wants some. Ooh, can I have a root beer too, Dad? Please?" Sean eyed his cousin's can enviously.

Ian hesitated. "I suppose so. But only half. You don't need that much sugar right now."

"I'll take care of it," Hawk said, taking a glass out of the cabinet. "You can bring that tea up. We'll meet you downstairs."

"Thanks." Ian placed a saucer over both mugs and carefully brought one of them up to his room. The door was ajar, and Leslie was nowhere to be seen. "Les?"

"I'm in the wardrobe!" her muffled voice called out. Ian walked through the large on-suite bathroom into the walk-in wardrobe.

"Tea is served," he said with a little bow.

Leslie finished securing a small stud earring and turned to smile at him. "Aw, thank you."

Ian handed her the mug. "I've just poured it, so you might want to let it steep a little."

"You're so sweet." Leslie kissed him on the cheek.

"Something happen to your earring?" he asked curiously.

"Oh, I was just cleaning them. They were looking a little dull." She laid the mug on the bathroom counter and checked her hair. Ian leaned in the closet doorframe and watched her closely. "What is it?" she asked, noticing his slightly worried expression in the mirror.

"Are you feeling okay?"

Leslie turned to face him. "Why do you ask?"

"Well, you just..." Ian sighed and fumbled to find the right words. "You've been looking a bit tired lately."

"My allergies have been bothering me some, but that's all. Nothing to be worried about," she reassured him.

"But it's not allergy season," Ian pointed out.

Leslie turned to look at him seriously. "Ian, you know I'm highly allergic to a lot of things. Yesterday, I made the mistake of taking Sean into the pet store because he wanted to look at the puppies. That's what was still bothering me this morning. Please, stop worrying. I'm fine." She looked at him pleadingly.

He gave her a gentle hug. "Alright, but—"

She placed a finger on his mouth. "No buts, Ian dear. Now, how did your little trip up to the Yard go?"

Ian followed her out the room and downstairs. "Vansant gave us a good deal of information, but he wasn't completely sure all of it was accurate. He thinks there's this secret headquarters used for illegal goods distribution that has the master key for the lock system. But I can explain it in detail in the office, if you care to join us."

"I would love to. Take me to your secret little Batcave." Leslie tried sipping her tea, but it was too hot and not strong enough for her liking, so she replaced the saucer to wait.

Ian rolled his eyes. "It's not the Batcave."

"It's more interesting than just saying 'the office.'"

"Sounds like Alex has been rubbing off on you!" he teased.

Down in the office, Ian and Hawk filled her in on what Vansant said, and what they intended to do. "We'll need to make accommodations for spending a day or two, and I'll work things out with our agent to let us in the castle after closing hours," Ian said.

"Who's all going?" Leslie asked.

"Well, us three guys, obviously," Alex said. "Flynn will want to drag himself along, and we wouldn't want to take the two munchkins along, so it just depends if Ian lets you tag along, Honey."

"Honey?" Flynn raised an eyebrow, taken aback at the nickname Alex had used for his aunt.

Ian rolled his eyes. "Yeah. We're not exactly sure how or when that one started. For some reason, Alex started calling her that a long time ago, and it's just sort of stuck."

Leslie smiled at the little exchange. "Of course I'm coming. Besides, it will look less suspicious. Lindisfarne Castle is a tourist sight, and it would look very odd for four guys to just show up for a day or two, scope out the castle, and leave. No, it's best if we go in two groups. You," and she pointed at Ian, "and Flynn and I will go together, and it will appear as a family holiday. Hawk and Alex can go together, since two random guys is less suspicious-looking than four."

"You have a point there," Ian agreed. "Very well, I'll ring the agent."

"And I'll take care of our rooms." Hawk turned his computer screen on.

Alex popped open his laptop and swung his legs up to rest on his desk. "Route calculations for me!"

"Flynn, you want to help me pack?" Leslie got up and motioned for him to follow.

"Sure."

"You haven't even finished unpacking, have you?" she asked as they headed back upstairs.

Flynn smiled wryly. "No, I haven't. No sooner here, than off we go again!"

She frowned. "I'm sorry about that, Flynn dear. This is not exactly what you—"

"Aunt, please, it's okay." He laid a hand on her arm. "I'm home, and I'm with you and Uncle Ian; what more could I ask for? I'm perfectly happy, and after the monotony of school, a little adventure is rather refreshing!"

~

"When are we leaving?" Flynn asked Ian later that night.

"Leslie's sister, Mary, has agreed to watch the boys, so we'll be heading out early tomorrow morning," Ian answered. "Hawk made reservations for us at The Ship Inn."

"Isn't that a pub?" Alex looked up from his laptop where he was busy checking his route calculations to ensure he'd found the shortest and fastest way possible.

"It's a pub and inn combined," Hawk replied.

"Oh goody, that means I can have a giant Ploughman's Lunch at least once, if not twice!" Alex grinned happily.

"Do you always think with your stomach?"

"No, but what's life without good food, eh? Just plain boring!" He tapped away at his computer. "Oh, and I got the best route figured out. If traffic isn't too much of a pain, we should get there in just over seven hours. Great, I love road trips! I'm calling a rematch on Vehicular Monopoly."

"What's that?" Flynn asked, raising an eyebrow in confusion.

"It's Monopoly played in the car. Duh."

"But how can you even do that? Don't the pieces go everywhere?"

Alex laughed. "My dear fellow, I've played Monopoly in the car for years, and I've only ever lost one little green house. It'll be great fun, you'll see. There's plenty of space in Ian's Mazda for it. But look out, 'cause I don't lose easy."

Flynn still didn't look convinced. "Just how exactly are we all going to play if we're in separate cars?"

Alex stared at him for a moment. "Oh. I didn't think of that." He looked over at Hawk, and a sly smile crept across his face. "We can always have that Risk rematch."

Hawk gave him a fist-bump. "You are so on! A bar of dark chocolate against a bag of Skittles says you lose horribly."

"You'd better buy those Skittles, ol' chap, 'cause you're going *down!*"

"We'll see about that. And hey," Hawk suddenly punched him in the shoulder, "you haven't gotten me those chocolate mints yet, have you?"

"Exactly when was I supposed to pick them up? During or after the raid on the Mallevilles?" Alex retorted, punching him back. "Stop your moaning. I'll get 'em to you, ol' chap by the end of the week. And if not, then I'll owe you two, deal?"

Hawk grinned at him. "Deal. Here's hoping you forget!"

~~

Chapter Seven

ALEX'S CALCULATIONS WERE proved correct, and it took just over seven hours for them all to drive to Holy Island. Hawk lost Risk, but demanded a rematch on the way back home, which Alex promptly accepted. They settled down in their rooms in The Ship Inn, which were next to each other and had a communicating door. Dinner was had at the adjoining pub, but the two groups sat at separate tables. Hawk and Alex sat at the tall counter and swapped stories with the sailors and other tourists, while Ian, Leslie, and Flynn took a table near a window and watched the comings and goings of the islanders.

When they were finished, the three decided to take a short walk on the beach to catch the sunset.

"It's so quaint here," Flynn said. "And I love the smell of the sea."

"Yes, it certainly is a smell like no other. I'll have to take you to Dover sometime," Ian said as he crooked his arm to let Leslie slide hers through.

Flynn pulled his Cambridge sweatshirt on as they walked. Sea breezes could be cold, especially at night. "That would be such fun! I've always wanted to see the cliffs in person. It seems the type of place that a picture simply does no justice to."

"They take your breath away," Leslie agreed. "Ian and I drove by them on our honeymoon, and I did wish we could've stayed longer. We really should plan a trip there. Maybe before you head off to university?"

Flynn never got the chance to reply, as a rolled-up flannel shirt whacked him in the back of the head. "Ow!" He reached up to protect himself against another assault.

"Flynn Tazer, I'm extremely annoyed with you! I ought never to speak to you again!" It was a girl's voice, and she did not sound happy.

"Von?" Flynn whirled to face her, and his arms dropped from his head. "*Von?*" he repeated incredulously, his whole face lighting up.

"Yes, you git, and I'm very put out. Not only did you disconnect your number, you gave me the wrong address for your uncle's flat." She put her hands on her hips and tried to scowl at him, but Flynn could tell she wasn't really angry at him, only pretending to be.

"Aw, come on, Von, I dropped my phone in the pond, and my uncle moved. That's not my fault, is it?" he wheedled. The corner of Von's mouth twitched. "I *suppose* not."

"You're not mad then?"

Von lost her composure and chuckled. "Even if I was, you know I couldn't stay that way for very long." Her face broke into a wide smile. "I'm ever so glad to see you again."

"You too, Von. Crikey, has it been awhile! But wait, I'd like you to meet my Uncle Ian and my Aunt Leslie." Flynn motioned to them as he spoke. They were regarding the two with rather amused expressions.

"I've heard quite a lot about you," Von said as she shook hands with them. "Mostly about you, though, Mr. Tazer. I've been told you're the best detective in the world."

"I'm afraid my nephew grossly exaggerates," Ian answered with a smile.

"I never exaggerate!" Flynn protested.

"Yeah right." Von smirked and wagged an eyebrow at him. "Remember that time with Mrs. Edwards—"

"Don't even, Von, or I'll bring up that time with Professor 'Plum'." Flynn looked extremely proud as his remark hit home.

"Oh, you naughty boy!" She lightly whapped his arm with her shirt.

"No, you're the naughty one. I'm going to have a headache from that shirt of yours. Aren't you sorry?" he teased.

"Not in the slightest. You deserved that." She unrolled her shirt and tied it around her waist.

Flynn crossed his arms. "Excuse me?"

Von shoved her hands in her pockets and said indignantly, "Do you realize what an utter fool I looked like, ringing the bell to your uncle's flat, only to be told you didn't live there?"

Flynn gaped at her. "You mean to tell me you went all the way to Windsor to see me, and I wasn't there?"

"Sort of. I have a cousin who lives out there, and she had a baby, so my dad and I went down to visit her a couple months ago. It was spring break, so I thought there was a chance you'd be there. I wanted to see you again, and suss out just why you disconnected your old number, so we drove by what I thought was your place. Only, instead of you, there was an old woman. She was as cranky as they come. Sharp as nails, let me tell you, and she yelled at me to 'clear off' — at least, those are my words. There's no way in the world I'm repeating hers." Von flipped her hair over her shoulder. "Needless to say, I was quite disappointed."

"I'm really sorry, Von," Flynn said seriously. "I had no idea! Here, you've got your phone with you?"

"Yeah. Promise me you're not going to go off the grid on me again?" She arched an eyebrow at him.

"Promise." Flynn gave her his number and new address as they continued walking down to the beach.

"I'm sorry I sort of barged in on you like this," she said, replacing her phone in her pocket. "I just saw that sweater of yours and couldn't believe my eyes."

Flynn slipped his hands in his pockets to warm them. "Don't be. I'm very glad to see you." He hardly noticed as his uncle and aunt moved to walk ahead of them, leaving them to saunter along the beach and talk by themselves. "The last half-year of school was boring, you know. I ought to be mad at you for ditching me like that."

"Well, it's not my fault my father got a job out here! But I agree with you. School wasn't half as much fun." She scuffed at the sand with her sandal. "It's easier to ignore the bullies and jocks with someone else."

"Were they that bad?" Flynn asked, giving her a sympathetic look.

She shrugged, as though it was no big deal. "It wasn't the end of the world, and I got through with flying colors, but...let's just say I'm happy not to be going back. But, enough of school." She shivered a little as a cold wind from the sea brushed past her bare arms. "Tell me about you. How are you settling in with your uncle? Is it what you'd thought it would be?"

"No," Flynn said honestly. "It's not at all what I thought, but it's really wonderful to finally get to live with him. Life can get a little crazy with his work schedule, but he's letting me help him out a bit, which is jolly good fun."

Von's eyes widened. "Have you been in any danger? I mean, he's still a copper, right?"

"He got promoted, so he does more detective work than regular policing," Flynn corrected. "And yeah, I've been in a little danger, but nothing too serious."

"Come on, out with it!" she begged.

"Well, we were hunting down this one guy who escaped from jail, only we found his crony instead. I was stupid enough to go running after him, but thankfully he only had a slingshot. He didn't hit me," he said hastily, seeing her look of concern. "And my uncle caught him, so now he's behind bars."

"Wow, that certainly sounds intense. Does your aunt mind?" The wind was too much for Von to continue as she was, so she untied her flannel shirt and slipped it on over her tank top.

"Uhm, aunt doesn't exactly know about the whole slingshot escapade," Flynn admitted. "She knows I helped catch a criminal, but that's about it. I think it worries her a little, but she hasn't really protested much to that effect. But what about you? How's life on the Island?"

"I like it. I'm allowed to roam the castle when there aren't any tours, and oh! I've been learning to row a boat!" Her eyes lit up with excitement. "I have to show you the little rowing boat that Dad got me for my birthday. I painted it myself, and I named her – don't laugh – HMS *Queen Anne's Revenge.*"

Flynn grinned at her. "May I inquire how a pirate ship can be in Her Majesty's navy?"

"Because mine is not a pirate vessel," she explained. "I know it was Blackbeard's ship, but I told myself when I was little that if I ever got a boat, I would name it after the famous ship in *Jack Ballister's Fortunes.* Do you like it?"

Flynn hesitated. "Yes, I like it, but you do know that wasn't the ship Blackbeard was sailing in when Lieutenant Maynard captured him...right?"

"What? It's not?" she cried.

"No. The *Revenge* ran aground, and Blackbeard was left with only the *Adventure.*"

Von made a face. "Well, I'm a bally idiot."

"You're actually admitting it?" Flynn teased.

Von flicked his arm. "Very funny, Flynn. Hey, what happened to your sweatshirt?" She took hold of his arm, stopping him from walking any further. Running her fingers

along the stich marks, she looked up at him expectantly. "Did
you catch it on a fence?"

"No, not a fence."

"What then? Did a dog get a hold of it or something?" she
pressed.

"Actually, it was a bullet." He felt a twinge of triumph as her
mouth fell open and her eyes widened.

She froze and started firing questions at him. "You were shot
at? How? Why?"

Flynn rapidly explained the whole airport incident, and rolled
up his sleeve so she could inspect the gauze that protected his
injury. "So you see, it's not really a big deal. Just is a little sore,
that's all."

"That's a wild story, Flynn. You could have been killed!" She
looked genuinely upset.

"Nah, they didn't want to kill me, just get me out of the way.
Besides, I'm fine, really." He looked up as his uncle and aunt
approached. "Oh, we kind of lost you, didn't we?" he said
sheepishly.

Leslie laughed softly. "Yes, but we knew you two would want
to catch up. We're heading back, now."

"I'll let you go. You probably had a long drive, and ought to
sleep. I'm guessing you all came to see the castle?" Von looked
from one to the other.

"Yes, we did," Ian assented.

"Well then, just you come over whenever you want, and I'll
make sure you get a private tour."

"Is that even allowed?" Flynn asked.

Von waved her hand dismissively. "My father is the tour guide, silly, and I know everything about the castle and the Island that he does. I can start your tour before one of the others, so we'll be ahead of everyone."

"That's incredibly sweet of you, but I wouldn't want to intrude on your father," Leslie said.

"Oh, it wouldn't be intruding. I've done it a couple times before for my cousin and a friend of hers, and Dad doesn't mind. And I can also introduce you to him. It's no trouble, so just come whenever you want," she said, rubbing her arms to stay warm.

"We'll see you tomorrow then," Ian said.

"It was so nice to meet you," Leslie added.

"You as well, Mr. and Mrs. Tazer." She shoved her cold hands in her pockets and smiled. "Goodnight, Flynn." She hesitated for a second, vaguely wondering if she ought to give him a hug, or a fist bump, or something, but as he didn't initiate anything, she opted just to head for home.

"'Night, Von."

"Von seems like a sweet girl," Leslie said as they returned to the inn. "Feisty, too."

Flynn laughed. "She certainly is that!" Leslie gave Ian a knowing smile, which was lost on the boy.

Once back at the inn, they found Hawk and Alex deep in the middle of another Risk game. "I thought you were going to play that on the way home." Leslie grabbed her shawl and wrapped it around her shoulders.

"We were, but we didn't have anything to do. It's not like we were going to make all our plans tonight, and after such a long drive," Alex said. "Now shush, this shake is very important!" He blew on the dice before shaking them and letting them drop to the board. "Oh come on, that is not even mathematically possible!"

Hawk grinned and motioned towards Alex's dwindling armies. "Sure is, mate, and it looks like Brazil is all mine. Time to invade the rest of South America."

"And I worked so hard for that Continent too," Alex complained. "Oh well. At least I've got all North America," and he gestured proudly to the board.

"Yeah, but not for long." Hawk picked up the dice and poured them from one hand to the other. "Does my bid for world domination need to wait for tomorrow?" he asked, looking at Ian. "Were you intending on making any plans now?"

"No, like Alex said, that wouldn't be the best thing this late. You two stay up as long as you like. Les and I are off to bed. We can discuss our plans in the morning." Ian said goodnight and both he and Leslie went into their room. Flynn watched the game until he couldn't keep his eyes open, and then headed to bed himself. Alex and Hawk were at a stalemate, and thus followed their friends' example. They all slept soundly, and, after getting dressed and eating breakfast, began discussing what course of action they would take.

"We bumped into Flynn's friend, Von, while on our walk last night, and she offered to take us on a private tour of the castle at any time during the day," Ian said. "That would give us the opportunity to see the inside layout and better determine where a secret entrance might be found."

"Ooh, Flynn's girlfriend is treating you to a private tour, eh? Very schnazzy!" Alex peered at Flynn over the top of his laptop.

"What? No!" Flynn cried indignantly. "I told you, she's my old school mate."

"But she's a girl and she's your friend, which makes her your...girlfriend," Alex continued mercilessly.

"No, she's— aw, come on!"

"As I was saying," Ian interrupted, "Leslie, Flynn, and I will head out there this afternoon and see what there is to see."

"I'll contact the agent and see about getting in the castle after dark," Hawk said.

"Shouldn't we alert SCO19, or whatever the Scottish equivalent is?" Alex asked before Hawk could continue.

"No." Hawk shook his head firmly. "We can't let Icabod even think there's a possibility we're on to him. Besides, this is our job. We're not called the Shadow Agents for nothing."

Ian leaned back on the couch and folded his arms. "Knowing Icabod, he'll have everything rigged up with traps and cameras, but if he's not currently engaged in some sort of transaction, then I doubt there will be anyone there. And even if there is, we're four, counting the agent."

"You mean five," Flynn interjected.

Ian frowned. "I don't know, Flynn. There's not really a place for you to wait until we know the coast is clear."

"Uncle, you said yourself that the chances of someone being there are very unlikely. Alex will get rid of all the cameras and traps, and I'm assuming you'll all be armed, so what's the harm in letting me come along?" Flynn looked at him pleadingly. "Please let me."

Ian didn't seem convinced it was a good idea. "I'll think about it," was all he said.

"Do you really think there is a secret entrance inside the castle?" asked Leslie. "I mean, if there was, wouldn't someone have found it by now?"

"Not necessarily," replied Hawk. "Old castles have lots of secrets. The agent told me he has seen some suspicious men around the castle lately, and there's been a rumor going around that there is a secret room in the castle. Not surprisingly, it started here, in this pub. The Islanders don't give it much credence, but it's an interesting rumor, due to what Vansant told us."

"Why aren't you referring to this agent by his name?" Flynn asked. "Am I not supposed to know, or something?"

"Force of habit," Alex said. "His name is Cade. Riley Cade. And he misses London."

"Does he now?" Ian turned his head to look at him.

"Yeah. Says he also doesn't see enough action and he's extremely bored of chasing wild stories told by the superstitious locals." Alex tapped away on his keyboard as he spoke in a rather absent-minded tone

"Are you reading something?"

Alex motioned towards his screen. "I'm messaging him. Can I tell him about Flynn?"

Ian hesitated. "Tell him I've brought a new recruit along, but that I want to introduce him in person."

"He says his curiosity is extremely piqued, and he's looking forward to tonight," Alex relayed a few seconds later. "He also called you a cryptomaniac, which I agree with whole heartedly."

"A what?" Leslie looked at him rather bemusedly.

"An extremely cryptic person who loves to give you less-than-straight answers until they deem necessary for you to know otherwise." Alex flashed Ian a wicked grin.

"That's Uncle to a T!" Flynn laughed, giving Ian a gentle punch in the shoulder.

"Tell Riley I'm extremely flattered," Ian said with a chuckle. "Now Flynn, suppose you text Von and ask her when's the soonest we can get that tour?"

~

Damian seated himself in an old wooden chair. He and the rest of the Mallevilles were in a cave of sorts. Water dripped dismally from the ceiling in various places, and everything was cold and damp. Damian hated caves. Not only were they nasty, dirty places, full of bats and bugs, they made him feel claustrophobic. His gaze wandered over the drab setting, finally resting on Tiernan who lay against the wall in a crumpled heap.

His face was a dead white and marred here and there by ugly, purple-black bruises. A lock of his sandy hair had fallen across his face, hiding his left eye. He looked awful. Icabod seemed to take a devilish delight in tormenting him, asking him what sorts of things the Metropolitan Police knew about them. Tiernan knew only what the papers said, as he had never been assigned to any part of the long and complicated Malleville Case, but whether Icabod believed him or not was irrelevant. If Tiernan couldn't answer him satisfactorily, Icabod hit him, kicked him, or backhanded him in the head.

Damian did not approve of this treatment. He had no love for the officer, but he did not have a cruel streak like his older brother. If he had taken the officer hostage — and he wouldn't have — he would at least treat him like a human being and just tie him up somewhere and let him alone. He was of no use to them, beyond being a bargaining chip, and it was absolutely pointless to injure him. If he couldn't sit up, or talk, or walk, then they'd have to drag him, and that made things complicated. Damian scowled. If only his older brother had a little more sense.

Icabod sauntered into the room and plopped into another chair off to Damain's right. "Is he awake yet?" he asked, jerking a hand at Tiernan.

"Obviously not," Damian replied drily. "I wish you'd just leave him alone."

"Why? Can't stomach a little rough housing?" Icabod sneered.

"It's a complete waste of time. You ought to be paying more attention to the plan at hand."

Icabod's eyes narrowed angrily. "Are you questioning my methods?"

"What methods? You're not accomplishing anything. You're just roughing him up for the fun of it. He doesn't know anything useful, and you know it." Damian was surprised at his own boldness, but he was seriously fed up with Icabod's antics.

"He's not your problem, is he?" Icabod snapped. "No, I didn't think so. He's my prisoner, I can do what I want with him, and I don't need any lip from you."

Damian huffed and left. This was a useless fight he couldn't win, and he knew it. Icabod grabbed a small tablet from a wooden table next to him and began messaging Lathrop about his latest activities. Lathrop had been sent out on an errand to get something Damian needed for the next phase of the plan.

Icabod laid the tablet aside just as Tiernan woke up. Opening his eyes slowly, Tiernan blinked several times, trying to focus. Every inch of his body hurt. His right eye was swollen, and he was sure he had several cracked, if not broken, ribs. He had no idea why the Mallevilles were still keeping him prisoner. He'd expected either to be used for some horrible scheme, or killed for knowing too much. But just kept for a punching bag? That didn't make sense.

"Well, hello there," Icabod said, bending over him. "Glad to see you're finally awake."

Tiernan glared at him. To him, Icabod wasn't a man, but a monster; a cruel animal who delighted only to inflict pain. Tiernan's temper flared, but since he was still gagged, he could do nothing beyond making unexplainable, muffled sounds that Icabod seemed to find quite amusing. So Tiernan smoldered silently. He was surprised when Icabod untied the gag and stepped back to survey him. "What, cat got your tongue?" he asked as Tiernan remained silent.

"No," Tiernan returned shortly. "I'm merely contemplating what new devilry you have in mind."

Icabod leered at him. "You still haven't learned your manners, have you? No, I don't think so," he answered his own question. "That's very rotten of you, you know." Tiernan had a difficult time keeping his tongue in check. He had no idea what Icabod was hoping to do to him, but he didn't want to give him opportunity. "It's even ruder to ignore me," Icabod continued, his voice losing some of its mockery.

"I'm listening," Tiernan said through clenched teeth.

"That's ever so good of you." Icabod flashed him a malicious smile. "Now, let me ask you something. Do you prefer to have this gag tied around your face, or thrown in the dustbin?"

"Isn't it obvious?"

"Of course, of course. But, in order for me to do that, you have to promise to keep a civil tongue in your head."

"And if I don't?" Tiernan challenged. He instantly regretted it.

"If you don't?" Icabod repeated, a dangerous edge creeping into his voice. "I'll do this." He unrolled the gag, bent down, and swiftly tied it over both Tiernan's mouth and nose. Tiernan was horrified to find he couldn't breathe. He began to writhe, but that irritated his ribs, making every movement agony. His tormentor laughed cruelly. "I could suffocate you, you know!"

Seeing the young man's mute appeal in his eyes, he asked patronizingly, "What is it you want? Need a little air?"

"That's enough!" Damian shoved Icabod to the floor and slashed the gag with a small penknife. Tiernan choked and drew breath in ragged gasps.

"You just…you just…" Icabod sputtered. He couldn't believe his little brother had snuck up behind him and knocked him down.

"Yes I just, and I'll do it again." Damian pointed the penknife at him. "I'm sick of this, Icabod. This is not part of the plan, and I will not have six years of painstaking preparation thrown to the wind because you want to monkey around with some prisoner we don't need. Leave him alone, and pay attention to what you ought to be doing for once in your life!"

A low growl sounded from Icabod's throat, like an angry dog, but he noticed Alvar enter the room from a side passage and thus refrained from any immediate retaliation. Icabod was humiliated. Nobody humiliated him and got away with it. He got to his feet and stomped away, muttering under his breath, "You'll pay for that…oh you'll pay for that!"

Alvar froze, unsure what had gone on and if he was intruding on something he shouldn't have been. Damian told him to get the maps and go over them with Icabod, and Alvar quickly left. Damian eyed Tiernan, who lay unmoving on the cold, stone floor. Going over to a large metal container, Damian withdrew a bottle of brandy and a roll of bread. Laying them on a side table, he knelt down and carefully propped Tiernan against the wall.

Tiernan hissed with pain. Damian slashed the ropes that bound the man's hands and then gave him the bread and brandy. "Don't try anything stupid," he warned. He doubted Tiernan would try to escape in his present condition, but he cautioned him nonetheless.

Tiernan eyed Damian for a few seconds before asking, "Why did you do that?"

Damian rose and began to walk away. "Because I don't want a dead body to dispose of, that's why. It ruins my plans even more than they already are. Now keep quiet, or I'll have to gag you myself."

Tiernan's arms ached from being tied behind his back for so long, but once the soreness had worn off a little, he managed to eat what Damian had given him. He was just replacing the cap on the brandy bottle when he heard Icabod's voice filtering through a passage from an adjacent room.

"Since Damian is so fond of mathematical equality, everything is done in multiples of twenty-six. Why he picked that number I haven't the slightest idea, and please don't ask. I don't need him rambling on about bloody maths for hours. Give me the Buckingham Palace map." There was a rustle of crinkling papers being shoved around. "Why isn't this labeled? There's supposed to be A to Z markings on here, for each level!" Tiernan realized he was hearing Icabod explain some of Damian's plans. The more he listened, the more horrified he became. Silently, he prayed that someone, somehow, would be able to rescue him before the culmination of the Malleville's plans. Tiernan possessed not only a very strong will, but the uncanny ability that some people have of remembering things on the spot. Everything Icabod said, whether Tiernan understood it or not, he committed to memory. He only hoped it would come in useful sometime soon.

~

Ian, Leslie, and Flynn met Von just outside the castle, and she proceeded to give them an extremely detailed tour. She knew just about everything there was to know about the castle, including all the previous owners and every barmy ghost story she'd heard from the locals. They all enjoyed the tour immensely, and Ian indicated silently to Leslie that he'd narrowed down which room had the potential for a secret room or passageway. Von introduced them to her father, Michael Henley, before another official tour started, after which Flynn offered to have Von join them for lunch.

"Oh, I don't want to intrude," she began, "it being your holiday and all."

"You're not intruding in the slightest," Leslie assured her as she slipped her arm through hers as they walked away from the castle. Lunch lasted well over an hour, as the foursome talked and laughed and became better acquainted. Finally, Von said she had to go, as she had some housework to get done that she'd been avoiding. She said goodbye, promising to stop by on the morrow before they left. "She's such a sweet girl!" Leslie said to her nephew. Flynn nodded absentmindedly as he watched Von leave. "She likes you, you know."

That caught his attention. Raising an eyebrow, he said, "Uhm, okay? What's that supposed to mean? Of course she likes me. I like her. We're mates, she and I."

"No, Flynn, that's not what I meant." Leslie laughed gently. "She's sweet on you."

"V-von? Sweet on, on *me*?" he stammered. "No, no, you're wrong, Aunt. Von and I are just mates, longtime mates. Nothing more."

"No, Leslie's quite right," Ian said. "Von's very sweet on you. I noticed it right away."

Flynn stared at them, and he felt his face get hot. "Well, this is awkward."

Leslie looked at him in surprise. "You mean to tell me you haven't noticed the way she looks at you, or the way she almost giggles at everything you say?"

"Uhm...no? She looks at me like she looks at everyone else," Flynn protested.

Ian chuckled. "Believe me, she doesn't look at me the way she looks at you! And I know you've got a good sense of humor, but did you really think you were that funny?"

"What do you mean?" Flynn was starting to get seriously annoyed. Not only did this blow his mind, it was extremely embarrassing, and they were in public to boot.

"You don't hear me laughing my head off at your knock-knock jokes, do you?" Ian ribbed.

"Okay, Ian, that's enough," Leslie admonished him gently. "You're making the poor boy blush."

"Uhm, no, I don't blush," Flynn lied, knowing his face probably was red as a cherry. "What time is it anyway? Aren't we supposed to meet that agent of yours this afternoon?"

Ian winked at Leslie, silently agreeing that the previous subject had been closed for the present. "He ought to be here soon, so why don't we go check on the guys?" he said. "Just let me pay for lunch and then we'll go."

~~

Chapter Eight

WHEN THE THREE RETURNED to their room, they found the communicating door wide open, and could hear Hawk and Alex talking with someone. Ian hurried into their room, a smile spreading across his face.

"Cade, it sure has been a while!"

A man in his early forties was seated on a couch, but rose upon hearing Ian's voice. He shook Ian's hand firmly. "It sure has, Tazer, and I'm delighted to see you again." His smiled widened as Leslie entered. "It's good to see you too, Miss Leslie. You're looking as well as ever, I daresay." His gaze shifted to Flynn, and he scrutinized him carefully. "This is your new recruit, I suppose?"

"In a way. Cade, I'd like you to meet my nephew, Flynn."

"Your nephew? I should have known. You two resemble each other." Cade stuck out his hand. "Pleasure to meet you, lad."

"You too, sir." Flynn shook his hand and smiled.

"Following in your uncle's footsteps, eh? It's not a bad job. Just make sure he doesn't exile you to the middle of nowhere to keep an eye on who knows what." Cade sat back down with a very straight face, leaving Flynn unsure if he was kidding or not.

Cade noticed his hesitation and chuckled. "Relax, I'm kidding. Though *please* take me back to London, Tazer; I'm *so* done here," he added, looking over at Ian. "Never let it be said I shirked my duties, but I assure you, there is no more counterfeit activity out here, and nothing but ghost stories to chase, beyond the usual bit of crime, and I'm extremely bored."

"Don't worry, you're coming to London with us. I wanted to bring you back early anyway," Ian said, seating himself and Leslie on the couch opposite. "Things have been heating up the past couple days with the Mallevilles, and I have a feeling we're closing in on them."

"Fire away, if you please. I am dying to hear something that's worth the telling." Cade leaned back on the couch, folded his hands, and shut his eyes. Anyone who had a close acquaintance with him knew that it was his posture of total concentration. Ian launched into a detailed explanation of everything that had happened, starting with the airport heist and finishing with their tour of the castle, Hawk and Alex interjecting their own views and extra details at various intervals.

"It's all very peculiar, if you ask me," Cade mused, opening his eyes. "Losing Axel at first sight seems a terrible loss, but to trade him for Vansant who is a veritable wealth of helpful information is probably the best thing that has ever happened to us on this case."

"I agree," Hawk said, propping his legs up on the coffee table.

"So, plan anyone?" Alex grabbed his laptop from off the floor at his feet. "You said you've narrowed the rooms down, Ian?"

"Yes. There's the entire basement, and there's also a room on the second level of the castle. I can't explain why, but something felt off about it." Ian was silent for a moment. "It just seemed smaller than it ought."

"And only you would notice that, Mr. Holmes," Alex quipped.

"Mr. Cade, how exactly are you going to get us in the castle without anybody noticing?" Flynn asked abruptly.

"Oh, I have an understanding with one of the employees there, a Michael Henley by name. I believe he thinks I am Mi6, and he informed me that he will leave the castle unlocked tonight." Cade raised an eyebrow ever so slightly upon seeing Flynn's look of astonishment. "Did I say something?"

"I'm just surprised that you know Mr. Henley, too, I guess. His daughter went to the same school as me."

Cade chuckled. "Ah yes, the feisty Miss Evonne. She is a very interesting sort of person, if I do say so myself. I have caught her trying to shadow me on *several* occasions." He crossed one leg over the other. "What time were you intending on going to the castle, Tazer?"

"After midnight," Ian replied immediately. "There will be less people around to notice our movements."

Cade nodded briskly. "And I am guessing our team consists of you, Nigel, Pierson, and myself?"

"Hawk," Hawk automatically corrected.

Cade blinked, staring at Hawk for a moment before light dawned. "Oh, sorry, I just get so used to using last names."

Hawk waved a hand dismissively. "You do it all the time, and I correct you all the time, and we'll probably do it forever."

"To answer your question," Ian said to Cade, "yes—"

"And me too," Flynn interjected.

Ian looked at his nephew and frowned. "I'm not so sure about this time, Flynn. If anything, this is far more dangerous than our raid two nights ago. We have no idea what we're dealing with. Although I don't think anyone will be there, like I've said before, we don't know that for sure."

"This ain't a tea party," Alex said, wagging his finger at Flynn.

"I know that, but I still want to go. I mean, I can guard the entrance or something, and wait for the all clear, right?" Flynn was desperate to find a way to be allowed to go.

"Yes, like in the cartoon *Robin Hood*, and we'll call you Nutsy. 'One o' clock, and allllll's welllll!'" he yelped in a perfect imitation of the vulture's voice.

Hawk elbowed him into silence. "And just how are you going to do that without a gun?" he asked Flynn.

Flynn felt himself turn a slight shade of red. "I...didn't exactly..." he sighed. "I'll stay away from the entrance then, until you say it's clear. Please, Uncle? I mean, if I'm wearing a bullet-proof vest, what can possibly go wrong?"

"Pretty much anything and everything," Ian replied seriously. "And before you protest about how it's just as dangerous for us as for you, that's entirely beside the point. We've been trained for situations like this, whereas you haven't. We will also be armed, whereas you won't." Flynn felt he was losing the argument badly.

He opened his mouth to say something, then shut it realizing it was useless. Either his uncle would let him go or he wouldn't, and arguing about it wouldn't help his case any.

"He didn't say no," Cade said, seeing his disappointment.

"I didn't say yes either." Ian lapsed into silence, thinking of all the hundreds of ways their midnight mission could go horribly wrong. He ran through the possible options of taking Flynn with, and wasn't satisfied with any of them. "I'll think about it, but we'll drop it for now." Flynn heard little of the conversation that followed. Going with would be ever so exciting, but he was beginning to see his uncle's side of the argument. He knew nothing of such situations, and his presence would be more of a hindrance than a help. Sighing inwardly, he resigned himself to staying behind, and resolved to tell his uncle so when they were finished making their plans.

When Ian got up and returned to their room to get ready for dinner, Flynn followed him and pulled him aside. "Uncle, if it's too much trouble, then I'll just stay behind. I want to go, desperately, but I don't want to complicate matters more than they have to be." He hated himself for saying it, but it was the truth. It was better for him to miss all the action if his being there put others in danger.

Ian put a hand on his shoulder. "I think it's for the best. Yes, I'd like to take you with, but I don't know what will happen, and I can't ensure your safety."

"Maybe next time, then?" Flynn said hopefully.

"That depends entirely on the situation of 'next time'. But don't worry your head about it. And as for tonight, enjoy yourself and get a good night's sleep for once. You've had several crazy days." Ian smiled wryly. "I'm sorry this isn't quite the homecoming you expected."

"Don't be. I'm enjoying myself immensely." As Flynn pulled on his sweatshirt, he couldn't suppress a grin. Three days ago, he could never have even imagined himself being here, in the midst of a group of secret agents plotting how they would infiltrate a potential criminal's base of operations. Life certainly loved throwing curve balls at him, but he had learned to roll with them, and he was glad to finally get a good one for a change.

~

Leslie coaxed Flynn to watch the first episode of *Foyle's War* while the guys worked out the last few details of their plan and made stock of weapons, ammunition, and other things needed for a potential raid. Flynn wasn't entirely sure if he'd like the show, but decided to give it a try since it revolved around mysteries and such. He found himself hooked after only half an episode, and at the end of it, begged his aunt to watch the second one; she complied, and thus both of them were very much awake when it was time for the guys to leave.

Ian prayed for their safety, Leslie hugged him goodbye, and out into the night they went. Hawk had their weapons stowed in Alex's jeep, and they drove out of town and into the wilds of the island. They parked in the middle of nowhere behind a bunch of trees and hiked down the beach to the castle.

"You couldn't have driven any closer?" Alex complained, letting his heavy satchel drop to the ground. He dragged it along behind him and shuffled through the sand.

"You could have left some of that gear behind," Hawk retorted. "And I wouldn't drag it through the sand, if I were you. Grit does your fancy equipment no favors."

Alex heaved the cloth bag over his shoulder and continued griping about the distance. "Please tell me someone grabbed the snacks," he said suddenly as they crested a large dune covered with weeds.

Ian stopped and looked over his shoulder. "Snacks? Alex, it's after midnight. If you're that hungry, you ought to have eaten before we left."

"I'm not hungry now, but I will be before this night is through." Alex groaned. "Well this is a fine pickle. No food, and a hundred mile trek ahead of us. Huzzah."

Cade kicked him in the shin. "Stop moping. Maybe the Mallevilles have a vending machine." Hawk snickered as Alex began moaning about how cruel it was to taunt him with an imaginary vending machine full of M&M's and Cheetos.

Ian shook his head. "What's gotten into him?" he muttered, more to himself than to Hawk.

"What's new, mate?" Hawk shifted the strap across his chest that held his AWM rifle on his back.

They could see the castle now, and Ian cautioned them all to speak only if it was absolutely necessary. Bathed in hazy moonlight, the castle had an almost eerie look to it. No light illuminated the windows; the beach was deserted, save for themselves, and the only sounds that met their ears were the occasional rustling as a small critter darted through the underbrush and the dull roar of the ocean as it crashed against the rocks. They made it across the beach and up the road without incident and entered the castle by the front entrance, Cade locking the door behind them. Ian led them up to the room he thought might hold a secret entrance. They had agreed the basement was too obvious and would be checked last.

"Fan out. Search the whole room for hollow spots," Ian instructed in a whisper. The group split up and began to scour the place, tapping lightly on the floors, walls, and even the furniture.

"Guys, I've got something," Alex said softly, holding up a little scanning device. "That wall there isn't completely solid." He pointed, and Ian instantly went up to it and began knocking gently on the stone.

"I can't hear a difference, but I don't doubt your equipment." He stepped back and surveyed the wall, hoping to find something that would indicate a doorway. The wall was entirely bare, save for an old chest that lay off-center. "Why is that not lined up straight?" Ian mused.

"Help me move it." Hawk took one end of the chest, and, with Ian's help, dragged it away from the wall. Getting down on their hands and knees, they examined the floor, feeling here and there amidst the cracks. Hawk's fingers snared a small indentation in the grout and he pulled his hand away with a little grunt of pain.

"What?" Ian asked.

"I don't know, but I cut my fingers on something. Metal, maybe? Alex, shine your torch over here, will you?" Alex complied and Hawk peered closely at the floor. Something glinted in the sudden light.

"It does appear to be a piece of metal in the floor," Ian said. Removing his flick knife, he snapped one of the blades open and tried prying the piece up. To his astonishment, a grinding noise met his ears, and part of the wall slid into itself.

"Well, I think you found it," Alex observed, shutting off the torch.

"Turn that back on," Ian said as he and Hawk stood up. It appeared to be a very tiny closet, only about 6dm[1] by 3dm, but there was no floor. Stairs could be dimly seen leading down into the hole.

Alex flicked the torch off and returned it to his satchel. "Before anyone goes down there, let me check for cameras and traps." Alex took out his equipment, set up his laptop, and began scanning the tiny room and hole. "Ah, just as I suspected. There's a little itty-bitty camera up in the ceiling of the...closet, or whatever it is. Wires are in the wall, probably." He activated his wrist device and swept the room. "No beams." He rifled through his satchel, took out some tools, and in no time had a small opening in the wall. It took him several minutes to figure

---

[1]Dm = decimeters. Six dm = about twenty-two inches.

out which wires he needed to connect to his equipment, and several more to successfully hack the camera and reroute it to his laptop. "There. All the cameras were attached to one another, so that was easy."

Cade raised an eyebrow. "How can you tell?"

"Once I hacked into the main line, my computer traced the rest of the wires. Everywhere they split off, there's another camera, which I now have possession of. Once I press this button, I will be able to see all the rooms the cameras are situated in. There. Oh. It's awful dark. There's got to be a light switch down there, otherwise this is absolutely useless. Oh, look, there's more split-offs and wires then there are cameras…odd. Maybe traps? Eh, let me just disable those… Bully for me. Whatever they are, they aren't going to work now! Okay, so who's going down first?" Alex stopped rattling on and looked from one to the other.

"Give me that beam detector of yours, and the torch," Ian said, holding out his hand. "Alex, Cade, you're on guard duty. If you see anything or anyone register either on the cameras or outside, alert us immediately. Hawk, you're with me."

Hawk drew his FN five-seven and followed Ian down the stairs into the inky blackness. Ian shined the torch along the walls until he located the light switch. Upon flicking it up, the stairway became flooded with annoyingly bright light from iridescent bulbs strung from the ceiling. At the bottom of the stairway, there was a meter long passage that terminated before a large wooden door. It had an old-fashioned lock which Hawk expertly picked, using a thin metal tool he kept in his pocket. Unbeknownst to them, the lock had been electrically rigged, but Alex had rendered it useless, so it gave them little resistance. The door swung open to reveal a short hallway and two more doors. One had the letters A.P. engraved on it, the other U.P. Both doors were secured with a heavy-duty lock.

"What do you suppose those letters mean?" asked Hawk.

After a moment's thought, Ian replied, "Authorized Personnel and Unauthorized Personnel. U.P. is most likely where the key would be."

Hawk examined the lock. "Aw, this is easy. Seriously, why can't they get better locks?" He holstered his handgun and took the tool out of his pocket, manipulating it for about a minute before the lock snapped open. He turned the knob and pushed the door inwards, but didn't go in, letting Ian shine Alex's detector across the doorway, which revealed nothing.

"This is way too easy," Ian said apprehensively.

"Not exactly. The locks were probably all rigged, but Alex disabled them. Not to mention no one is even supposed to know it exists." Hawk stepped into the dark room and flicked the lights on. "Whoa..." The walls of the room were lined with cabinets that reached from floor to ceiling. Several dirty lightbulbs hung from the ceiling, illuminating a large metal table that sat in the center of the room covered with containers, boxes, and papers. "Where do we even start?"

"I haven't the slightest idea." Ian scanned the room, wishing there was a bright red label that said *Master Key*. He knew he wouldn't find it, but the sight of all the cabinets and containers was rather daunting. "Let's start with the table, and if we don't find anything there, we'll work our way through the cabinets."

Hawk shoved the tool back into his pocket and advanced towards the table. Soon, he and Ian were engrossed in opening every box and cylinder and rifling through every piece of paper. They found records of illegal shipments, cases of illegal weapons, and an abundance of illegal substances. "This is a gold mine of evidence," Ian said, closing the top of a metal container filled with what appeared to be drugs.

"No kidding." Hawk shoved a cardboard box aside and reached for a small, metal case off to his left. "Hullo, this won't open," he said after fiddling with the clasp.

"Is there a keyhole?" Ian asked, making his way over to Hawk's side of the table.

"Yeah, a very tiny one." Hawk inserted his tool and began working at it. "Stupid, stubborn little thing," he muttered after several failed attempts. He tried once more and a satisfying click met his ears. Laying the case down on top of a shoebox, he lifted the lid and peered inside. "Mate, I think we just hit the jackpot."

Ian leaned forward for a closer look and grinned. "I think you're right!" A large, silver M lay nestled in red velvet in the case. It shone and sparkled brightly as the light reflected off of it.

Hawk shut the lid and handed the box to Ian. "We've got what we've come for, but we can't just let this place go. Cade ought to ring Henley and tell him there really is a secret passage and rooms down in the castle. He should then swear him to secrecy, and make it look like Henley found it by accident. Henley rings the police, *et voilà*. We can get our hands on all this evidence without anyone knowing we were involved."

"Good idea. Let's go." Ian turned the lights off, closed the door, and replaced the lock. He hesitated before the other door. "Do you suppose we should see what's in there first?"

Hawk considered his suggestion and finally gave a short nod. "Why not? We're here, we might as well see." Picking the lock and opening the door, they found themselves in a room larger than the other one that was outfitted like a warehouse. Boxes and file cabinets and containers filled every inch of the room. There was another door on the far wall, and Hawk hastened to open it to reveal a dark tunnel. "This is probably another way in and out. Let's see where it goes." Ian followed him down the tunnel without a word. The tunnel wove for several hundred meters before ending with a trap door in the ceiling and a metal ladder leading up to it. The trap door stuck horribly, however, and nothing Hawk or Ian could do would make it budge.

"You might have to unlock it from the other side," Ian said, panting from the effort.

"You think?" Hawk snarked. "I guess we leave it to the local police," he added resignedly. He was disappointed that they couldn't open the door, and dearly wished he had a crowbar of some sort to force it. He and Ian made their way back through the tunnels and doors and on up the stairs to where Alex sat, watching everything on his laptop.

"Pretty neat, fellas. Looks like you had all the fun," he remarked as he began shutting some programs down. "Too bad you guys weren't strong enough to bust the trap door though." He looked slyly at Hawk.

Hawk whapped him on the back of the head. "It was locked on the outside, and you know it." Alex swatted at him and messaged Cade to come back from his lookout post in one of the towers.

"You got it, I trust?" Cade asked as he reentered the room.

Ian held up the metal case. "We did. Time to ring Henley."

~

The next morning, Ian recounted to Leslie and Flynn all that had transpired. "And so, if you were to go outside just now, I'd bet you the castle is all roped and taped off, and absolutely swarming with police and the press. Henley cooperated brilliantly, and he has no idea that anyone else was with Cade last night. The press will get its facts just the way we want them, and the Mallevilles will be none the wiser. God blessed this trip tremendously."

"Yes, He did. He kept you all quite safe, too, and that is most important of all." Leslie drew a light sweater on as she spoke. "You ought to sleep more, m'dear; you had such a long night."

"I'm really not all that tired. I've waited far too long for a break like this, and there's a ton to do."

Leslie frowned. "Yes, but you're no good to anyone when you're tired. A few more hours won't hurt you, and it won't hinder your investigation any."

Ian sighed resignedly. "Very well. But we're leaving before noon."

Ian took Leslie and Flynn to a small café before he headed back to the Inn to sleep a little. Leslie wanted to get a souvenir for Sean, and Flynn accompanied her. They had just finished their shopping when they ran into Von.

"Good morning, Mrs. Tazer, Flynn. Have you heard the news? There really *is* a secret passage in the castle!" She shivered with excitement, her eyes shining. "My father found it only this morning, and it's apparently been a criminal hide-out. What a *story* this will be! Why, the locals will be telling it for years and years."

"Are you serious?" Flynn asked, doing his best to act surprised.

"Oh yes, quite! The whole place is chockablock with coppers and important-looking men in business suits and armored guys with large guns. It's not something you see every day!" Von grinned. "This place needed a little livening up, you know. Oh, and you'll never guess what the rumor is of who used the hideout." She lowered her voice conspiratorially. "It's not confirmed, but it's said it was used by the notorious Mallevilles themselves."

Leslie gasped. "You're jesting, surely. The Mallevilles, all the way up here? They plague us in London!"

Von nodded emphatically. "That is what I have heard, and that is the rumor about town, and I'll bet you it's as true as the stars that shine."

"What are you betting me?" Flynn teased. "A new torch?"

"A new...ohhhhh." Von blushed to the roots of her hair. "I still owe you one, don't I?"

"You most certainly do, Miss Henley, and don't you forget it." Flynn crossed his arms.

"How could I, when I have you to remind me?" She laughed and winked at him. "Well, I'd love to stay and chat, but I promised to bring my dad a cup of hot coffee, so I'm off then." She hesitated, then blurted, "I don't know when you're leaving, so, if I don't see you again, I do hope you have safe travels. It was good to meet you, Mrs. Tazer." She stood there, almost awkwardly, wondering if she ought to shake Leslie's hand or give her a quick hug.

Leslie came to her rescue and gave her a hug. "You as well, Evonne. You will look us up the next time you're in London?"

"You're ever so kind. I will, I promise." Turning to Flynn, she shoved her hands in her pockets and gave him a smile. "It was good to see you, Flynn. Don't lose my number again."

"I won't." The previous day's conversation with his aunt and uncle flashed across his mind, and suddenly, saying goodbye became very awkward. "Uhm, well, see you, Von."

"Yeah, see ya, Flynn." She ducked her head, hopped off the sidewalk, and walked away.

Flynn was quiet as he and his aunt returned to the Inn. He'd never thought of Von as being...well, someone...someone...agh. It was all too complicated. Why couldn't things stay as they were, just old school mates and nothing more? He looked over his shoulder to catch a last glimpse of her as she disappeared into the café, and he felt something akin to regret. Why, or of what, he couldn't say.

"Missing her already?" Leslie teased, softly bumping into him as they walked down the sidewalk.

Flynn felt his face get hot again as he said, "Aw, come on, Aunt."

"And what's with the torch business?" she inquired.

"Oh, she dropped it from the school roof," Flynn replied with a grin, the color in his face slowly returning to normal. "It didn't stand a chance against the pavement, and shattered into a hundred little pieces. That was what…almost two years ago?"

"And just how did she manage to drop it from the roof?" Leslie gave him a searching look.

Flynn appeared almost guilty as he said, "We got super bored at the school dance, so we climbed the roof to star gaze. No one knew we did it, not even Grandmama. She would've fainted."

"I ought to scold you," Leslie said, trying to look serious.

"Well, it's not like Grandmama never said I couldn't," Flynn said defensively. "And neither did any of the school staff."

Leslie stopped walking and stared at him, as though a thought had just hit her. "If you were at the school dance, how in the world did Von climb on the roof in a dress?"

"Oh, it was kind of cold, so she had leggings on, and knee-high boots. Boots make for excellent climbing gear." Flynn shrugged. "We found a ladder, too, so it was fairly easy."

"Kids never change," Leslie said, shaking her head. "But don't you even think about climbing the roof at home." She shook her finger at him. "It's far too dangerous, and I will not have you needlessly putting yourself in harm's way."

"I won't, unless Uncle takes me up," Flynn said with a mischievous smile.

Leslie sighed. "You are so incorrigible!"

~

"Icabod, how in the world are we going to get past security?" whined Otto. "Shouldn't we just kidnap them or something?"

"No, you idiot. You can't just kidnap hundreds of guards and not have somebody notice. Besides, we've been infiltrating the key points, so stop whinging!" Icabod snarled.

Tiernan felt his heart racing. This evil plan had to be stopped. But what could he do? Nothing. He was trapped. *Please, God, protect her and stop these evil men! And please, set me free somehow, someway, so I can expose their plans,* he prayed inwardly.

"I don't believe it!" Alvar growled.

"What?" Icabod snapped, angered at the interruption.

"One of the tour guides found our headquarters at Lindisfarne Castle." There was an ominous silence as this news sunk in.

"What?" Icabod asked in a low, dangerous tone.

Alvar hesitated. He knew that tone, and he did not want to be on the receiving end of it. He handed Icabod the tablet he was reading and quickly backed away. Icabod scanned the report. The veins on his neck bulged, and his face turned almost

purplish-red with rage. Otto cowered in the corner as Icabod
stormed out of the room and hollered for Damian. This day
most certainly was *not* going how any of them had planned, and
it showed no signs of improvement.

~~

Chapter Nine

IAN AND THE REST LEFT JUST AFTER noon and didn't get home until around eight in the evening. Cade did not return with them, as he needed to gather his things at the motel he'd been staying in near Edinburgh, but he promised to show up at Ian's house within a day or so. On the way back home, Hawk and Alex played a third game of Risk. Alex lost a second time, and found himself owing Hawk quite a bit more sweets than he'd originally planned.

Sean and Lukas were still up, seated on barstools at the counter, eating slices of an apple pie that their Aunt Mary had baked earlier. The minute the garage door opened, both of them tumbled out of their seats and rushed for the door. Hawk opened it just as both of them ran into him.

"Dad!"

"Uncle Hawk!"

"Hey, boys." Hawk hugged them both. "Did you have a good time with Aunt Mary?" he asked as Sean ran to hug Ian and Leslie.

Lukas nodded vigorously. "She made a different pie every night. It was *so* yummy! We had apple and pumpkin and cherry."

"You're looking tons better." Hawk removed his shoes, ruffled the boy's hair, and stepped aside to let the others in the house.

"I *feel* better, and Aunt Mary says I'm good as new." Lukas looked very pleased. "I wish I could've gone with you. I missed you, and castles are so cool!"

"I'll take you there one day," Hawk promised. "I might enjoy it more myself, knowing it'll be a holiday and not work." He laid an oblong package on the counter and shed his sweater. Lukas scrambled up onto one of the barstools and eyed the package curiously.

"What's that?" he asked, reaching out to poke it.

"Ah-ah-ah, don't touch." Hawk slid it out of reach.

"Ooh, I want to see!" Sean cried. Having said hello to his parents and cousin, his attention was completely distracted by the strange package. He got up on another seat next to Lukas. "What's in it, Uncle Hawk? Sweets?"

"Sweet boxes aren't shaped like that," Lukas said.

"Maybe it's a tube of sweets," Sean suggested. "Like, a totally different kind of sweets. Sour, maybe? I love sour!"

Ian made a face as he hung his keys on the little key rack by the door. "Sour sweets are disgusting," he said emphatically.

"No they ain't!" Alex protested as he shut the door and juggled his laptop, satchel of equipment, and Risk game box. "Sour sweets sounds pretty good just about now. And no, it's not sweets, boys."

"You know what it is?" They both looked at him expectantly.

Hawk laughed and whisked the package off the counter. "He does, but he's not going to say a word. It's a surprise, and you can open it, Luke, once I've dumped my stuff in my room." Hawk brought the package into the living room before taking his suitcase upstairs. Both boys hopped up on the couch and eyed it in utter fascination. Their excitement was heightened by the little bag Leslie added to the coffee table, and the brown paper sack that Alex tossed next to it.

"It's presents for us, 'cause we didn't get to go," Sean whispered loudly to his friend.

"Don't be so sure," Lukas cautioned. "It could just be a cool souvenir or something for everyone."

Sean shook his head. "No, I bet it's presents. And Alex got sweets. He always gets us sweets."

Lukas giggled. "Yeah, he does. I wonder what kind he got us this time!" They fidgeted on the couch impatiently while their parents, Alex, and Flynn brought their things up to their rooms, and while Leslie thanked her sister for watching the boys. Finally, the travelers came into the living room; to the boys, it had seemed like ages, when in reality it wasn't even ten minutes.

"I suppose you can guess what mine is," Alex said. He picked up the sack and dropped it between them.

"Sweets?" Sean asked.

Lukas pulled out a clear plastic confection bag filled with brightly colored, wrapped candies. "Ooh, saltwater taffy! Ta, Uncle Alex! I love saltwater taffy. Dad, can I have some now?"

Hawk shook his head. "You've already had pie. That's quite enough sugar for one night."

"I suppose that goes for me, too?" Sean gave his mother a wistful look.

"Yes, Sean dear, it most certainly does. You and Lukas can split it up tomorrow." She picked up the little bag and handed it to him. "That is a little something we got for you, since you couldn't come along."

"I told you so!" Sean gave Lukas a little punch on the arm.

Lukas rolled his eyes. "I never said it wasn't. Just open it."

Sean pulled out two little somethings wrapped in packing paper. He tore the paper apart and threw the bits and pieces at Lukas. When the tattered pieces of paper had settled, he found a hard-plastic figurine of a knight decked out in elaborate black-and-burgundy armor and weapons, along with a war horse in the same colored gear. "Aw, this is so *dench!*"

"He's Rupert's brother," Lukas declared firmly. "The second oldest, and he resents that."

"Yeah, totally, and he's got a bad streak, and he gets tricked by the Desert Lady." Sean put the knight on the horse and galloped him along the air. "Thanks, Mum, thanks Dad! He's so cool, and he's perfect for our game!" he said, referring to the years-long game he and Lukas had been playing with their small action figures and plastic animal figurines.

"I'm glad you like him. Flynn picked him out, actually," Leslie said.

"You sure know what a fellow likes!" Sean said with a grin. "I'll have to show you the rest of my guys."

Flynn leaned on the back of a chair. "I look forward to it."

"And that's for me?" Lukas asked Hawk suddenly, pointing to the strangely-shaped package.

Hawk got up from his chair and carefully placed it in his son's lap. "Yes it is, but open it slowly."

Puzzled, Lukas pulled the brown paper away as gently as he could. As he revealed what was inside, his eyes widened and he gave a little gasp of awe. There, in his lap, lay a glass bottle with a beautiful little three-masted ship sailing inside. The ship had crisp white sails, and flew the Union Jack from the crow's nest. "Oh Dad!" was all he could say. He picked it up with both hands and stared at the ship. "It's so neat! I wish I could sail on it. Oh thank you!"

"I'm glad you like it," Hawk said with a smile. "I know it's not exactly a toy like Sean's, but—"

"But I wanted a model ship!" Lukas interrupted. "And I wanted one in a bottle, like Mum's, and it's just perfect, Dad. So perfect." He sighed contentedly.

Sean laid his knight down and leaned closer to Lukas to see the ship better. "Wow, that's ace. How did it get in the bottle though?"

"Whoever made it used very special tools to build it inside the bottle," Hawk explained simply.

"That had to take hours and hours," Lukas murmured as he shifted the bottle slightly to get a better look at all the intricate details.

"No kidding! I'd probably break the bottle by accident before it was finished." Sean broke off and tried to stifle a yawn, but was horribly unsuccessful.

"Time for someone to head upstairs," Ian said, fighting a yawn himself.

"A few someones from the looks of it," Leslie said. "Pick up those papers, Sean, and then up you go."

"Are you headed to bed?" Flynn asked his aunt.

She arched an eyebrow at him. "I was, why?"

"We-ell, I didn't know if you wanted to watch another episode of *Foyle's War*?" He looked at her sheepishly.

"Somebody's hooked!" Alex said in a high, sing-song voice. "And are you kidding? After that long drive? You'll fall asleep in the first five minutes."

"My thoughts precisely," Leslie said. "Besides, you don't want to watch all the seasons in a couple weeks, do you?"

"I guess not," Flynn grudgingly admitted.

Ian yawned again. "You can all dither about watching shows as long as you want. I can't stay awake, so goodnight."

They all said goodnight to each other and went upstairs. Leslie tucked the two boys in, and it wasn't long before the house fell silent. Flynn sank into bed, a well-worn paperback copy of *The Hound Of The Baskervilles* in hand. He didn't think he was quite ready to go to sleep just yet, but he'd hardly read a page before his eyes began to close. Laying the book aside, he turned off the lamp and was drifting off to sleep when Von flitted across his mind. He thought this rather odd, but didn't have time to think any further of it as sleep claimed him for the night.

~

Flynn got up early the next morning, and, after showering and getting ready, set to unpacking his suitcase and carry on. He left his door ajar, and Hawk leaned in to say good morning before heading downstairs to help with breakfast. Flynn was just finishing putting his clothes in the dresser when Lukas pushed his door open wider.

"Whatcha doin'?" he asked.

"I'm finally unpacking all my stuff," Flynn said as he shut the dresser drawer.

"Can I watch?"

Flynn shrugged and bent down to see what was left in his suitcase. "Sure, if you want." He took out a little cardboard box and set it on the dresser.

"What's in there?" Lukas hopped over to him, gripped the edge of the dresser, and stood on tiptoes to get a better look.

Flynn took his penknife out of his pocket and slit the tape that held the top flaps down. "Just a few breakable things."

"Like?" Lukas peered into the box and noticed that everything was wrapped with brown packing paper.

Flynn drew out a rectangle shape and peeled back the paper. "Like this." He held a small picture frame in hand and gently set it down on the dresser.

"Ooh, she's really pretty. Can I?" Lukas held out his hands and Flynn nodded. Lukas picked up the frame and examined the woman closely. "Is she your Mum?"

"Yeah." Flynn unwrapped another frame. "And this is my Dad."

Lukas took that one, too, and held them side by side. "Hey, he looks like Uncle Ian."

Flynn cracked a smile. "That's because they were brothers."

"Oh, right. My dad told me that." He carefully set the frames back on the dresser. "Can I ask you something?"

"Anything you like." Flynn swiped the paper onto the floor; he'd pick it up when he was finished.

"What happened to them?"

Flynn stopped unwrapping another item and turned to look at Lukas. "They died," he said softly.

"I know. Dad told me. I meant how, I guess, and when. If you don't mind, of course," he added quickly. "I don't want to make you sad."

"No, you won't. They were killed in a car crash when I was five." Flynn glanced at the photos rather wistfully. "I wish I could have known them."

"I'm really sorry about that," Lukas said sympathetically. "My mummy was taken away by evil bad guys. Do you want to see her?"

"I'd love to." Flynn had met her before, but he didn't say as much.

Lukas dashed out of the room and returned moments later with a small frame in hand. He gently set it on the dresser. "There. That's my mum. Isn't she pretty?"

Flynn picked up the frame and looked at the woman who was smiling back at him. She was indeed beautiful, with dark brownish-blond hair, hazel eyes with a hint of green, and an extremely faint smattering of freckles across her little nose. "That she is, Lukas. Your dad never did find out who took her, did he?" He set the frame down as he spoke.

Lukas's face fell. "No. And he says we might not ever." He sighed loudly. "I miss my mum. Lots." A tear trembled in his eye. "Do you miss your mum?"

Flynn knelt down in front of him to give him his full attention. "Yes, but not like you I'm afraid. You remember yours. I don't."

Lukas swiped at his eyes and looked very surprised. "You don't? Nothing at all? But that's so sad! I couldn't imagine not remembering my mum."

Flynn gave him a sad sort of smile. "Well, not exactly nothing. I have one memory that's very clear. It was my birthday, and she brought in a dark red and white cake, and she was wearing a yellow dress. She had a big smile on her face, too – she was always smiling. But that's about all I remember. I'm sorry about your mum, Lukas. Who knows, though? Maybe God will bring her back to you one day."

Lukas tried to smile back. "I hope so. I miss her so much. Dad does, too. But it helps to talk about her, because then she seems closer, you know?" Flynn nodded absently. Lukas reached up and grabbed the frame. "I'd better go put this back." He returned seconds later and asked if he could help with anything, and soon he and Flynn were busy rearranging things on the top of the dresser.

"Dad said Mum's favorite color is blue, like his. Though he likes a sea-blue, and she likes a brighter or darker blue. I like blue, too. What about your mum?" Lukas gathered up loose bits of packing paper and began folding them as neatly as he could.

"I don't know," Flynn said rather flatly.

Lukas's eyes widened. "You don't? How come?"

"I told you, I never knew her."

Lukas was still confused. "But...didn't Uncle Ian ever tell you? Or your grandma?"

"I never asked Uncle, and my grandmama didn't talk about Mum," Flynn said shortly.

"That's silly," Lukas declared, not noticing Flynn's tone. "I mean, yeah, it hurts to talk about it sometimes, but it's better to do it. That's what Dad says." He was interrupted from saying any more as Ian came in the room to tell them breakfast was ready. They both had no idea he had overheard the latter part of their conversation.

"What's the plan for today?" Alex asked as he dumped a very generous portion of brown sugar into his oatmeal.

"I rang Grant, and we're going to raid the Malleville's headquarters at nine this morning. He's putting together a team of SCO19 and so forth, and we're to meet him like we did before," Ian explained. He cut up an apple into tiny pieces and dropped them in his oatmeal as he spoke.

Leslie poured several cups of tea and passed them around. "You will all have a very crazy day, whereas I intend to stay home and make a roast for dinner," she said, shifting the conversation for the sake of the little boys.

"And maybe help us with my new LEGO set?" Sean asked hopefully. "It came in the mail yesterday, and it's super ace looking!"

Lukas nodded vigorously and grinned. "Yeah, and it's got panthers and trucks and snakes, and cool stuff. Do help us, Aunt Leslie, please?"

"I would love to. I have a few chores to do, and then I'll join you both, okay?" Leslie reached for what she thought was the sugar dish and accidentally filled her tea cup with brown sugar instead of white.

Alex held out his hand to stop her, but was too late. "Uh, Honey...oh dear."

"What?" she asked, stirring her tea.

"That wasn't white sugar. You know that, right?"

Leslie's gaze flicked to the dish and she gasped. "Oh no, I thought...oh." She looked sadly at her tea. "Well, it can't taste *that* awful, can it?" She took a tentative sip, wrinkled up her nose, and started coughing. "It can!"

Ian switched her cup out with his. "Drink mine; I was on my second one already." He stared at her cup a minute, then took a sip himself. "Ooh, you weren't exaggerating, were you?

That's…uhm, I don't even know what that is. How in the world did you put brown sugar in it instead?"

"The dishes look the same, and I thought the white was in front of me, so I didn't exactly look at it. I hate ruining tea." She held the cup back out to him. "Are you sure you don't want this? I can go get another one."

"I'm sure." He washed the taste out of his mouth with a last bite of a jellied English muffin. "Okay guys, meet me in the basement. We have to get going."

Flynn was also finished with his breakfast and followed his uncle downstairs. "Please let me go with," he said in a rush. "I'll stay in the car like last time, and I won't ask to go into wherever the door leads unless you say it's safe. Do let me, please."

"You can go, but it might be very tedious. If it's an entire bunker or cave system, you could be left there for at least an hour or two, if not longer. Are you sure you want to stick it out?" Ian opened the door of the storage closet and began to collect their gear.

"Are you kidding me? Of course! I'll just bring a book or something."

In less than ten minutes, the guys were all suited up and ready to go. Leslie begged them to take care of themselves, and warned Flynn to listen to his uncle and stay in the car, no matter what. He duly promised, and they went on their way.

The seriousness of the situation gradually began to sink in, and Flynn was suddenly nervous for his uncle. "Uncle Ian, just how dangerous is this going to be?" he asked.

"It all depends. By now, they have in all certainty learned that the Lindisfarne headquarters is no more. If they fear the master key has been discovered for what it really is, then they may have gone. If they don't, then..." Ian's voice trailed off.

"Then there's a possibility of fireworks," Alex finished for him. "Which is why I'm staying in the house with SCO19. I'll monitor the cameras, and relay info to you, but I'll let you fellows take out the bad guys all you want."

Flynn remained quiet as the guys discussed potential situations and what they would do in each one. This was far more dangerous than he had originally thought it would be. "How can you stay so calm?" he finally blurted.

Ian broke off his sentence and glanced at Flynn in the rear-view mirror. "I'm sorry?"

"How can you stay so calm going into something like this? I mean, you've just gone over fire-fights, collapsing tunnels, traps, and explosives, yet you don't seem ruffled in the least."

Ian saw the fear in his nephew's eyes; fear, not for himself, but for those he loved. "Sometimes what we show on the outside is not an accurate portrayal of what's on the inside," he began. "In this type of job, you have to force yourself to control your emotions. That doesn't mean suppressing them; it simply means not allowing them to control you. At the same time, I remind myself that my life is in God's hands. Nothing will happen that is outside of His control."

Flynn managed a rather strained smile. "I guess you're right."

"It's easy to say, but not so easy to do," Hawk added. "It often requires an extreme conscious effort, a mental fight even, to trust in God and keep your cool. It becomes a little easier, however, the more you do it."

They met up with Grant and SCO19 just like they had before, and in no time at all, Flynn found himself saying goodbye to his uncle. He gripped Ian's shoulder tightly. "Take care of yourself, Uncle, and may God be with you."

"And with you, Flynn. Try to relax, okay? I'll text you the all clear before I come and get you. And remember: do not get out of the car for any reason, alright?"

Flynn rolled his eyes. "Come on, Uncle, I'm not Sean. I'm not going anywhere until you come and get me. Promise."

"Guard the car well, Nutsy." Alex winked at him and slammed the door shut before Flynn could say anything in his defense. Flynn let his head fall into his hands and sighed audibly. Why did all the worst nicknames stick like Gorilla Glue?

Raising his head, he watched as Ian, Hawk, Alex, and Grant vanished into the house, along with a swarm of SCO19. Once they were gone, he hopped into the front seat and leaned back. He stared out the window for what seemed like a very long time, but when he glanced at his watch, it had only been six minutes. Scowling, he reached into the back seat for his book, but found he just couldn't concentrate. He absent-mindedly fanned the pages, laid it aside, and stared back out the window. SCO19 guarded the house at all points of exit and entry, and absolutely nothing was happening that he could see. How he wished he could be down there, helping his uncle with whatever the tunnel revealed! Doing nothing was driving him insane. He wondered how his aunt could possibly stay home and stay sane at the same time.

When he couldn't stand it anymore, he picked up his phone and texted his aunt, asking her just how she could handle the waiting. Her reply: *I pray, a lot. It's the only thing that keeps me calm. And when I must go on with my daily duties, I concentrate fully on those. Whenever thoughts of Ian and the rest come back to my mind, I pray again, and then force myself to think of something else. When you pray for someone's safety, you are putting them into God's hands. Worrying about them is like trying to take them back. Leave them there; they're safer times infinity in His hands than in your own.*

Flynn sighed heavily, then texted her a quick thank you. She was right, and he knew it. Closing his eyes, he prayed fervently for his uncle and the others, and then turned his full attention to his book. It took some effort, but he eventually was lost deep in the pages of *The Eagle of the Ninth*.

~

The beam in the front door had been completely dismantled for evidence, and the kitchen trap door had been left as it was, so it took hardly any time at all for them to descend into the tunnel. Ian produced the master key, removed the outer casing as Vansant had instructed, and inserted the pendant into the wall. Alex, who had memorized the combination lock numbers, rattled them off one by one and Ian pressed them accordingly. Both of them stepped back, expecting the wall to open in some fashion, but nothing happened.

"Uhm, maybe we're supposed to punch it or something?" Alex suggested. He suited his words to the action before Ian could protest, slamming his left fist into the M. "Ouch! That thing is...*whoa*..." His mouth dropped open as, with a creak and a groan, the wall slid open to reveal an inky black tunnel. "I feel like I'm in a sci-fi movie," he muttered.

"Scan it," Hawk broke in impatiently.

"I'm getting to that." Alex opened his laptop and ran through his different software programs after checking the opening with his wrist device. "No beams, only a camera further down. I can either wait for you guys to make sure the tunnel is clear as far as the camera so I can disable it, or I can just manually shut everything down, including the lights, by blowing the fuse in the breaker." He looked expectantly from Ian to Hawk to Grant and back again.

"I don't think blowing the fuse is a good idea," Grant said disapprovingly.

"Okay, but I'm going to need something to work off of, and I've got to get that camera disabled," Alex began.

"Let me," Hawk said, drawing his Beretta which he had equipped with a silencer before heading out. "Somebody have a torch so I can see my target?"

"How does a lightbulb sound instead?" Alex flipped the switch on the wall. "I mean, of course, a torch is less light, so it makes your shot more impressive, but we have to turn the lights on anyways, so—"

"Shut up." Hawk raised his handgun, lined the camera up with his sights, and fired.

"Do you ever miss, ol' chap?" Alex asked as the camera lens shattered and fell to the stone floor.

"You're actually asking?" Hawk stood back to let SCO19 advance down the tunnel, then waved Alex ahead of him, still gripping his handgun. "Do your stuff, Tuck."

They had to get a chair from the kitchen for Alex to stand on, but he was soon busy hacking into the camera system via the wires from the shattered device. They couldn't wait for him, however, and the bulk of SCO19, along with Grant, Ian, and Hawk continued down the tunnel. About five minutes later, the tunnel widened and the walls became rougher, the ceiling more jagged.

"Looks like they tunneled into a natural cave," remarked Grant.

"And this is where they broke through." Ian flicked the next set of wall switches, activating the string of bulbs ahead of them. "Tuck, how's the camera coming?" he asked, speaking into his smart watch.

Alex's voice filtered through a Bluetooth earpiece. "Eh, almost got it. Just need to attach another wire or two, press a couple buttons, and we'll be good to go. Oh crud, I hope I didn't need that..."

They hadn't gone far when SCO19 stopped, and Hawk said to Alex over his own watch, "The tunnel splits here. That camera would be really nice right about now."

"Yeah, sorry, but the bloody thing hates me, okay?" Alex responded in a frustrated tone. "Give me a second here..."

"If he can't do it within the next minute, we will have to split up," Grant said firmly.

"Just wait," Ian cautioned, confident in his friend's ability.

Grant muttered the seconds under his breath and had just reached forty-seven when Alex cried triumphantly, "Okay, got it! Smile, fellows: you're on camera."

Ian rolled his eyes. "Tuck, cut the gab and tell us where to go."

"Sorry, uhm, oh gosh, I can actually see Tiernan!" Alex scanned the maze of cameras, trying to configure a basic outline of the tunnel system. It wasn't easy, especially since half the cameras were pitch black, indicating the lights hadn't been turned on yet. "Okay, there's nobody that I can see anywhere else, he's by himself, head right. There doesn't look like another fork comes up until you actually get to the room, but I could be wrong. It's not like I have a map here."

"To the right," Ian relayed to Grant. With SCO19 leading, they hurried down the tunnel, which split off into two more tunnels and the large room where Tiernan was being held. Hawk pushed past SCO19 into the room and saw Tiernan slumped against the far wall. Tiernan's eyes slowly opened and widened in disbelief as he took in the heavily armed officers, but his mouth dropped opened when they fastened on Hawk.

Hawk was on his knees next to him before he could say anything and hissed, "Sparrow. Call me Sparrow, okay?"

"Okay, but...what...how?" Tiernan shook his head slightly, not fully comprehending the situation. "I must be hallucinating," he muttered, closing his eyes.

Hawk laid a hand on his shoulder. "No, Skyndar," referring to the man by his first name, "you're not hallucinating. We've come to get you out of here. Are you hurt beyond those bruises?" he asked, glancing at the injuries on the man's face.

Tiernan grimaced. "My ribs. I'll be surprised if any of them are still intact."

Hawk's face darkened dangerously, but before he could reply, Alex's voice came over his earpiece. "Bad news, bad news, bad news! There's another entrance, guys, and three of the Mallevilles have just shown up. Get out, will you?"

"Where?" Ian demanded.

"A ways down, but they're headed your way. Looks like they're coming down the tunnel on your left. They don't know you're here yet." Alex's voice became increasingly high pitched. "Get out of there, seriously, and let SCO19 handle it. Axel's carrying his Glock, and Alvar's got a shotgun. Can't see what Damian's carrying. This is not going to be pretty. Get out!"

"Tuck, I can't just leave Tiernan here," Hawk started as Ian rapidly explained the situation to Grant.

As Tiernan grasped what was happening, he gripped Hawk's arm tight, his face contorted with fear. "They're coming?"

"Yes, but don't you worry. SCO19 will handle it," Hawk reassured him.

Getting up and shoving everything off of the wooden table in the middle of the room, he flipped it on its side and slid it over towards the far exit where the Mallevilles were most likely to come through. With the help of an SCO19 officer, he moved the three large, metal containers that were in one corner over to the table, and motioned for Ian and Grant to grab the wooden chairs and tip them over next to the containers, thus completing the make-shift barrier. He and the officer crouched behind it, guns at the ready, while Ian and Grant sat with their backs to the containers and relayed messages back and forth.

"Tuck, I need to know where that other entrance is," Ian cried urgently. "Now!"

"Working on it, Cap…"

The ominous silence that filled the room was suddenly shattered by the sounds of yelling and gunfire. "Tuck, *now!*"

"Got it! It's in another clearing, about a third of a mile off to the right of the house."

Ian relayed this to Grant, who instructed half of the remaining SCO19 left upstairs to rendezvous and intercept anyone who came out of that entrance. The lights suddenly died, as did the gunfire and shouts, and the caverns became eerily quiet. "Tuck, talk to me," Ian demanded. "What's going on?"

"I don't know! Everything's out! Lights, cameras, everything." Alex's voice was panicky. "Are you guys okay? What's going on? I can't see anything!"

"Tuck, get to the breaker and see if you can fix it," Ian commanded. "And stay calm. Panicking will not help."

"Yes, Cap." Alex took a deep breath. "Let's just hope it's a blown fuse or something."

~

Flynn finished a chapter and stifled a yawn. He was starting to get hungry, and vaguely wondered what snacks Alex had packed. He figured he could take a peak, and worked his way to the very back. Leaning over the back seat, he popped open the lid of the cooler and fished around inside. He lighted upon a small cloth lunch box, and after unzipping it, found several snack bags filled with some type of cereal and chocolate chips. It looked good, so he closed everything back up and began to return to his seat. He was about to hop into the front when he noticed the officers stirring around the house. Several of them ran out of the house, got into their ARV's, and drove away. Something important was happening, and suddenly all his former anxiety came flooding back.

The rest of SCO19 ran into the house, leaving no one outside. That was unusual. Essentially, he was completely alone, and for the first time he felt vulnerable and uneasy. Sinking into the middle passenger seat, he continued to stare out the window.

He jerked his head to the windshield as his peripheral vision caught movement near the edge of the forest line. A man was slinking from tree to tree, staying far away from the house itself. Flynn couldn't tell who it was until he stepped out into the empty clearing and ran for Ian's Mazda: Quentin Lathrop.

Flynn slid down the seat and onto the floor, desperately hoping the man hadn't seen him and wasn't going to try and steal the car. His horror mounted as he heard Lathrop fiddling with the outside lock. The scratch-scratch of his tool slowly frayed at Flynn's nerves, and he shut his eyes, willfully keeping the panic at bay. In less than two minutes, Lathrop had opened the door and taken possession of the driver's seat.

Flynn felt his heart pounding in his chest. What in the world was he supposed to do? His uncle had told him not to leave the car for any reason, but surely he hadn't counted on an impromptu kidnapping. He heard Lathrop working on the dash, presumably trying to manually start the car without a key. Rapidly, he began to form a plan of escape. If Lathrop did manage to start the car, he'd have between three to five seconds to jerk the passenger door open and roll out before the man hit the gas. Swallowing hard, Flynn shut his eyes and silently prayed that he would be able to get out in time, and that Lathrop wouldn't have a gun. Flynn didn't relish the thought of getting shot at again. He couldn't make a sound, lest Lathrop should become distracted, and he kept his body rigid in anticipation of what he had to do. As the minutes ticked by, his tension mounted, threatening to suffocate him.

The car's engine roared to life, shattering the stillness in an instant. Yanking the door handle viciously, Flynn threw himself out of the car and scrambled to get clear. "What...!" Lathrop exclaimed, pulling out a compact handgun and firing out the open door; Flynn, however, had reached the back of the vehicle. Snapping open his penknife, he buried it into the back tire in the hopes of slashing it, but before he could finish the job, Lathrop slammed his foot on the accelerator. The blade stuck in the tire and the penknife ripped from his hand; all he could do was watch dejectedly as the car roared out of the clearing. SCO19 ran out of the house, and while several began firing their rifles at the vehicle, others jumped into one of the remaining ARVs and tore after it.

Three SCO19 officers hurried over to Flynn, shouting, "Are you alright? Are you hit, sir?"

Flynn got to his feet and brushed himself off. "No, I'm not hit. I'm fine." The adrenaline rush wore off as quickly as it had come, and he was suddenly dazed and shaky. It had all happened so fast. He stumbled, breathing heavily, and one of the officers steadied him.

"Come with us, please, sir. It's not safe out here." SCO19 hustled him into the house and instructed him to stay in the living room. Two officers remained with him while the others went back outside.

"What's going on?" Flynn asked as he leaned against the wall of the dirty, bare room. His legs felt weak, but there was no way he was going to sit on the floor. "What happened?" The officers didn't reply, which Flynn found extremely annoying. "I need to know what's going on," he demanded.

"I'm not entirely sure myself," one of the officers finally said, noticing his distress. "We'll know shortly. Why don't you sit down—"

"No thank you, not on that floor." Flynn closed his eyes and tried to calm himself. He couldn't voice concern for his uncle, since SCO19 wasn't supposed to know their identity, and that was making him feel even more jittery. He also couldn't stop shaking, which he found super annoying.

The sound of someone pounding up the collapsible stairs in the kitchen met his ears, and in mere seconds Ian barreled into the living room. He motioned imperiously for the officers to leave and grabbed Flynn by the shoulders when they were gone. "Are you okay? What happened? Why, you're shaking!" he cried, scrutinizing his nephew with concern.

"I'm okay, Uncle. I'm guessing it's just the adrenaline rush wearing off. You're not angry with me for getting out, are you?" Flynn asked almost guiltily as he tried to control the trembling in his limbs.

"Angry? No, oh no!" Ian hugged him impulsively. "Thank God you're safe...what happened?" he repeated urgently, pulling back to look at him anxiously. "No, wait, let me get you a chair or something. You can hardly stand."

Flynn held onto his uncle's arm. "No, it's okay. I'm not going to fall over or anything. Besides, it's not so bad anymore. Stupid adrenaline..."

Ian hugged him again fiercely, and held him tight for a minute or two until Flynn stopped trembling. "Oh my gosh, I can't believe you're okay. SCO19 said first the car was taken, then that you were down on the ground and I...oh Flynn, I'm so glad you're safe!"

"Same goes for you," Flynn said as his body slowly relaxed and returned to normal. "I figured something bad must have happened, since everyone just left, and nobody would tell me what was going on."

Ian gripped Flynn's shoulders. "They left you?!" He shook his head, unable to comprehend how that could be. "Tell me what happened," he pleaded.

Flynn took a deep breath and rapidly relayed the last few minutes to his uncle. "I saw SCO19 go into the house, and then Lathrop came out of the trees. He broke into the car and somehow managed to start it without the keys. He didn't see me, because I hit the floor when I saw him approaching, and when he started it, I opened the door and threw myself out. He fired at me, but missed. I got my penknife in the back tire." He suddenly looked distraught. "That's the one you gave me for my twelfth birthday. It's probably ruined, now...and I lost my book, too, dang it. But what am I saying?" He smacked his forehead. "You lost your car! That's way worse."

"Never mind about that. It's just a car. You're the one I'm concerned about." Ian passed a hand over his face and sighed heavily. "I could never forgive myself if something happened to you...I can't believe you're safe." He grimaced. "How shall I ever explain this to your aunt?"

Flynn thought about that for a moment and drew a blank. "Oh, we'll think of something, but what happened down there? Why did so many of the SCO19 leave? Why was I left alone in the first place?" He fired the questions at his uncle thick and fast.

Ian held up his hands to allow him to explain. "There's another entrance, and the Mallevilles paid us a visit. Alex figured out the location of the entrance, and Grant sent some officers to intercept anyone who came out of it, but I have no idea if anyone has been caught yet. As to why they left their positions I don't know, but I am going to chew them out!" Anger laced his tone, and his eyes sparked. "They oughtn't to have left the outside unguarded, and they should have seen Lathrop and apprehended him before he even got into the car, let alone start it and drive away!"

"Uncle, nobody's perfect—" Flynn began.

"I know, but their actions were unacceptable!" Ian snapped. "They had no business all coming in the house. They were instructed to guard the exits and entrances and apprehend any trespassers, and they failed. Miserably." He sighed again and looked at his nephew seriously. "You do realize this is the third time in a week that you could have been killed? I may have to rethink this whole in-the-field-training thing."

Flynn's eyes widened. "Oh please don't, Uncle. You said yourself the job comes in waves. This just happens to be a particularly crazy time. And besides, what better way to be prepared for dangerous situations than to learn first-hand?"

"I'm not so sure about that, but we'll talk about it later, okay? No," and he raised a hand to stop Flynn from protesting, "I'm not saying you can't come with me anymore, or anything like that. I'm only saying we may need to rethink a few things. The idea is for you stay alive."

"I've stayed alive so far," Flynn replied archly. "Looks like I'm doing just fine."

Ian groaned. "That's not what I meant, and you know it. Oh hang on, repeat that, Tuck, would you?"

Alex huffed. "Fine, but I hate giving bad news twice. The Mallevilles are gone. They disappeared before SCO19 got to the second entrance. They've got such a head start, and no one knows what their vehicles look like, there's no chance of catching them. The only good thing to this whole mess is that Tiernan's in one piece. I got the breaker up and running, but, well…"

"Well what?"

"There's at least three officers down. Can't tell if anyone's alive, either…" he added heavily.

Ian massaged the bridge of his nose. "Can this mission get any messier," he muttered. "Have you called an ambulance?"

"I did." Hawk's voice filtered through the earpiece. "Tiernan's going into shock. I just hope it gets here fast. I'm guessing Flynn's okay?"

"Yes, just a bit shaken up," Ian replied back. "He can fill you in later."

"Oh, and I'm sorry I freaked SCO19 out," Alex added.

Ian's brow furrowed in confusion. "Huh? What do you mean?"

"The breaker shocked me, and I kind of yelped..." Alex's voice was rather sheepish. "It hurt, but I guess I sounded like I was getting attacked or something, because they just suddenly appeared in vast numbers."

"So that explains why they all left their posts outside," Ian muttered.

"What?"

"Nothing," he said hastily. "Don't worry about it."

"Okay, Cap."

"What?" Flynn wished he could hear the conversation. Ian explained briefly, after which Flynn asked, "Why would Tiernan go into shock? He wasn't shot, was he?"

"No, but he's been through a lot of trauma," Ian said. "The thought of the Mallevilles coming back, combined with the firefight, probably terrified him, and in his weakened state he just couldn't handle the stress, so his blood pressure dropped, thus causing shock."

Flynn considered this before asking, "Is this mission a success, or not?"

Ian frowned and folded his arms across his chest. "It's more of a draw. We came to get Tiernan, and we succeeded. We also came to capture the Mallevilles, and we failed. We hoped to come through with no casualties, but as you know, that's not the case."

"What do we do now?" Flynn asked feeling rather discouraged.

"Right now, all we can do is wait to hear if SCO19 caught Lathrop. If Tiernan's injuries aren't too serious, we can question him on what he might know tonight. If not, then certainly tomorrow. I'll also have to ring forensics to see what can be found in the tunnels. Chances are there's a good deal of evidence that may prove useful." The call didn't take long, and Ian had just hung up when several ambulances arrived.

Grant went out and instructed the paramedics before coming into the living room. "I have both good news and bad news," he said. "The good news is SCO19 apprehended Lathrop. The bad news is your car is destroyed. The windows have been shot to pieces, and Lathrop threw himself out while it was still running, so it totaled a tree. I'm really sorry about that. Can't imagine how he got it running without the keys."

"Lathrop is a dab hand with keyholes and locks; he found a way with something," Ian said.

Grant shifted his gaze to Flynn. "Had a bit of a rough morning, eh lad?"

Flynn gave him a wry smile. "It wasn't too bad. Certainly more eventful than I was originally thinking."

Once it was ascertained that the tunnels were entirely free of danger, Ian allowed Flynn down into the tunnels to help them look for evidence. "We want papers and electronics. Leave everything else for forensics. They might complain that we're nosing in here before they arrive, but we have full right to do it, so don't mind them. Stick close to me," Ian instructed. They scoured the passages and rooms, but found very little to take with. There were two tablets, a laptop, and a box of papers. Everything else was either weapons, food, clothes, or illegal substances.

Alex was not optimistic about the electronics. "Knowing Damian, he'll have tons of safety features activated. And assuming I can get past them, they will either be encrypted or wiped clean."

"You can unencrypt them, right?" Flynn asked.

"Yeah, but you can rig a file to recognize when it's been broken into, and then it will manually delete itself. Like a self-destruct button, basically. I'm counting on everything being wiped." He stuffed the electronics into an empty cardboard box that he'd found as he spoke.

"How could he do that?"

"Easy. You set up your phone with an outside account that allows you to wipe your phone if you lose it, right? Damian probably implemented that on the laptop and tablets. I have that on all my equipment and stuff. It's simple, really." Alex stopped. "You look lost."

"Uhm, just a little?" Flynn replied sheepishly. "I've never exactly paid attention to an outside wiping thing."

Alex smacked his forehead. "It's not an outside wiping thing. It's a— oh, never mind. It's easier to show you, but I don't have time right now." He picked up the box and hollered over his shoulder, "Cap, you ready?" A forensics guy glared in his direction, and Alex made a face right back.

"Yeah, I'm right behind you," Ian called. "Do you have some tape in that satchel of yours? This box is falling apart."

"Heads up!" Alex grabbed a roll of duct tape and tossed it to his friend.

Ian caught it with one hand and started to unroll a piece. "Thanks." He raised an eyebrow at the Star Wars villains printed on the tape, but refrained from comment. Only Alex would have Star Wars duct tape stashed in his satchel

When they returned to the kitchen, they found Grant conferring with one of the SCO19 officers in charge. "Ah, Cap, I was just about to go down and see if you were ready to go. Since your car is destroyed, you guys can ride with me. It'll be a tight squeeze, but we'll manage."

"Good. Tuck, just stow this in the trunk, huh?" Ian held out the box.

Alex looked down at all the stuff he was carrying – laptop, satchel, the Mallevilles's electronics, all the camera feeds – and stared at him. "Do I look like I have a free hand?"

"Allow me," Hawk said, coming up behind them. He knew what his friend wanted to do, and hustled both Alex and Flynn out of the house.

"I want a word with you," Ian began, addressing the SCO19 officer in charge.

The man held up his hand. "I know, sir. Detective Chief Inspector Grant has explained the situation to me, and I want to sincerely apologize for the actions of my men. I know that doesn't fix what happened, but I can assure you, my men will be dealt with. They heard one of your agents scream inside the house, and thought the Mallevilles had broken through, when he'd only been shocked by the breaker. However, what they did was unacceptable, since they did not have orders to leave their position, and they had full knowledge that another of your agents was inside the vehicle."

Ian gave a short nod. "I accept your apology, and I am relieved you understand the seriousness of what occurred, for not only did they abandon their posts, but allowed a suspect to escape. Make sure the discipline you give ensures this will never be repeated. In our line of work, we can't afford errors of any kind." The officer agreed heartily before they parted.

When he and Grant got in the car, Flynn looked at his uncle apprehensively. "You didn't...you know, tell him off or anything?"

"No. He was very apologetic, and as upset about what happened as I was, so I did not give him the piece of my mind that I was originally intending to."

"Wise idea. You've already given away enough pieces, I don't know how many you have left," Alex jabbed.

"Ha ha, very funny." Ian pulled out his phone and stared at it, contemplating what exactly he ought to tell his wife. He would tell her the story in full when he got home, of course; but how much should he say before then? He didn't want to worry her out of her wits, so he quickly texted her, saying they had Tiernan and Lathrop, nobody was hurt save for a couple SCO19, and they were headed home to go through some papers and electronics that the Mallevilles had left behind. She instantly texted him back, saying she was relieved to know they were all okay, and hoped they would get home both safely and quickly.

He put his phone on standby just as he heard Alex say to Flynn, "You had one job, Nutsy: guard the snacks. That was seriously too much for you?"

"I'm *not* Nutsy!" Flynn protested. "And how do you expect me to protect snacks from getting kidnapped if I have nothing but a penknife?"

"Excuses, excuses." Alex clucked his tongue.

"Stop complaining," Grant said as he pulled over on a side road and motioned towards Ian's Mazda. "You can salvage the snacks all you want."

Flynn's mouth dropped as he took in the scene. Several ARV's were parked around the dark grey vehicle that was little more than a mass of crumpled metal and shattered glass. "How is Lathrop even alive?"

"He jumped out, remember?" Grant explained as they got out. "He sustained serious injuries nonetheless, but they don't appear to be fatal; we'll be able to question him in a few days or so once he's stable."

It took some maneuvering, but Ian was finally able to get the vehicle registration and proof of insurance out of the glove box, along with his Baroque CDs and Flynn's book. Alex's cooler and snacks had somehow survived the crash without a noticeable scratch, and he managed to stuff them in Grant's trunk. Flynn went over to the back tire to see if anything was left of his penknife, but found nothing at first glance.

"I'm sorry about the knife," Hawk said, getting down on his hands and knees for a quick once-over, to ensure it wasn't in the near vicinity.

Flynn shrugged, trying to appear as though it didn't affect him all that much. "Aw, it's okay. I can get another."

"Still won't be the same," Hawk continued. His hands brushed against a broken piece of the blade that had fallen out of the tire when the car impacted the tree. He held it out to Flynn sympathetically. "Trust me, I know. Most people think one knife is the same as any other, but when you get attached to a specific one, there's nothing quite like it."

Flynn nodded and pocketed the broken blade. He remembered exactly where he was when his uncle had given it to him, the dull green paper it was wrapped in, even the shiny blue ribbon tied around the package. He had felt almost like a man, being given something so important. His grandmama had argued that he wasn't old enough for a knife, but Ian had gently and firmly disagreed, and insisted upon her not interfering with his choice of a gift. Ian rarely crossed Flynn's grandmama, but if he did, he always got his way.

Flynn was quiet on the way back home. Alex noticed, and elbowed him, saying, "You okay? You're as silent as a Stormtrooper."

"Huh? Oh, yeah, I'm fine." Flynn lapsed into silence again and fingered his book, smoothing out the creases the cover and pages had sustained in the crash. He was trying to process the events of the morning and was starting to feel a little overwhelmed by it all.

When they arrived home, Ian thanked Grant for the ride and hurried to open the front door. Leslie came out of the kitchen, drying her hands on a towel, and regarded them with a bemused expression. "Ian, what are you..." She noticed Grant wave to Alex as he drove away and her confusion mounted. "Why did Grant drop you off? Where's your car?"

"Oh my gosh, he's got my snacks!" Alex dropped all his stuff in a heap in the doorway and took off down the driveway after Grant's car.

Ian gave his wife a hug as Flynn and Hawk went down into the basement to put away their gear. "That's kind of a long story, m'dear, and probably best told all at once. Where are the boys?"

"Upstairs, putting Sean's new set away; they had it spread all over the living room. Can you tell me now? Please?" She gave him a pleading look and laid a hand on his arm. "I was worried already when you said some of SCO19 were injured, and now that your car is missing...please, Ian, unless you absolutely have to go over something with the guys."

"Of course, m'love. Why don't I tell you upstairs so I can change out of these things and freshen up a bit? I'm covered in cave dust." Ian led the way to their bedroom and closed the door in case the boys came down looking for them. Leaving his bulletproof vest by the door, Ian changed into a fresh pair of dress slacks and a starch white buttoned-collar shirt. "We got into the tunnels with little trouble," he began. "Alex took care of the cameras, and there was no one but Tiernan to be found at first. We'd just gotten to him when some of the Mallevilles showed up from a different entrance."

Leslie sat on the edge of the bed and watched him while he inspected his hair in the mirror and made sure his undershirt was tucked in properly. "Oh my...how many?"

"I'm not entirely sure." Ian turned to look at her and began buttoning up his shirt. "Alex saw Alvar and Axel in the lead. SCO19 went to intercept them and there was a little fire-fight, which is how three of the officers were hit. Grant instructed some of the remaining SCO19 around the house to find the entrance and prevent the Mallevilles from retreating. We barricaded the room we were in, in case the Mallevilles broke through, but the breaker blew, and all the lights went out."

Leslie's hands flew to her mouth. "You mean you couldn't see a thing?"

"No, not at all. The Mallevilles retreated in the dark and SCO19 didn't find the entrance in time." Ian turned back to the mirror and adjusted his collar.

"And the car?" she asked. Ian sighed and lightly gripped the edge of the bathroom counter, wondering how he could explain it to her without scaring her badly. "Ian, what is it? What happened next?"

Shutting the bathroom light off, Ian stood in front of her and folded his arms. "Alex lightly shocked himself while he was fixing the breaker, and according to SCO19, he yelled pretty loudly, more out of surprise than anything else. They assumed the Mallevilles had somehow broken through, run through the tunnels, and entered the house without Grant being able to contact them, and all of the remaining officers who were stationed outside went into the house." He stopped, and his jaw clenched in anger. "They left their positions without orders."

"Okay...then what?" When Ian didn't reply right away, she burst out, "Ian, please, stop trying to find the gentlest way to tell me. You're scaring me. What happened?"

Ian sighed again and rubbed his forehead. "I'm sorry, I'm just...I'm still a little rattled myself. But I assure you, no one was hurt, okay?"

"Ian, stop. Just spill it," Leslie pleaded.

Ian shoved his hands in his pockets and continued. "I don't know where he came from or what he was doing, but Lathrop was in the woods near the house. When SCO19 ran into the house, he made his way over to my car and broke into it."

Leslie let out a little choking gasp. "Flynn! Wasn't Flynn in the car?"

"Yes," Ian said heavily. "Lathrop didn't see him, as he hit the floor when he saw Lathrop advancing on the car. Lathrop manually started the car somehow, but Flynn threw himself out before Lathrop could leave."

"But, *how?*" Leslie's eyes were wide with angst. "Is he okay? Oh Ian…" She held her head in her hands.

Ian moved forward, and gently laid his hands on her arms. "Hey, hey, it's okay. Flynn's fine. He yanked the door open, which startled Lathrop enough to give him time to get out and slash the back tire. SCO19 came out of the house and got Flynn into the living room, and I ran up to make sure he was okay. He was a bit shaken up, but otherwise fine. SCO19 did catch Lathrop, but not before he totaled a tree. M'dear, please don't get so upset." Ian stopped his narrative and softly brushed a hand across her cheek as Leslie shuddered and fought to hold back tears. "Nobody was hurt, m'love, and it's all over now." He was a little surprised when she started to cry, as she wasn't usually so upset when he relayed their missions, but he said nothing and simply gathered her in his arms and held her until she calmed down.

"I'm sorry, I don't know what happened…" Leslie wiped at her eyes and frowned. "Oh dear, I've ruined my mascara, haven't I?"

"It's not that bad. I like that raccoon look. It looks good on you." Ian followed her into the bathroom and grabbed her a Kleenex. Leslie wiped at her eyes and checked to make sure she hadn't smeared mascara all over her face.

"Thank you. Sorry, I just…Ian, please don't take Flynn with anymore. He could've been killed. I mean, what if Lathrop had a gun?" Ian winced, remembering what Flynn had told him. Leslie took hold of his arm. "Are you saying he did have a gun? No."

Leslie shook her head firmly. "No, Ian, he can't go with anymore. Not until he's had some proper simulation training. Promise me, Ian, please."

"I can't exactly promise that," Ian started, but Leslie cut him off.

"Ian!" she remonstrated, almost angrily. "He could have *died!* Don't you get that?" She tightened her grip on him.

"Yes I do, Les. And I told Flynn myself that we may need to rethink a few things. If the situation is not dangerous, then yes, I'll let him come. But," and he held up his hand to keep her from arguing, "if it is dangerous then, well, I guess it just depends on what 'dangerous' means."

"No," Leslie disagreed. "I don't care what 'dangerous' means. If there's any danger, however miniscule, he oughtn't go, not until he's been properly trained and has some idea of how to protect himself. Please, Ian, surely you see the wisdom in that."

Ian nodded in assent and hugged her. "I know it will disappoint him, but you're quite right..." He let his voice trail off. "I was terrified, Les, when Grant relayed SCO19's message."

"I can't even imagine. You frightened *me*, and I wasn't there!" She gently rubbed his back and gave him a kiss on the cheek. "Have you contacted the Emperor about your car yet?"

Ian laughed softly as she used Alex's term for his superior. "No, I haven't had a chance to. He'll probably be able to get us a new one in a day or two. Until then, we'll be stuck using Alex's jeep."

"Aw, come on, that's not the end of the world," she said, noticing his expression.

Ian wrinkled his nose. "It's so old, it smells like McDonald's, and I swear he hasn't cleaned the floor mats since he bought it."

"Hey, at least he scrubs the dash and doesn't leave trash everywhere, right? A little dirt on a floor mat isn't going to kill you. And you can always open the windows for some fresh air." Leslie checked her eyes once more, and wasn't satisfied with what she saw. Pulling open her cosmetic drawer, she selected her mascara and began to touch up her eyelashes. She noticed Ian's searching look and stopped. "What? Why are you looking at me like that again?"

Ian appeared almost sheepish as he answered, "You just, well, seem a little off."

"Off? Off how?" Satisfied with the final touch-up, she closed her mascara and returned it to the drawer.

He hesitated before replying. If he told her she was acting way more emotional than usual, she'd probably take it the wrong way. It wasn't that being emotional was bad – far from it! – it just wasn't like her normal self to burst into tears when he relayed a mission. He opted, however, to voice his other concerns instead. "You had a horrible headache last night, you're allergies have been bothering you in the middle of summer, and you were dizzy this morning."

"No I wasn't," Leslie lied.

Ian crossed his arms and raised an eyebrow. "You're a terrible liar, m'love."

Leslie sighed and leaned back against the counter. "Okay, fine, but I just got up out of bed too fast, that's all."

"I'm hearing way too many 'that's all's'," Ian said with a little frown. "Have you thought about getting yourself checked?"

"No, I don't need to. You know I'm highly allergic to just about everything." Leslie tried to explain away how she was feeling, but sensed she was losing the argument badly.

"You've said that before, and I get that, but I still think you ought to get yourself checked. If it *is* your allergies, then maybe you just need your medicine adjusted. I'm not going to force you to go, unless it gets serious, but I'm worried about you. Promise me you'll think about it?" Ian asked gently.

"I will," Leslie promised. "And please don't be worried, okay? I'm fine, really." A knock on the door stopped her from saying anything more.

"Dad?" Ian opened the door and Sean threw his arms around him. "Hi, Dad! Whatcha doin'? Ooh, that's your new shirt, isn't it? Neat! Mum helped Luke and I with my—"

"Luke and me," Leslie corrected.

"Yes, Mum. Anyways, my new set is finished and it's so ace! Can you come see it? Ple-ease?" Sean bounced up and down and gave his father puppy eyes.

"I've got some work to do with the guys, but I'll come take a look first. It was a pretty big box, wasn't it?" Ian let Sean lead him up the stairs. He always enjoyed hearing Sean's random commentaries as he explained his new LEGO sets and toys.

Sean bobbed his head. "Yeah, and there's so many trucks and creatures, it's *so* cool! There's a spotted panther but Lukas thinks it's a leopard, but I think he's wrong." Lukas ran into the room behind them, having said hello to Hawk, and soon the two of them were busy showing Ian all the bells and whistles of the intricately designed jungle ruins.

~~

Chapter Ten

"WE STARTED WITHOUT YOU, ol' chap," Alex said as Ian entered the office. "Hope you don't mind."

Ian sat down in his desk chair and reached for the box of papers that hadn't been opened up yet. "That depends on if I've missed anything interesting."

"Nope. The laptop was wiped, and I'm just finishing up checking the hard drives on the tablets to confirm the same." Alex tapped away on the devices.

"I was nice and waited to open the box of papers," Hawk said with a straight face. "Ow," he complained as Alex lightly hit him on the side of the head with one of the tablets.

Ian took out his flick knife and slit the tape holding the top flaps down. "I'm not exactly sure how we want to go through all this," he said, picking up a stack of the loose papers of all sizes and shapes and setting it down on his desk.

"You do that pile, I'll do another, and when Alex quits monkeying around, he can finish off the rest." Hawk ducked another hit from Alex and took his own stack of papers out of the box. "Half of these are receipts for electronics and clothes," he said after a few minutes.

"And the tablets are useless too," Alex piped up. "All they're good for now is to sell on eBay."

"You can't sell evidence, mate." Hawk motioned to the almost-empty box. "Now make yourself useful."

"I hate going through papers." Alex made a face and put the box in his lap. "They're so boring, and hardly anything makes sense. They're either in code, or chicken scratch, or a foreign language."

"What about you, Ian? Got anything?" Hawk asked, ignoring Alex's griping. "Ian?" He looked up as his friend didn't answer. "What is it?"

Ian had unrolled a map and was staring at it with wide eyes. "This is a map of Buckingham Palace," he said finally.

"Buckingham Palace? Why the dickens would they have a map of Buckingham Palace?" Hawk got up to peer over Ian's shoulder.

"I have no idea. And look, it's all marked up." He pointed to sets of letters scrawled in corners, doorways, and other odd intervals across the map.

"I don't understand." Hawk raked a hand through his blond hair. "It would be stupid to try and steal something from there. Yeah, there's a lot of valuables, but the security is ridiculous."

"Whose security is ridiculous?" Flynn asked, coming into the office. He had been intercepted by his aunt in the hall when he'd gone upstairs to put what remained of his knife in his nightstand, and had missed everything so far.

"Buckingham Palace's," was the not-very-enlightening reply.

"O-kay?" Flynn sat down and waited for a more detailed explanation. "And why is that very obvious fact important?"

"The Malleville's have several maps and blueprint copies of it," Ian said, laying aside one and pulling another from his lap. "They're all marked up. The question is, why?"

"Maybe Tiernan knows," his nephew offered. "He was with them for a few days. Perhaps he overheard them or something."

"He may have, but I doubt we'll be able to learn anything from him today," Hawk said with a frown. "He was in pretty rough shape. Liam said he ought to be able to talk tomorrow, but he would text me to confirm it."

"They're planning something big, and I don't like it," Ian said abruptly. "They're capable of anything, even murdering the Queen herself."

"Ian!" Alex gasped, looking very aghast. "How could you even think of such a thing? They wouldn't dare! They'd have no reason to."

"I don't get their reasons anymore, Alex. I don't know what they're up to, and I don't know why they're doing it either. Everything is coming to a head, and I can't figure it out, but danger is screaming at me in the face." Ian tossed the blueprint aside with a frustrated sigh.

"It's terribly maddening, but all we can do is focus on what we do know versus what we don't. Let's categorize all this stuff so we know what's what." Hawk shifted the conversation and slid the pile of receipts aside. In a quarter of an hour, they had several little stacks spread all across the desk and floor. There were purchase orders and receipts, maps, diagrams, and blueprints, random notes, and mathematical equations.

"It looks to me like a heist of some sort," Alex finally said as they leaned back in their chairs and surveyed the papers. "I mean, you don't buy half that electronic stuff unless you want to bypass security measures and hack into alarm systems."

"But what could they possibly want? And why Buckingham Palace? I mean, for the amount of security they're dealing with, I'd rather hit the Tower and go for the Crown Jewels," Hawk pointed out.

Ian massaged his temples, his eyes shut. "We're missing something. We've got most of the puzzle, but we're missing just enough to leave us in the dark."

"Let's hope Tiernan has the other piece," Leslie said from the doorway. They all jerked to look in her direction.

"Oh, sorry m'dear, I didn't know you were there. You haven't been standing there long, I hope?" Ian asked.

Leslie shook her head. "No, I just came down to tell you dinner's ready."

"Dinner? Isn't it kind of early for dinner?" Flynn checked his watch in case he'd totally missed the time.

"Only by an hour or so, but I know you all didn't have a proper lunch, what with the raid and all, and I figured you would be hungry," Leslie explained.

"Right you are, Honey! I'm as hungry as a bear. You said you were making a roast, right?" Alex got up and shut his laptop as he spoke.

"Yes indeed, along with some fresh, hot garlic rolls." Leslie smiled as Alex got a dreamy look in his eyes.

"Garlic rolls...with so much butter...and a hot roast..." he moaned in delight. "I could eat that every day and not grow tired of it. Last one up does dishes!" and he took off up the stairs.

Ian chuckled and turned his screen off. "It sounds wonderful, Les. Lead on, m'lady!"

~

Beyond making detailed lists of the information disclosed in the papers, there was little else they could do. Hawk got a text from Liam after dinner that Tiernan was doing very well. There was a good chance of talking to him on the morrow, but as to when, Liam couldn't say.

Flynn watched the third episode of *Foyle's War* with his aunt before going to bed. He enjoyed it, but Leslie noticed he was quieter than usual. When asked if he was okay, Flynn replied in the affirmative. He really was fine, but had an underlying sense of unease. He forced it down and ignored it, though, telling himself there was no reason for it. By the time the show was over, he appeared to be very much himself again, but when he went to bed, his unease returned.

It took him a while to fall asleep. Getting rocks slung at him from an unknown enemy was totally different than getting stuck in a car with a dangerous criminal and being shot at — again. When he did drop off, it wasn't peaceful, and he tossed and turned fitfully.

Around midnight, Hawk groggily opened his eyes. Something had woken him, he just wasn't sure what it was yet. Straining his ears, he heard a low moaning sound. He swung his feet over the side of the bed and started towards Lukas' and Sean's room, but stopped in the hall as the sound came from Flynn's room. Opening the door softly, he saw Flynn jerk in his sleep, and softly moan the word 'no'. He went over to him and laid a firm hand on the boy's arm. Flynn gasped, his eyes flew open, and he batted Hawk's arm away, still not fully awake.

"Hey, hey, it's just me. You were having a nightmare," Hawk whispered soothingly.

Flynn sat up and shook his head, as if to clear his mind from what he'd been dreaming of. "Hawk?" he asked uncertainly.

"Yeah, you okay?"

Flynn rubbed his eyes and sighed. "Yeah. Sorry I woke you."

Hawk shrugged. "Don't be. I'm a light sleeper, and I keep my door open in case the boys need something."

Flynn fell back and felt his eyelids droop. "'Night," he murmured sleepily.

"Goodnight." Hawk closed the door and was just drifting off to sleep when he heard Flynn moaning again. This time, he had to gently shake Flynn to wake him. Flynn jerked up with a cry, and grabbed the man's arm, his eyes wide. It took him a minute to realize his dream was over, and he sank back on his pillow with a shaky sigh.

"I'm *so* sorry," he muttered, turning his head away and shutting his eyes.

"You want me to get your uncle?" Hawk asked as Flynn shivered involuntarily.

"No! I'm not five," Flynn whispered back almost savagely. He was knackered, humiliated and unnerved; he hadn't had nightmares in years.

"Hey, look at me," Hawk said firmly in a low tone. Flynn turned his head and grudgingly opened his eyes. "Having a nightmare doesn't make you a coward, or a wuss, or any less of a man than you are now, okay? Everyone gets them at some point in their life. So don't feel embarrassed. And," he added kindly, "I only asked if you wanted your uncle since I know from experience that it helps to tell someone about it so you can get it out of your system and sleep, and I didn't know if you'd feel comfortable telling me."

Flynn sighed, sat up, and leaned against the headboard. "I'm sorry I snapped. I'm just...humiliated, I guess?"

"Why?" Hawk sat on the edge of the bed.

"You guys always keep your cool in dangerous situations. I get put in just one, and I'm a nervous wreck," Flynn said bitterly. "I thought I was fine, but at first I couldn't sleep, and then I started dreaming. I was in the car, but I couldn't get out. The lock wouldn't budge, and the door stuck, and I could see Lathrop coming, but I couldn't get out early. And once he got in the car, the door still wouldn't open. I was trapped. And my efforts to open it got his attention, and he pointed his gun at me. But he didn't shoot me. He moved his arm and shot out the window. My uncle was coming out of the house, and he...he shot *him* instead." Flynn shivered again. "It just kept looping itself over and over, and I couldn't do anything."

"You want to know something?" Hawk asked.

"Sure."

"Keeping your cool and getting rattled are two totally different things," he explained. "Do you remember what your uncle told you about controlling your emotions?" Flynn nodded. "You did that this morning. You were terrified, but you kept your head and you got yourself out of a very sticky situation. You stayed cool, same as any of us, and that's something to be proud of. Not everyone can do that," he said encouragingly.

"But I got all shaky afterwards, and now I'm dreaming about it," Flynn pointed out.

Hawk raised an eyebrow as though it was no big deal. "So? You had a huge adrenaline rush. Getting a little shaky is normal. It's happened to all of us guys on numerous occasions. After one of my first fire-fights, I got violently sick, and shook so badly I couldn't stand up."

Flynn's mouth opened in surprise. "You? Seriously?"

"Seriously," Hawk answered with a wry smile. "An adrenaline rush simply means your blood is getting pumped to your head, legs, and arms to help you in a fight or flight situation, and a whole bunch of hormones and stuff is pumped into your system too, kind of like dumping tons of caffeine into your body. Once the rush is over, your blood pressure drops, and anything can happen. You can throw up, have tremors, pass out, whatever. It's not your fault and it's nothing to be humiliated about, okay?"

"Okay." Flynn sighed. "I guess I didn't realize just how much it upset me. That's not, you know…silly or anything. To be upset, I mean."

"No," Hawk assured him. "If you weren't upset, that'd be a problem. You could've died, your uncle could've died, a million things could've happened. You've never been in situations like this before, and you've been bombarded with them more than once in the past week. You've handled the stress terribly well, if I do say so myself." Hawk stifled a yawn.

Flynn smiled and dropped his eyes at the praise. "Well, thanks." He, too, tried to stifle a yawn, but failed. "Sorry to keep you up."

"Hey, no apologies. And let me pray before you nod off, huh?" Hawk closed his eyes and prayed, "Dear God, please calm Flynn's mind and take away his nightmares. Thank You for protecting him, and for keeping all of us safe today. Please help him to sleep well and peacefully. In Jesus' name, amen."

"Amen," Flynn echoed. "Thank you, Hawk."

Hawk stood up and smiled. "Don't mention it. Get some sleep."

Flynn slid down onto his pillow and pulled the blankets back up. He remembered when he was little, not long after he'd lost his parents, he'd had a particularly horrible nightmare, and his uncle had softly spoken the words of an old hymn to calm him down. Flynn had never forgotten the words, and he mentally recited them to himself as he drifted off to the land of slumbers.

Trials dark on every hand, and we cannot understand, all the ways that God would lead us to that blessed promised land; but He'll guide us with his eye, and we'll follow 'til we die. We will understand it better by and by. By and by, when the morning comes, when the saints of God are all gathered home, we will tell the story of how we've overcome, and we'll understand it...better...by and...by...

~

"Ic's gonna be furious!" moaned Axel as Alvar wrapped his arm tightly with a thick gauze bandage. He, Alvar, and Damain were seated in a dirty motel room in the outskirts of London. Axel had been shot in the arm, and was doctoring himself with Alvar's help. Damian was typing madly on a laptop, but paused as Axel spoke and glared at him over the top of his screen.

"*I'm* furious! My plan is supposed to culminate in three days. Three days! And nothing is going as it ought." Damian slammed his laptop shut, got up, and began pacing the room. "What I want to know is, how did the coppers get in?"

Axel grunted in pain as Alvar fastened the bandage tightly. "Vansant probably told them about the key, and they must have gotten it from Lindisfarne after the raid. Is there any way to silence him?"

Damian gave him a *drop-dead* look. "Do you think I have the time and resources to come up with a plan for that? I'm having all I can do to keep my original plan together, thanks to..." Damian trembled with fury and shut his eyes. He felt like flying into a rage, cussing up a storm, and throwing a royal tantrum.

But that wasn't professional. He couldn't act immature in front of his men; that's what Icabod would do, and never let it be said he stooped to the actions of his older brother! He took a deep breath and calmed his mind. Opening his eyes and turning to look at Alvar he said in an even tone, "Ring Icabod, and inform him what happened. Axel, is your arm still usable?"

Axel stared at him incredulously. "You asking? 'Course." He flexed his arm — and stifled a wince — to prove his point.

"Meet up with Otto, make sure he's gotten everything I sent him out for, and give him this list." Damian handed him a sheet of paper covered with items listed neatly in little rows. "These are all the absolute necessities that we lost in the cave. I need them by tonight."

Axel scanned the sheet and whistled. "What about the expense?"

Damian shrugged. "What about it? Otto's using a credit card Lathrop swiped earlier this week. There shouldn't be a problem, and if there is, then it's up to you to swipe another one. Now ring him. We don't have all day."

~

Flynn blinked sleepily at the clock. *7:00 AM…what?!* He sat up, rubbed his eyes, and stared at the clock, hoping he was wrong. He was horrified to find he was not. "Oh gosh, and it's Sunday, too!" Jumping out of bed, he hurried to shower and dress, and took the stairs down two at a time, making it to the dining room just as Ian finished praying for breakfast.

"Guess you slept well, huh?" Alex teased as he speared a waffle with his fork and put it on his plate.

Flynn made a face. "Yeah, sorta. Sorry, I didn't mean to sleep in." He reached for the bowl of strawberries as he spoke. "Are we going to be late?"

"We'll miss Bible Study, but we'll make it in time for the late service. But don't worry, it's not your fault – we all slept in a little," Ian added, seeing his apologetic look.

"Not me!" Alex protested.

"Then why are you still here?"

Alex stared at him as if he'd lost his mind. "Ex-*cuse* me? Do you think I wanted to miss fresh waffles for breakfast? Uh, noooo!" He finished buttering his waffles and held out his hand. "Syrup, please."

Hawk handed it to him and changed the subject. "I texted Liam this morning, and he said he thinks we can talk to Tiernan this evening. He's going to move him to his house so we can talk in private." He reached out and snitched a strawberry off of Lukas's plate. "He said Tiernan's improving marvelously, but the transfer will probably wear him out, and he'll need time to rest, which is why he suggested this evening."

"Hey!" Lukas laughed and tried to steal his dad's toast in retaliation, but Hawk caught his hand. "Aw, missed."

"Do it when he's not looking," Sean whispered loudly.

Ian lightly buttered his English muffin and said, "That works for me. I'm picking up my car after church, and I have something to do this afternoon, so the evening will be fine."

"I thought you had to wait a day or two to get the car." Flynn sliced an unusually large strawberry in half with his spoon.

"So did I. But I'll explain that later. Sean, no, you don't need sugar on those strawberries." Ian whisked the sugar dish out of reach.

"Aw, come on, Dad, they taste better that way! Mum puts sugar on 'em sometimes. And whipped cream. Can I have whipped cream?" Sean was ready to jump out of his chair and dash for the kitchen.

"No, Sean," Ian said, shaking his head. "You don't need any more sugar of any kind for breakfast. Waffles and syrup is quite enough."

"Yes, Dad." Sean sighed a little and forced himself to eat his strawberries plain.

"Can we go to the grocery store on the way home, too?" Leslie asked, refilling her mug with tea and motioning for Ian to hand her his cup.

"I don't see why not," Ian said. "Was there something in particular you wanted?"

"Yes. I wanted to make a German chocolate cake for dessert tonight, and I don't have all the ingredients." She gave him his newly-filled cup back.

"German chocolate cake!" Alex cried. His whole face lighted up. "Honey, you're the best person I know. I was just craving that."

"You crave every sweet all the time," Hawk ribbed him.

Alex shrugged and grinned. "It's in my DNA."

"What's DNA?" Lukas scrunched up his face at his dad inquisitively.

"According to the Encyclopaedia Britannica," Alex said, before Hawk could reply, "'DNA is the abbreviation of deoxyribonucleic acid, the organic chemical of complex molecular structure that is found in all prokaryotic and eukaryotic cells, as well as many viruses.'"

Lukas stared at him. "What? Is that even English?"

"DNA is like a code," Hawk explained. "It's a whole bunch of cells and stuff all connected together, and it's what makes you who you are. Every living creature has DNA, and it's all different. Human DNA is different than the DNA of Uncle Alex's Betta fish. DNA makes his fish a fish, and your DNA makes you human. Does that make sense?"

"I think so. Where is it inside me? Is it near my heart, or is it in my brain?" Lukas asked seriously.

Hawk chuckled and ruffled the boy's hair. "It's in every single cell in your body, so it's really everywhere. It's not like a specific organ, such as your heart or brain or lungs."

"Oh. That sounds complicated." Lukas scratched his head, trying to understand.

"You'll learn about it in science soon enough."

"I hate science," Sean complained loudly. "It's too complicated. Legos are funner."

"Sean, that's not the right attitude, and funner isn't a word," Leslie reprimanded gently. "Science may be difficult, (it's certainly not *my* strong point,) but you shouldn't hate it. God created science, and it is a very important subject. Science is in everything, including the waffles you are eating."

Sean's eyes bugged. "Science teaches you how to make waffles? Okay, I don't hate it. Can I learn that kind of science, please?"

"Me too!" Lukas begged. "It can be our 'speriment. I like 'speriments. Dad, we showed you our volcano, right? It had baking soda and red food coloring, and everything, and it went boom! All over the place!"

"Yes, you did, and it was pretty dench," Hawk said. "Ian and I made one of those years ago, and we made a huge mess all over his mother's kitchen."

Ian grinned at the memory. "We sure did. And stained her new white tea towels, too. We were in deep that day!"

"You had it worse," Hawk reminded him. "It was your idea to wipe it up with white towels! I told you to use the red ones in the laundry closet, but—"

"I know, I know!" Ian pointed his fork at Hawk. "And I had to forfeit my allowance to buy new ones. You really owe me half for that."

Hawk smirked. "I don't owe you a red cent. It wasn't my idea, so I didn't have to pay for them then, and I'm certainly not paying for them now." Ian rolled his eyes. The towels were an old joke, one his mother enjoyed immensely, and it wasn't about to die any time soon.

"Okay, guys, finish up. I don't want to be late for the late service." Leslie got up and began clearing the plates, and they all pitched in to help her.

They drove to church separately: Alex in his Jeep, Hawk and Lukas in the MGB, and Ian, Leslie, Sean, and Flynn in the BMW. Before leaving, however, Ian instructed his nephew to bring his sweater and trainers. Upon inquiring why, however, Ian refused to give him an answer, and Flynn was forced to obey without any explanation.

After church, Leslie wanted to drive Ian to the car dealership but he would have none of it. "Not while I'm here."

"But I have to drive it after you pick up the Mazda, so it makes sense for me to already be in the driver's seat," Leslie protested.

"We've been over this," Ian said firmly, yet kindly, as he started the car. "I don't feel right about being in the passenger seat and letting you drive unless I'm completely worn out or injured. It's as bad as me not opening a door for you, or not pulling your seat back at the table. It simply isn't done."

Leslie conceded defeat silently and then leaned over to kiss his check. "You're a true gentleman, m'dear, and I wouldn't have it any other way. Do you have all the papers you need?"

"I think so." Ian gestured to them at her feet. She quickly thumbed through them, making sure he had his proof of insurance and other important documents necessary for procuring the vehicle.

"You never did say how you got the car so fast," Flynn observed from the back seat.

"I contacted my superior last night, and he informed me this morning that he had already purchased one and I could pick it up whenever I chose," Ian explained

"Your boss must have a lot of money!" Sean piped up.

Ian shrugged as Leslie folded the papers and handed them to him. "Not necessarily, Sean. He works for the government, same as I do, and the expense did not come out of his pocket."

When they arrived at the dealership, Ian told Flynn to get their sweaters and shoes from the trunk and follow him into the building. It took less than ten minutes for Ian to get his new Mazda, and soon he and his nephew were back on the highway. "Now are you going to tell me where we're headed?" Flynn asked.

"You'll see," was Ian's vague response.

"Oh, come on, that's no answer. Where are you taking me?" Flynn demanded.

"I'm taking you somewhere special, and that's all I'm saying for now." Ian took an exit onto another main highway and set the cruise control. "I have a confession to make."

"A confession? Ooh, this is gonna be good," Flynn teased.

"Ha, very funny. I overheard the last bit of your conversation with Lukas yesterday morning." Ian glanced at his nephew as he spoke, and noticed the smile fade from his face.

"Oh, uhm, okay. And?" Flynn crossed one leg over the other and waited for his uncle to continue.

Ian leaned back in his seat, one hand resting on the top of the steering wheel. "What did you mean about your grandmama not talking about Elise? She didn't forbid you to speak of her, did she?"

Flynn shifted his position uncomfortably. "Uhm, well, sorta. It hurt her too much. Grandad too."

"What? Flynn, you can't be serious!" Ian looked at him incredulously, completely taken off guard. He'd only asked the question to confirm such wasn't the case, and was not expecting the opposite answer.

Flynn shrugged. "Everybody handles grief differently. Grandmama, as you know, was never one to show much of any emotion at all. She smiled or frowned, but wasn't...emotional. She prided herself in that, I think, but she couldn't control it where Mum was concerned, so she just asked that the subject be avoided all together. Grandad agreed with her, and..." Flynn nervously ran a hand through his hair. "I couldn't mention Dad either. Because that implied Mum."

"I can't believe it." Ian gripped his steering wheel, and Flynn was surprised to see his knuckles go white.

"Like I said, everyone handles things differently. If Grandmama couldn't control something, she made it nonexistent." Flynn idly ran his fingers along the ledge of the car window. "It wasn't so bad, most days. It just hurts sometimes because I don't know much of anything about them. Lukas knows his mum's favorite color, and all that stuff, but I don't," he said rather wistfully.

"Why didn't you ever ask *me*?" Ian asked, his anger mounting, not at Flynn, but at the boy's grandparents.

"I did ask you some things, on a few occasions, but most of the time either Grandmama was around, or I just, I just…" Flynn fumbled with his words, trying to explain himself. "Either I forgot all my questions when you were there, or I didn't feel like asking them, because sometimes it made me sad, and I wasn't supposed to be sad around Grandmama and Grandad for no reason, since that meant I was thinking about Mum. Or I just wanted to stay happy. Whenever you came to get me, it was like Christmas, and who likes to be depressed on Christmas?" He stopped, seeing the furious look on his uncle's face. "Uncle, did I say something?"

"They had no right!" Ian exploded. "No right at all! I ought to have gone through and sued them. I'm sorry, Flynn. I almost did, many times, but I didn't want to mess up your life any more than it already was. How *dare* they!" Ian smote the steering wheel, just missing the horn.

"Whoa whoa whoa, sue them? Whatever are you talking about?" Flynn held up his hands to stop Ian's flood of angry words.

"Yes, sue them," Ian said sharply. "Sue them for custody of you. I thought about it a lot, but I didn't want to disrupt your life. You were settled in a home, a school, and a church, and you didn't need any more crazy circumstances turning your life upside down, so I refrained." He clenched his teeth. "I'm sorry, Flynn, I really am."

Flynn fixed Ian with a look of seriousness. "Uncle, you don't have to apologize for anything. God put me where He wanted me, and anyways, it wasn't practical for you to take me in at the time. You were newly married and living in a tiny flat. And living with my grandparents wasn't bad. I'm making it sound all wrong. I had stability, and I found a friend at school, and you were always there when I needed you. Always." He stopped, unsure how to continue. "My life has been different, but it's been good; so please, don't feel bad, and don't apologize."

Ian was silent. He felt the anger draining out of him, but was still very much upset. "Flynn, I miss Jack and Elise every bit as much as your grandparents, if not more so, but don't you ever feel like you can't mention them or ask about them because it might hurt me, okay? Yes, there are days when it *does* hurt, but when someone is taken away, all we have left are the memories. God gave us those memories, and they aren't supposed to be filed away." He sighed heavily. "I don't even know where to start, but I promise you, I will tell you everything and anything you want to know."

Flynn's whole face lit up. "Thank you, Uncle, so much."

"You don't have to thank me, Flynn. It's your right." Ian took an exit off the highway and braked at the stop light. Turning to look at his nephew, he said, "I'm actually taking you to a very special place that Jack took me to all the time when we were young. We'd sneak away from our parents whenever we went to Chilterns Hills, and they never could find us. And by the time Jack got his driving license, well, we must have spent a third of our lives out there."

"A secret place? Aw, that's cool!" Flynn's eyes danced with excitement, but as the stoplight turned green and Ian started forward, some of the light died. "Uhm, your secret place is going to be fun, so, can I ask you a heavy-ish sort of question first, instead of later?"

"Of course," Ian said. "Like I said, you can ask me anything."

"Okay, well, I've always kind of wondered this, but…why wasn't I with Mum and Dad in the car that day?" Flynn twisted his hands in his lap as the memories came crowding in. "And why was I at Aunt Mary's, instead of with you?"

Ian's own memories hit him like a brick wall. He remembered that day as if it were yesterday. He knew exactly what he was doing, and where he was sitting, when he got the call that his older brother and sister-in-law had been t-boned by a lorry. His voice was quiet as he said, "Leslie had a horrible cold, and I was working late on a case, so Jack dropped you off with Mary," he explained, referring to Leslie's older sister. "They were just out on a date night. They had made reservations for a fancy dinner, and had tickets to the cinema, and were leaving the restaurant when it happened." Pain flickered in Ian's eyes as he parked the car, shut off the engine, and turned in his seat to face his nephew. "I still to this day do not understand why God took Jack and Elise home, but I do know that He purposely spared you, and for that I am so thankful. More thankful than I can ever express," he said huskily.

Both were silent for a few minutes, until Flynn said softly, "I suppose that's why I don't really like going to Aunt Mary's house. And she grates on my nerves," he added suddenly. "She treats me like a lost puppy."

Ian lost the sober look on his face and began to chuckle. "Mary thinks everyone is a lost puppy!"

Flynn's face broke into a smile and he, too, began to laugh. "I guess I can't really argue with that."

"She drove Jack batty." Ian shook his head and smiled. "She mothered him, and lectured him on how to treat Elise, and was constantly giving him advice on how to be a better husband in general. She didn't mean it unkindly, it's just her. She's lectures everyone on everything."

"She's like Mrs. Bennet," Flynn interjected.

Ian lost it, and couldn't stop laughing. "That she is!" he gasped. "I'm so telling Les you said that. What a kick she'll get!"

When the mirth had subsided, Flynn gestured out the window. "So, secret hideout. Where is it?"

Getting out of the car, Ian popped the boot and shed his suitcoat. "We have a bit of a hike, but it's not too far. You'll want to switch your shoes, though." Both of them changed out of their dress shoes, and since it was a little chilly, Flynn traded his vest for his sweatshirt. Ian sent his tie after his suitcoat, unfastened the top button on his dress shirt, and slipped on a dark blue sweater. Into the forest and gently rolling hills they went, Ian leading the way with confidence. Not a quarter of an hour later, he held up his hand to stop Flynn from coming any further. "Welcome to my hideout." Moving some over grown underbrush aside, he led Flynn onto a hidden path, and in a few seconds they found themselves on a small hill overlooking a thin, windy river.

"Oh Uncle, it's beautiful!" Flynn gazed out at the peaceful landscape and slowly sat down. He couldn't tear his eyes from the gorgeous view before him, and was left quite speechless. Ian sat down on the grass next to him.

"Jack found this years and years ago. I was, oh, I don't know, six maybe? He found it by accident. Jack was always wandering off the paths, and I, of course, followed him." He laughed softly. "I got a lot of scraped knees and bruised elbows thanks to Jack's escapades."

"What else are big brothers for but to get you in trouble?" Flynn teased, shoving his uncle lightly.

"Yeah, that about sums it up."

"Did Mum ever come here?" Flynn asked suddenly. "Or was it just your and Dad's special place?"

"We asked her to come many times, but she wouldn't, save once. She said it was our, as you put it, special place, and all brothers needed that." Ian plucked a piece of grass and rolled it between his fingers.

"What was the exception?" Flynn prodded.

Ian smiled and tossed the piece of grass to the wind. "That day is forever etched in my memory, because it was the day she found out she was pregnant with you. She was so excited, she drove out here, unbeknownst to us, and rang Jack in the parking lot, begging to know how to get here. He told her it was kind of complicated, and went and brought her here himself, and that was the only time she ever came."

"What were they like?" Flynn asked, letting himself fall onto his back. He put his hands behind his head and pulled his knees up. "Okay, that's kind of vague. I guess I mean, were they funny? Serious? Fashionable, or laid back? You know, stuff like that."

Ian thought for a moment before replying. "Both your parents had a very good sense of humor, but Jack was a bit of a prankster. Elise was gentle, sweet, and quite the girly-girl, and Jack loved to get her new clothes and different shades of lipstick."

"Lipstick?" Flynn wrinkled his nose. "Dad went shopping for lipstick?"

"Of course," Ian answered, as though it were the most natural thing in the world. "Your mother was a daring soul, and wasn't afraid to try any shade in the make-up department, and Jack liked treating her. He knew what looked good on her, too."

"That's weird," Flynn declared.

"Just wait until you get married, young man. Going shopping for your wife is extremely fun." Ian whacked the boy's shoulder.

"Oh shut up!" Flynn tried hitting him back, but Ian shifted out of reach.

"Trust me, you'll learn really fast what does, and does not, look good on your girl," Ian said with a grin. "And also keep in mind, that your girl likes to please you, so if you tell her something looks good on her, she's very eager to wear it again."

Flynn sat up like a shot. "Okay, why are you telling me this?" he demanded. He was blushing horribly, but couldn't figure out why.

"Oh, no reason." Ian laid himself back on the grass and deliberately placed his hand behind his head. "But you do need to be aware that when you compliment Von on her outfit, she is going to remember that, and she will wear it again."

"*What?!*" Flynn didn't think his face could get any hotter.

"Don't tell me you didn't notice how she lighted up when you told her you liked her sweater?" A corner of Ian's mouth turned up.

"N-no, and she didn't, like, light up, or whatever that means," Flynn stammered. "That's, well, that's silly."

Ian stifled a laugh and continued to rib his nephew mercilessly. "Oh she lighted up alright, and I'll bet you she'll wear that sweater the next time she sees you."

"Stop it!" Flynn cried, getting seriously exasperated. "Just because I said she looked cute in a certain sweater doesn't mean—"

"So you *do* think she's cute!" Ian raised himself up on one elbow. "Finally, you admit it."

"No, I...I didn't...ugh!" Flynn rubbed his forehead, feeling extremely self-conscious. He had no idea what to think anymore. "Von is my school mate," he said, more to reassure himself than to argue with his uncle. "And yes, she looks, uhm, nice, but we're mates, and that's all."

Ian responded with a short laugh. "Just mates? In your dreams."

"Stop it!" Flynn cried, wishing he had a pillow to launch at his uncle. "This is so...discombobulating," he moaned.

"Okay, fine," Ian conceded, seeing how embarrassed Flynn looked. "But there's no shame in admitting you like her."

"Of *course* I like her! I've known her since primary school. Happy now?" Flynn crossed his arms, feeling very ruffled.

Ian smirked. "For now, I guess."

Flynn got up and walked over to the crest of the hill, hoping the conversation would stay closed. He tried to shove thoughts of Von from his mind, but couldn't. He kicked at a rock in frustration. Trying to sort through all his emotions was like trying to undo the Gordian knot – physically impossible. His gaze flickered to the river, and he asked, abruptly, "Have you ever gone fishing down there?"

Ian got up, brushed the loose grass from his dress slacks, and stood next to him. "No, I don't really like fishing, and neither did Jack, so we never bothered to find out if we could or not." They were silent for another minute or two, before Ian said, "There's something you and I have to discuss."

Flynn turned to face him. "You mean about going out in the field, right?"

Ian shoved his hands in his pockets and gave him a short nod. "I'm guessing your aunt has said something to you by now?"

"Yeah." Flynn scowled in remembrance. "She told me she didn't want me going with anymore, because it was too dangerous. But she's not serious, right? I mean, how else am I supposed to properly learn how to do things? Obviously it's not smart for me to go along when there's imminent danger, but never to go again? That's a bit extreme."

"No, she doesn't mean you'll never go again," Ian corrected. "We talked about it, and we agreed that if there is any danger involved, you will have to remain behind, but," and he held up his hand to stop Flynn from speaking, "that is only temporary. You need to have a good dose of simulation training, and you will get some over the summer before you head off to university."

Flynn's eyes widened. "Really?"

"Yes. Simulation training may save your life one day, and if this is what you want your path to be, you're going to need a lot of it."

"Come on, I'm not that incompetent!" Flynn cried, misunderstanding what his uncle said.

"I didn't say that," Ian corrected gently. "You've handled yourself very well, but you've only been in three dangerous scenarios. There are hundreds of which you maybe even can't conceive of, situations where you're going to need to know exactly what to do, and you only have seconds in which to do it." Ian slipped his hand in his sweater pocket and removed a small, compact revolver. "And that includes learning how to both use and carry weapons. That will probably make your aunt nervous, but it's part of the job."

"I thought you said I wasn't supposed to think about weaponry for a while yet," Flynn said, eyeing the revolver and wondering if his uncle always had it on him.

"I did," he replied, returning the weapon to his pocket, "but I meant more you actually using one outside of a shooting gallery. Besides, there are many scenarios to run in simulation that do not involve firearms, and we'll start with those. You'll also need to learn to drive. I don't believe your grandmama let you practice, did she?"

Flynn looked confused. "Uhm, I'm supposed to get lessons from a certified instructor, not my grandparents, so no."

"We'll fix that," Ian declared. "And forget the instructor, I'll teach you myself."

"That's not legal," Flynn started to say, but Ian cut him off.

"I applied for that a long time ago, I'm just not on any list because I don't want random people trying to hire me to teach them. I'm officially certified, so it's entirely legal."

Flynn stared at him. "You're kidding."

A corner of Ian's mouth turned up. "No, I'm not kidding."

"What *can't* you do?" his nephew demanded.

"Well, I can't walk into Buckingham Palace while the Queen's in residence," Ian said drolly.

Flynn lightly punched his shoulder. "Duh, nobody can do that. Wow, you never cease to amaze me, Uncle. Driving instructor...never would have guessed! When can I start?" he asked eagerly.

"After this Malleville business is over and done with," Ian answered firmly. "I want to make sure you have my full and complete attention, and that I don't have to run off in the middle of a lesson to follow up on a lead."

"Do you really think it's all coming to a head?" Flynn asked.

Ian sighed and viewed the river pensively. "Yes, I do. I'm just missing a few important pieces. If I can just get my hands on them, we could wrap this up fairly soon." He rubbed his forehead. "It's been so long, Flynn. Two grueling years, and I can almost taste victory, but it eludes me." He lapsed into silence, his thoughts drifting over all the crazy and complex points of the case.

"God does promise judgment for evil doers," Flynn said. "No, He doesn't promise it in this life, but I seriously doubt He would allow you to chase them all over the country for two years, and then have them vanish. Don't give up hope, my dear uncle; we'll get them yet."

Ian squeezed the boy's shoulder. "I won't. I get frustrated with our progress, but I do know, ultimately, that God is in control, and He will put them in my hands when the time is right." They gazed out over the landscape for a few moments, until Ian suddenly pulled up his sleeve and glanced at his watch. "Unfortunately, we're going to have to head back if we want to talk to Tiernan."

"We?" Flynn looked at him hopefully, pouncing on the plural adjective.

"Yes, we; I can't imagine what can possibly go wrong at Liam's house, unless a Malleville sniper showed up." Ian's teasing look became serious. "And that was a joke, so don't repeat that to your aunt." Flynn simply laughed.

"Thank you for taking me here," Flynn said as they headed back. "Can we come again sometime?"

"Often, if you like." Ian replaced the underbrush just so before taking the lead down the trail.

"I would, very much."

They walked in silence for a few minutes, until Ian said over his shoulder, "Oh, and by the way, your mother's favorite color was purple. She preferred a dark violet, or a light lavender, and she looked wonderful in both. As for Jack, he liked red. The brightest, deepest red you can think of. And burgundy."

"That's my favorite color," Flynn said softly, his eyes reverting to his beloved sweatshirt.

When they were in the car, Ian said, "Hey, I forgot to ask how you slept last night, after what happened."

Flynn ducked his head sheepishly. "Uhm, I ended up having a couple nightmares, and I guess I was kind of loud because I woke Hawk up." Ian gave him a concerned look as he continued. "I felt bad about waking him, but he was fine with it and made me spill it, and that helped."

"I wondered if you would. I'm sorry about that," Ian said sympathetically.

Flynn shrugged it off. "Aw, it's fine. I was humiliated at first, but then he told me that everyone gets them, and it's nothing to be ashamed of. He reminded me what you said about controlling your emotions and stuff, and then prayed I'd actually sleep, and I did. But only after reciting that old hymn you told me all those years ago."

"What, you actually remember that?" Ian asked, shocked.

"Of course I do. Why wouldn't I?"

"You were just a tiny little thing, not even six years old."

"Yeah, well, for some reason I can remember every detail about it, plain as day. Do you really get nightmares like Hawk said?" he asked abruptly.

Ian made a face. "Sometimes. It depends on the circumstance. My job does not consist entirely of examining empty headquarters and interrogating prisoners. I've seen a lot of ugly things, Flynn, very ugly things, and some of them still haunt the recess of my mind. We live in a fallen world."

"Yes, and 'tis 'a wretched hive of scum and villainy'," Flynn interjected lightly.

Ian rolled his eyes at the reference. "Yeah, something like that."

"But it's worth it, isn't it?" Flynn asked.

"I'm sorry?"

"What you do, it's worth the nightmares, right? I mean, you're helping people, and bringing criminals to justice, and setting wrongs right. Do you ever regret it?" Flynn eyed him curiously.

Ian shook his head. "No, I've never regretted it, and in my mind, the reward is worth it. I hate injustice, passionately, and I don't feel fulfilled if I'm not doing something to combat it. Like I've said before, this life isn't for everyone, but I do think it is what God made me for, and thus I will throw myself into it wholeheartedly until either I'm too old and infirm, or God takes me home."

"Somehow, I can't imagine you being old, let alone infirm," Flynn said, picturing his grandad in his mind and comparing him with his uncle. "Nope, I can't see it."

Ian grinned impishly. "You will one day, only by then I expect to have a little army of great nieces and nephews to keep me busy."

"Uncle Ian!" Flynn whacked his uncle hard this time.

"What?" Ian looked at him innocently. "It's the truth! I mean, you do intend to get married one day, don't you?"

Flynn groaned and massaged the bridge of his nose. "Well yeah, but that's a long way off. I haven't even gone to university yet, let alone met the right girl to eventually marry."

"I agree with you as regards university, but as for the girl..." Ian allowed his voice to trail off as he flashed his nephew a teasing look.

Flynn turned a cherry red and just sat there, staring out the windshield. "You're incorrigible. And hopeless. I refuse to be affected by certain people's remarks."

Ian gave a short laugh. "Lighten up, I'm messin' with you. You hungry? Me too." He took an exit off the highway and gestured towards a sign that indicated some of the fast food restaurants in the area. "Let's see if we can't find something to eat."

~~

Chapter Eleven

HAWK CALLED IAN NOT LONG after the two had finished their lunch, informing him of the details of their upcoming talk with Tiernan. "Liam has moved Tiernan to his house. He said Tiernan's extremely suspicious and confused, and I don't blame him. How exactly are we going to handle the conversation?"

"You wanted to recruit him, right?"

"Yeah, I think he'd be a good addition," Hawk replied. "You and I have worked with him before, and I like what I see."

"As do I," Ian agreed. "What does he have for family connections?"

"Nothing to speak of, really, save for his elderly mother."

"Doesn't he have an aunt and some cousins in Liverpool?"

Hawk made in indescribable noise. "Yeah, but they aren't exactly on speaking terms, and haven't been for years."

"Hmm." Ian thought for a moment before continuing. "Obviously we can't tell him everything right now, especially since I'd have to clear a few things with my superior, but...oh, let me do the initial talking, okay?"

"Fine. I'll meet you at Liam's, then," Hawk said before hanging up.

It wasn't long before Ian pulled up in the driveway, and he and Flynn were met at the door by Liam's wife, Gwen. "Hi, Ian, good to see you. Ah, you must be his nephew. Flynn isn't it? A pleasure to meet you! I know you've come to question Tiernan; he's down the hall. Hawk hasn't arrived yet. Do either of you want any gingersnaps? They're fresh out of the oven."

Ian wasn't a big cookie eater, but if Gwen offered him a gingersnap, he usually couldn't refuse her. They were her specialty, and he found he couldn't get enough of the sweet-spiced treat, and thus it was with great reluctance that he said, "As tempting as they sound – you know I'm a sucker for your gingersnaps – I honestly don't think I can eat one right now."

"Oh, don't worry about it – how about I package some up for you to take home?"

"If it's not too much trouble. That sounds wonderful."

"I'm on it." Gwen left for the kitchen and Ian led his nephew to the little recovery room Liam and his wife had set up in an extra bedroom on the ground floor. The door was ajar, and Ian lightly tapped on it before entering.

"Come in," Liam called out. He was busy making sure Tiernan was comfortable before Ian and Hawk started questioning him. "Hey, Ian. He's been anxious to talk to you since this morning, but the transfer from the hospital wore him out, and I almost said no."

Skyndar Tiernan regarded Ian with a rather bemused expression. He sat in a recliner that was tipped back just enough to take the pressure off of his broken ribs. The cuts and abrasions on his face had been plastered, the bruises had begun to heal, and though obviously tired, he looked much improved since Ian had seen him last. "You were there at the headquarters with Hawk weren't you?" Tiernan blurted. "I know you were," he added, not letting Ian answer the question. "I heard your voice." He was almost challenging the man to disagree with him.

"Yes, I was there," Ian assented, sitting down in a plastic chair Liam had brought earlier. "But we'll get to that later. Hawk ought to be here any minute now; I'm surprised I beat him here. This is my nephew, Flynn."

Tiernan was about to say something when Hawk walked in. "I got stuck in traffic, due to an accident, that's why you beat me. Hullo, Sky! You're looking a mite better than when I saw you last." Hawk shook the man's hand before straddling another plastic chair and resting his arms and chin on the back.

"I feel much better. I've never been so thankful for pain meds in my life," Tiernan said with a wry smile.

Hawk gave a short laugh. "Broken ribs do hurt like the dickens, don't they?"

"Yeah. Okay, I don't mean to be blunt or anything, but I'm super confused. Why did you ask me to call you Sparrow? Why were you and you," indicating Ian, "with SCO-19? That's not protocol. And why was I moved here? What *is* this place?"

"Skyndar, things are not always what they seem," Ian said cryptically. "You're here, at Liam's house, because it's the safest place for us to discuss what you know about the Malleville's plans. There are no cameras, or listening devices, or anything of that sort."

"Wait, this is somebody's house?" Tiernan's look of confusion mounted.

"Yes, but he has permission to set up hospital equipment here in case we need it," Hawk explained.

"I'm lost." Tiernan massaged his temples. "Are you guys spooks or something? Because that's the only thing that would make any sense here."

"Uhm, if you mean Mi6, or Mi5, then no," was Ian's vague answer.

Tiernan scowled. "That is not helping."

"Hawk and I do some undercover jobs, and nobody is supposed to know about it, which is why he asked you to refer to him as Sparrow. I would rather you not have learned about us, but it was inevitable due to circumstances, and I trust you to keep silent on the subject, understand?" Ian said firmly.

"Yes, sir," Tiernan replied solemnly. He involuntary saluted, felt silly, and let his hand drop.

"Good. Now, our undercover work of late has been revolving around the Mallevilles. Unfortunately, we're at a bit of a stalemate, and we were hoping you might have overheard something as regards their plans."

Tiernan's eyes widened as all the information he had committed to memory flooded his brain. "I don't even know where to start. Half of the information I don't even understand, but I memorized everything I heard."

Ian pulled out his cell phone. "You don't mind if I record this, do you?"

"No, not at all." Tiernan waited for Ian to open the app and hit *record* before speaking. "I guess I ought to start with what they're intending to do. Next week is the 26th week of the year, and that is when the Mallevilles intend to kidnap the Queen of England. If their demands for her ransom are not met immediately, they will blow up the Palace of Westminster, and if the ransom isn't met after the bombing, they will kill the queen. They will not, however, specify their target in the ransom demand. They will simply state they plan to blow up something in London; that way, there will be no time to evacuate the people inside the Palace of Westminster. The reason for the bombing target isn't political necessarily; it's both an important landmark and a vital government seat, not to mention filled with hundreds, if not thousands of innocent people. Blowing it up makes a huge statement that they have no qualms about killing anyone, including the queen."

The silence that ensued could have been cut with a knife. It was eventually broken by Flynn. "You're joking," he said, unable to comprehend such an act.

"No, I'm not. I wish I was, but I'm not." Tiernan launched into a detailed explanation of the Malleville's plans, citing maps, and figures. Some of what he said didn't make sense, and he acknowledged it. "I accidentally dozed off a few times," he said apologetically. "And sometimes, I could only hear snatches at random intervals." It took several hours for him to divulge everything he knew. When he was finished, he sighed heavily and closed his eyes. He felt drained and mentally exhausted, and was distinctly aware that the pain medicine was wearing off.

"Thank you, mate," Hawk said, laying a hand on his arm.

Skyndar opened his eyes and smiled wanly. "Yeah. I just wish I knew more." He shifted his position and winced.

"If you knew any more, you'd be a Malleville yourself," Hawk joked. He started to get up, but Tiernan suddenly grabbed his hand in a vice-like grasp. "You guys will be able to stop them, won't you?" He looked anxiously from Hawk to Ian and back again.

"Don't you worry your head about it," Ian said gently. "God is on our side, and I can promise you we'll do everything we can to stop them."

"Get some sleep," Hawk said. "And yes we'll keep you informed," he added as Tiernan was about to say something more.

"Ta. I appreciate it."

Liam entered the room as Hawk, Ian, and Flynn left, and gave Tiernan another dose of medicine before closing the blinds to shut out some of the sunlight that was streaming through. As the door closed and he was left to himself, Tiernan stopped fighting his drooping eyelids and drifted off to sleep.

~

Leslie sat on the edge of her bed and let her head fall into her hands. She felt absolutely miserable. She had a headache, was drowsy and spacey, and having weird abdominal pain. She still had no idea how she'd made it through church, or how she'd managed to hide it from Ian. At least, she assumed she had, since he hadn't said anything, and hadn't been eyeing her with concern during the service. Sighing, she raised her head to look out the window. She wished Carliss was here; she missed having her best friend to confide in. For a fleeting instant, she thought of telling her sister, but pushed the thought aside. Mary meant well, but she worried far too much and couldn't keep her mouth shut.

This most definitely was not her allergies, and she began to have a gnawing thought in the back of her mind that maybe, just maybe, she was pregnant. But what if she was wrong...again? Leslie loved children, and had dreamed of having at least five or six. But after Sean, she and Ian had only met with problems, having first a miscarriage, and then twice thinking she was pregnant, only to find out it was hormonal imbalances. She and Ian hardly ever talked about it now, almost silently accepting the fact that maybe God had decided Sean would be their only child. Now, however, Leslie had room for doubt. Only she was afraid to tell Ian of her suspicions. He wanted another child just as much as she did, and she would hate to disappoint him if she was proven wrong for a third time. No, she mustn't tell him anything until she was absolutely sure one way or another. Getting up, she grabbed her phone and made a doctor's appointment. She had just hung up when Ian entered.

"Hey, m'love. Who were you talking to?" he asked as he threw his sweater on the bed and washed his hands in the bathroom sink.

She laid her phone down almost sheepishly. "I took your advice and made a doctor's appointment."

"Oh, good. At least now we'll know if it really is just your allergies, and you need your medicine changed, or if it's something else." He dried his hands and made sure to fold the towel just right...or, at least, what Leslie thought was right. He personally didn't care how a hand towel was folded, but she certainly did, and he made a point to make sure he did it exactly how she liked it. "What made you do it?"

Leslie shrugged non-committedly and gave him a tired smile. "I just got fed-up with feeling off, and saw the wisdom in your advice, that's all." She sat back on the edge of the bed and folded her arms. "How did your time with Flynn go? Did you have a good talk?"

"Yes, we did. Actually talked about some heavy stuff, as regards his horribly incompetent grandparents—"

"Ian," Leslie interrupted gently. "You don't have to call them names because you disagree with them."

Ian's eyes sparked dangerously. "They forbade him speak of Elise and Jack because it upset them, so calling them incompetent is about the nicest name I can come up with right now."

Leslie gasped. "Ian, you're kidding! They wouldn't. They couldn't." She sat there, utterly stunned. "Why, that's the most selfish thing I've ever heard of!" she burst out.

"My thoughts exactly." Ian shook his head indignantly. "I've half a mind to ring them up and tell them just what I think of it, but I know that isn't the most Christian way to handle it." He leaned up against the wall and crossed his arms. "It infuriates me, Les. He has every right in the world to talk about his parents whenever he wants, and to learn as much about them as he can, and all because Miss Hoity-Toity can't keep a stiff upper lip, she bans the very mention of their names. It makes me so angry I could...I could..." Ian wasn't actually sure what he could do, and let his voice trail off. "It's cruel, Les. Just plain cruel. And I feel horrible for not knowing a thing about it for thirteen years."

"Ian, it's not your fault," Leslie began.

"I ought to have guessed it, though." Ian frowned ominously. "I always did think it odd that he didn't bring them up very much." He sighed. "What am I supposed to do? I feel like I should tell those two old coots off, but..."

Leslie was quiet for a minute or two as she considered the situation. "I think you ought to say something to them, both of them," she said slowly, "but you should do it as civilly as possible. What they did was wrong, but flying off the handle into a rage will not mend matters. Besides, our words are to 'be with grace, seasoned with salt,' and we are supposed to rebuke each other gently, since we could fall in same area. And, of course," she added, "you and I must pray about it first. Remember, it wasn't their intention to be mean. They love Flynn very much, it's just their awful way of dealing with emotion."

Ian pushed himself off the wall and gave her a hug. "You're right as usual, m'love." He kissed her forehead. "God certainly knew what He was doing when He put the two of us together. I have no idea what I would do without you."

"Nor I without you," she replied softly. Pulling back a little as a sudden thought hit her, she asked, "Hey, how did the talk with Tiernan go? Did he know anything?"

Ian released her and gave her a very serious look. "Yes, he most certainly did; way more than I think even the Mallevilles realized. We've got our missing pieces, m'dear, and now all we have to do is put them together and pray God blesses this final effort."

Leslie's hands flew to her mouth. "Are you serious? Are you saying you know what they're going to do, and you...you actually have an idea of how to stop them?"

Ian nodded grimly. "That's exactly what I'm saying."

A soft ringing tone interrupted them, followed by Sean's scream of, *"Mum!! Doorbeeeeeeell!"*

Ian grinned and stifled a laugh as Leslie stuck her head out the door and called, "Thank you, Sean."

"Apparently our doorbell has an echo," Ian observed as he headed down the stairs. He looked out the window first to see who it was, and then threw the door open. "Cade! Well, it's about time. What took you so long?"

Cade clasped Ian's arm and held it firmly. "Sorry, Tazer, but things got a little topsy-turvy with my motel landlady and— oh, it's complicated! Never mind, but suffice to say I'm here, and I hope I haven't missed too much."

"Actually, you're just in time for the fireworks." Ian stopped as his son came running down the stairs to meet the newcomer. "Sean, you remember Riley Cade, don't you?"

"Yeah! He always has caramels." The boy grinned and nodded vigorously. "Hi, Mr. Cade!"

"Sean!" Ian scolded.

Cade laughed. "Don't scold, Ian, he's quite right. Would you like one now, youngster?"

"Oh yes! Please, Dad, may I?" Sean threw Ian a pleading glance. "I'll eat it at the table, and I'll wash my hands when I'm done, I *promise*."

"Yes, but only one, and don't forget about that hand washing," Ian consented as Cade fished in his pocket for the desired treat.

"I won't. Ooh, can I grab one for Lukas? Thanks!" Sean availed himself of the caramels, shouted for his friend at the top of his lungs, and vanished into the dining room.

Cade chuckled and shook his head. "I knew he'd ask for them, so I made sure to have some on me," he said. "Hullo, Miss Leslie, you're looking as well as ever today, if I may say so."

"Why, thank you, Riley. You're looking well yourself. Glad to be back in England?" Leslie came down and followed Cade and Ian into the basement.

"You've no idea! I missed even the smell of this city. There really is no place like home." Cade stopped at the top of the stair and motioned for Leslie to pass him.

The office door banged open and out came Alex, looking both flustered and pleased. "Hi, Cade, glad to see you're finally going to pull your weight around here. And Ian, seriously, will you get down here already? Hawk refuses to tell me anything until you get here, and I'm starting to wonder if I missed out!"

Flynn laughed as he gave up his chair for his aunt and leaned back against the desk. "You ought to have come with if you were so worried about it."

"My point exactly." Hawk shook Cade's hand in greeting before nodding to Ian and saying, "You want to tell it, mate, or shall I?"

"Go ahead." Ian sometimes preferred to listen, instead of relaying the latest info, because it gave him time and space to think about it. Hawk complied, and quickly gave the group a run-down of their conversation with Skyndar, which, needless to say, left them all stunned.

"This always happens!" Alex complained. "I stay home, and you guys hear all the cool info."

"Kidnapping the queen and blowing up the Palace of Westminster is hardly what I'd classify as 'cool info'," Ian remarked drily.

"What I want to know is, if they have a bomb rigged in the cellars of the Palace of Westminster, how come the security staff hasn't discovered it yet?" Leslie asked.

Alex shrugged. "Tiernan said the Mallevilles have been infiltrating the place from the top down, so the security can't be trusted." He tossed a rubber band ball into the air and tried to catch it with his left hand. He missed, and it dropped and rolled around Hawk's feet.

Hawk bent down to pick it up and tossed it lightly between his hands. "For now, we have to assume all the guys on security are corrupted. None of them can be trusted, and none of them can be alerted."

"Whoa, you're not...going to tell anyone?" Flynn's eyebrows reached his hairline. This was the Queen's life they were talking about; hers, and all those in the Palace of Westminster.

"Not exactly," Ian replied. "Secrecy is of essence, but we have to be able to get into the Palace without raising a ruckus. We'll work out our plan of action, and then I will bring Grant and the Head of Security at the Palace into our confidence in order to pull off the plan successfully. As we know, the cameras themselves will not be in possession of the Mallevilles until Tuesday, but the bomb will probably have been already been put in place. We have to, somehow, disable the bomb, maintain control of the cameras, and guard the Queen, all without the Mallevilles knowledge, and with the hope of catching them." Rubbing his forehead, Ian sighed deeply, his brain working furiously.

"Yeah, the only question is: how?" Alex said, reaching out to steal the rubber band ball from Hawk, who flipped it tauntingly into the air before batting it back to him.

Leslie had been looking down at her hands, processing the information she'd just heard, and idly noticed she wasn't wearing her watch. It was a slim gold-colored band which she always wore, and she couldn't believe it had taken her this long to realize she didn't have it on. That's when she remembered dinner. "I'm sorry, this is rather random, but what time is it? I forgot to put my watch on, and I need to check on dinner around six."

Alex glanced at his watch, but before he could say anything, Ian answered, "Five."

"Oh come on, stop ribbing me," Alex complained. He always forgot to change the old battery in his watch, and thus it never actually worked, and was frozen on five o'clock, something his friends teased him relentlessly about.

Ian raised an eyebrow. "I'm not. It's actually five."

"Really? Well, would you look at that. See, I told you my watch is right!"

"Yeah, only twice a day," Hawk teased. Alex stuck his tongue out at him.

Returning to the issue at hand, the group threw suggestions around, some of them crazy enough to draw laughter. After a while, Ian's gaze flickered to Hawk. He'd noticed his friend had been quiet for some time, and wondered if he was forming something of a real, workable plan. "You got something, Hawk?"

"Possibly. Something you said just a minute ago, Flynn, started to make sense." Hawk paused. "It's a little on the barmy side, but it just might work."

"Spill it, mate," Ian said impatiently. After he explained, Ian nodded slowly, mulling over the unfinished details. "You're right; that just might work." Pulling out his phone, he rang Grant and gave him a rough outline of their plan, refraining to mention it was still in the works.

Grant was silent for a few seconds. "It will take a ridiculous amount of set-up and coordination. You sure you can pull this off?"

"I'm sure. Obviously, I'm going to need a lot of help from you, but I do think this has the potential to work." The more he thought about it and talked about it, the more Ian liked it.

"Okay then. Send me all the details and I'll have everything ready when it needs to be."

Hanging up, Ian laid the phone aside, a grim look on his face. "If we're going to do this, we're going to need to work out a lot of details immediately. This is probably the craziest thing we've ever done. I'm not entirely sure how it will play out, but I do know God put us on this case for a reason, and He has revealed the Malleville's plans several days ahead of time. Let's pray first, and then get down to business."

"To beat the Huns!" Alex sang in a horribly off-key voice.

"Beat the Huns? What Huns?" Cade asked, raising an eyebrow in confusion.

Alex stared at him like he had two heads. "Haven't you ever watched Disney's *Mulan*?"

"What does a Disney princess movie have to do with arresting the Mallevilles?" Cade was at a complete loss and couldn't find any connection between the two.

"I made an inadvertent song reference, that's all," Ian said hastily before Alex could launch into a long-winded and detailed explanation. Cade rolled his eyes. References weren't exactly his strong point.

~

That evening, Leslie kept Lukas and Sean occupied while the guys spread out maps and diagrams all over the dining room table. The office was too small for all of them to do what needed to be done in so short a time, and thus the dining room became their temporary headquarters for the night.

"Where'd Alex vanish to?" Ian looked around after they had set everything up.

"I have no idea," replied Hawk. "Probably the pantry."

"I'm right here!" Alex hollered. He banged a few things in the kitchen before entering the dining room, plate in hand. "Care for a piece of fudge or a cookie?"

Despite the fact that they had all had generous slices of German chocolate cake, none of them could resist Leslie's fudge. After it was passed around, they set to working out a more coherent plan.

"It's all a big mess!" Cade burst out as they finished calculating an estimate of the number of SCO19 officers needed for their plan.

"I know," Alex said mournfully, eating the last gingersnap and eyeing the crumbs on the plate.

"I mean, we have the bare facts, but not the details," Cade continued. "We don't know what surprises Icabod and Damian may be cooking up in their evil brains."

"Good phraseology!" Alex interjected, munching on the last piece of fudge. Hawk rolled his eyes.

"Right now, we can't worry about that," Ian said firmly. "I highly doubt they've set up traps or anything of the sort. They have literally no idea we know of their plan, and they will not be expecting any resistance, let alone infiltration. Yes, it's messy, but what case isn't?" He slid two diagrams into the center of the table. "This is Buckingham Palace," and he lightly tapped it with his fingers, "and this is the Palace of Westminster. Hawk, you and Cade are taking the Palace of Westminster, and I'm going to Buckingham Palace with Grant."

"Sounds good to me, mate." Hawk crossed his arms in his peculiar fashion as he leaned back in his seat

Looking over at Alex, Ian continued. "According to Tiernan, the cameras and security measures are to be taken care of at the Palace of Westminster first and Buckingham Palace second. Alex, you are certain you can manually take control of one system while you're stationed at the other, correct?"

Alex gave Ian a thumbs-up, his eyes never leaving his computer screen. "Sure thing, ol' chap. Wouldn't have said I could if I couldn't." He tried to make his voice sound confident, almost cocky, which was the exact opposite of what he was feeling inside. Just dealing with computers and cameras and wires didn't bother him – it was the impersonation of Damian's right hand man that freaked him out. Not to mention the entire plan of both the Mallevilles and Ian rested on him. He wasn't used to that much responsibility, and he wasn't all that gung-ho about it either. However, he would never admit that, and thus he put on a brave face and tried to keep his eyes focused on his computer as much as possible.

Flynn listened intently, throwing in his own two-pence-worth every now and then, and asking as many questions as he dared without being a nuisance. Part of him could hardly believe this was actually happening, yet the other part of him wanted to yell with excitement. The discussion went long into the night, and as the clock struck one, Flynn found himself struggling to keep his eyes open. He didn't realize he'd fallen asleep until he felt his uncle gently shaking his arm. Once upstairs, he tumbled into bed, vaguely wondering if all the plans had been figured out but not being fully awake enough to care very much. Sleep claimed him, and all thoughts of the Mallevilles faded away.

Everyone got up late Monday morning, save for Leslie and the two little boys, but despite the less-than-early start, the guys renewed their planning with vigor. Alex and Cade ran out in the afternoon to get some last minute equipment, while Hawk and Ian laid out the last few details with Grant.

Towards the evening, Leslie managed to pull Ian aside. "When exactly will everything start?" she asked anxiously.

"Tonight, or rather, very early this morning, around two-thirty, Alex is supposed to show up at the Palace of Westminster to take care of the cameras and alarms. We won't start getting into position for another hour or two. The Mallevilles plan to have the Queen kidnapped by six in the morning, but, of course, we intend to stop them before then." Ian stifled a yawn behind the back of his hand.

"You'll want to all go to bed early tonight, won't you?"

Ian nodded with a tired smile. "Yes, indeed." A thought struck him, and he asked abruptly, "When is your appointment?"

"Tomorrow at nine," she replied. "Do you know when you'll be home?"

"No, m'love, I don't," Ian said, sighing a little. "If this succeeds, there is going to be quite the mess to sort through, what with arrests and interrogations and the outrage of the trustworthy security staff at both locations. I'm guessing it will be sometime around or past dinner time. Don't worry about food or anything like that, okay? We'll get home when we get home, and I'll text you when it's all over." He gently wrapped his arms around her and held her for a few moments. "I don't know what will happen tomorrow, but I pray all goes well. We've been waiting for this day for two long years, Les, and I can hardly believe the end is in sight. It seems surreal."

Leslie looked up into his face, her expression calm and encouraging. "Don't dwell on it too much, Ian. Just take it one step at a time, and know that I will be praying for you and all the guys as hard as ever I can."

"I know m'love, and you don't know what a comfort that is." He gave her a light kiss before releasing her and heading upstairs. He found his nephew sitting on his bed, staring out the window. "Hey, you okay?"

Flynn jerked at the sound of his voice, having been deeply lost in thought. "Huh? Oh, yeah, sorry. Just thinking, that's all."

"May I inquire as to what?" Ian leaned on the doorframe and waited.

Twisting his hands in his lap, Flynn hesitated a little before replying. "I was just...going over in my head everything you guys have been planning the last two days. I guess I'm starting to get a little overwhelmed by it all." He stopped and looked furtively at his uncle. "I'll be honest. I'm scared. Not, like, frightened, or terrified, or anything like that but...I mean, this could go horribly, horribly wrong, and I don't...I don't want anything to happen to you. And I know you know the dangers, but I'm still getting used to it, you know? Agh, I'm not explaining it right." Rubbing his forehead, he sighed and let his gaze drop to the floor.

"No, no, you're explaining it just fine," Ian reassured him. "I have completely turned your life upside down in a very short amount of time, and I'm not surprised at all that you feel a little muddled, or scared even. Like you said, there is the potential for this plan to go really wrong really fast." Coming fully into the room, he stood in front of his nephew and continued. "But there is also the potential for this plan to succeed, and that is what you and I have to dwell on the most."

"I know." Flynn rubbed the back of his neck and said rather sheepishly. "I really wish I could go with you. I prefer being in the thick of things versus waiting to see how things turn out."

Ian gave a short laugh. "You'll get your chance soon enough! But for the time being, enjoy your evening, and your morning tomorrow with the boys. I'm guessing they're roping you into building with LEGOs?"

Flynn smiled. "Yeah, that's the plan. They also wanted to show me all their knights and stuff, so it looks like I'll be having a playdate for the first time in several years. Oh, I forgot to ask Aunt about lunch..." He swung his legs over the side of the bed and got to his feet. "I'd better check if we're fending for ourselves, or if I need to make something for her as well. Shouldn't you be off to bed?

"Yeah," Ian admitted grudgingly. "I hate going to bed when it's still light out, but I know I'll be thanking myself later. Goodnight, Flynn, and I'll see you tomorrow, okay?"

"You promise to text me when it's over?" Flynn stopped in the doorway and cast his uncle a pleading look.

"I promise," Ian answered firmly.

~

"Reporting for duty, sir." Otto gave Icabod what he thought was a smart salute.

"Don't act ridiculous. Is everything set for this morning?"

"Yes, sir. I contacted Lachlan, and he's all ready to go. Said he was going to get some shut-eye in anticipation of such an early start." Otto shifted nervously from one foot to the other. Icabod always seemed so angry and short, and Otto hated getting yelled at.

He was surprised when Icabod threw back his head and let loose a deep, evil laugh that reverberated through the room. "Tomorrow I shall become the richest and most famous man in all of the UK and her provinces! Victory – I can taste her sweetness on my tongue!"

"Don't gloat yet," Damian cautioned. "Victory is still several hours away."

"Oh, don't be such a spoil sport," Icabod said irritably. "What could possibly go wrong?"

Damian stared at Icabod's back. If looks could kill, his brother would be dead on the floor. Almost everything that could have gone wrong with his plan in the past week had done so, and at the moment, he wasn't entirely optimistic about the outcome of his plan's culmination. He most certainly would not be celebrating until it was all over and done with. Sighing internally, he concentrated on completing his contact with the rest of their crew. It appeared everything was a go for tomorrow; he only hoped it would stay that way until the very end.

He chided himself for depending so heavily on just one person: Peter Lachlan. Lachlan had run a series of complicated heists solely with technology, which is how the two had met. Damian had known him for well over ten years, and though Lachlan wasn't officially part of the Mallevilles, he often helped out whenever there was complicated tech involved. His knowledge of the latest technology was second to none, and he was one of the few people Damian actually respected. It was Lachlan's job to take control of all the security systems at both the Palace of Westminster and Buckingham Palace.

Damian realized that, technically, everything hinged on Lachlan. If just one camera wasn't hacked, or one alarm disabled, or one guard in the wrong place at the wrong time, everything could fall apart. He didn't like it, but there wasn't anything he could do about it now. His only comfort lay in Lachlan being, well, Lachlan — he always followed the plan, and always came out successful...unlike Ichabod. Damian shivered. Thank goodness his plans did *not* hinge on his older brother.

~

The sun still hadn't decided to wake up yet when Alex, disguised in heavy amounts of make-up and a security guard's uniform, approached a side gate to Buckingham Palace on foot. A name tag pinned to his uniform said "Peter Lachlan". Thanks to Tiernan, the real Lachlan had been apprehended earlier by Grant, but, of course, his arrest was kept hidden and thus the Mallevilles were completely in the dark.

"Fada beo an Banriona[1]," muttered the guard on duty.

"Fada beo an Mallevilles[2]," replied Alex boldly, yet in a low tone.

"You're a little late, Lachlan," growled the other, scowling. "They're waiting for you in the security base."

"Sorry." Alex, a.k.a. Lachlan, shrugged. "I had a lot to do at the Palace of Westminster, and it took me longer than I thought. You wouldn't believe the security they've got in that place!"

"Fine, fine, just get going," grumped the man as he let him in.

Lachlan was instantly joined by another supposed security guard the minute he stepped foot on the grounds. "You must be

---

[1] Gaelic for "Long live the queen."
[2] Gaelic for "Long live the Mallevilles."

Lachlan. I'm Jake. Damian said you were a whiz at hacking into stuff, but you sure took your sweet time at the Palace of Westminster."

Lachlan frowned. "I don't think you realize the depth of the systems we're dealing with here. This isn't like getting into a school computer system."

"Whatever. Follow me." Jake led Lachlan to the big room where all the cameras, laser detection beams, and security panels were. "We own half the cameras and sensors. You need to hack what's left — I've done the easy stuff. Got it?"

"Just leave it to me."

Jake watched him pull out his equipment for a minute or two. "Well, I've been up all night at this thing, so I'm going to catch a little shut eye before the big excitement starts."

"Okay," Lachlan said, watching him go, and muttering under his breath, "Only you're not gonna be so excited when *they* all jump out." Humming some old English sailor ditties, he began hacking the devices. So far, everyone he'd met had bought his disguise, hook, line, and sinker, and some of his nervousness had begun to fade, but not completely. All it would take was one person to realize he wasn't the real Lachlan, and everything would go down the drain.

"How's it going?" Ian's voice filtered through his earpiece.

"Fine. I've finished the Palace of Westminster and I'm in Buckingham Palace. Once I've hacked everything — sensors, alarms, cameras, etc. — I've got to re re-route them to my laptop. The Palace of Westminster took me longer than I thought, but

Damian already had a guy take care of the preliminary stuff here, so I can promise you everything will be set by five."

"Great work, Alex. If you need something, let me know and I'll see what I can do."

"I could use a full English breakfast."

"That's not what I meant, and you know it." Alex could hear the smile in Ian's voice.

"Well, you asked!"

It didn't take him long to finish hacking into the security systems. The difficult part lay in re-hacking everything so the Mallevilles thought they were in possession of all systems, when in reality, all it took was a switch and button and they would be out of commission.

Jake came to check on Lachlan a few minutes before five. His eyes were glossy, and he rubbed his face sleepily. "You finally done?" he asked, stifling a yawn.

"Yeah. I was just tuning a few things up."

"Then shut up and watch the screens," a foreign-sounding voice snarled from the doorway. It was Alvar Currito.

"O-kay!" Lachlan squeaked, dropping into a chair and gluing his eyeballs to the screens in front of him. A moment of panic swept over him. There was a good chance Alvar had met Lachlan before, unlike all the other Malleville members who he'd dealt with that morning. To Alex this was the ultimate test; if he could fool Alvar, he could fool anybody. Not that that made him feel any better...

"And if you see anyone," Currito continued, "and I mean anyone, who's not supposed to be there, you radio one of us immediately, *comprendo*? You have the sheet of positions, no?"

"Yes sir, that I do." Without tearing his gaze from the monitors, Lachlan held aloft two detailed maps of the Palace of Westminster and Buckingham Palace.

"*Excellenté*. Jake, get to your position. Icabod will be arriving soon, and I want everything in place when he does." Jake saluted and hurried away. Alvar scrutinized the screens for a moment or two before he himself left. He wasn't a computer person by any means, and he sincerely hoped Lahclan knew what he was doing.

Lachlan leaned back in his seat, reached down into his satchel with one arm, and removed a small bag of jellybabies. Technically, they were Ian's, but he couldn't hog them all for himself. Besides, he probably wouldn't even miss them.

The screens refreshed suddenly, and Lachlan glanced at his watch, a half-smile spreading across his face. His hacking had gone off without a hitch; all the security systems were now in his control, and he could set off any alarms needed and observe all movements of the Mallevilles inside both buildings.

Activating communication on his watch, he radioed Ian, saying, "It's a go. All systems are mine, and all the alarms ought to work. Obviously, I haven't been able to test them, but I'm confident it will work out."

"Good. Standby for those alarms."

"Right-O, Cap!" Alex dug into his ziploc bag and amused himself by tossing jellybabies up in the air and catching them in his mouth. He was pretty adept at it, having had many years of practice, but a few missed their mark, leaving him to get down on his hands and knees and find them. After no less than three of these mishaps, he refrained, knowing he needed to be keeping a steady eye on the consoles in front of him. Any unease still left in him had fled. He was completely alone, no Mallevilles were looking over his shoulder, and suddenly his job didn't seem all that scary any more.

~~

Chapter Twelve

IAN, STANDING INSIDE A SECRET ROOM within Buckingham Palace, switched his communication frequency to Hawk's and proceeded to relay Alex's message. "You and Cade are free to move in. Alert me when you've finished with that bomb."

"Here's hoping this doesn't take as long as I think it will. Bombs are tricky things." Hidden behind a clump of trees and bushes on the grounds of the Palace of Westminster, Hawk gave Cade a thumbs-up, and then radioed the SCO19 officers to begin moving in. Though simple, their plan had to be executed perfectly in order for it to succeed. Since they had a general idea of where some of the Mallevilles's gang would be stationed, thanks to the maps found at their headquarters, they essentially had to have SCO19 take them out, one by one, swiftly and silently. Once they reached the cellars and had located the bomb, it was Cade's job to disable it, after which Hawk would radio Ian to move in on the Mallevilles at Buckingham Palace.

Cade was an expert with explosives of any kind, and thus Hawk wasn't worried in the slightest about the man's ability to disable the bomb. Neither was he worried that the bomb could go off early if something went wrong, because it wouldn't. The Mallevilles had to save it in order for their kidnapping to happen successfully. He was, however, worried that if something went wrong at the Palace of Westminster, Icabod and the rest of the main gang would be alerted and get away before Ian and Grant had a chance to catch them.

"But it's a risk we have to take," he muttered to himself.

"Huh?" Cade whispered.

"Nothing." Hawk waved forward the first wave of SCO19, who carefully entered the Palace of Westminster through a side window. No alarms went off, thanks to Alex's careful hacking, and no Mallevilles streamed into the empty room, since Alex had complete control of the cameras and relayed no messages to Damian and his crew.

SCO19 did not question Hawk's authority, as he was posing as an officer with the same rank as Grant. To avoid being recognized, he'd been forced to have something of a make-over like Alex, though not as drastic. To say Hawk disliked it would have been an understatement. Make-up and disguises were not his thing, and he avoided them as much as possible. This time, though, it couldn't be helped; he only hoped he didn't look as ridiculous as he felt. Actually, he knew he didn't, since Alex and Leslie were dab hands at "doing them up", as they called it, but it still bothered him.

Cade was posing as none-other than…himself. Everyone in Scotland Yard knew he was an explosives expert, so there was no need for him to take on a different identity, let alone have to suffer in the make-up department. Hawk silently envied him.

The two men waited by the window, both on pins and needles. No yelling or bursts of gunfire met their ears as the minutes ticked by with painful monotony. Hawk kept glancing irritably at his watch, wishing this part of the mission could be over. He would feel infinity more at ease once they had just a bomb to deal with.

Five minutes. Ten. A half hour slipped by.

"Is it supposed to take this long?" Cade whispered.

"Yes. They have to take out the guards one at a time, and move them to a different area of the building where they will be held until everything's over and done with at Buckingham Palace, remember? Icabod can't have any idea anything unusual is going on over here." He stopped abruptly as a voice filtered through his ear piece.

"The coast is clear, sir. We have eliminated all targets, and have checked the cellars thoroughly. We located the bomb, sir, and are awaiting further orders." The voice was clipped and confident, with a hint of triumph. It was the same officer whom Ian had spoken with at the Malleville's old headquarters.

"Excellent. I shall be there directly; wait for me."

"Yes, sir."

"We're clear," Hawk relayed to Cade. "Follow me." The two men entered the building via the window and hurriedly made their way to the cellar entrance, which was guarded by four SCO19. They moved to let the two pass, and soon Cade and Hawk found themselves descending the steps into the cold tunnels. The lights had been turned on, and it didn't take them long to find more SCO19 guarding the bomb.

The officer who had spoken to Hawk minutes earlier, (Arthur Colman by name,) stepped forward, saying, "As you can see, sir, it's a very sophisticated bomb. I'm not entirely sure you can disable it without setting it off."

Hawk eyed the device, which was set in the corner of the foundation and had been hidden by several large barrels. These had been rolled aside with some difficulty, and several of the SCO19 were still panting from the effort. "I'm no dab hand when it comes to explosives of that caliber," he said, motioning towards it with his hand. "Have at it, Cade."

Cade slung a light satchel of tools off his shoulder, knelt down on the stone floor, and rummaged through what he'd brought before selecting a few interesting-looking gadgets and inspecting the bomb. "Arthur's right," he said after a few minutes. "I can take the bomb off the wall, but I can't turn it off without detonating it." He softly tapped the intricate wires. "Whoever made this really knew what they were doing."

Hawk scowled at the device, several plans running through his mind. "We have to get it out of here. Can't you...put it on stand-by or something?"

Cade chuckled mirthlessly. "That's one way of putting it, and yes I can. It's rigged up to a mobile phone remote, which Icabod probably has possession of. Or Damian. Probably Damian, but anyways. I can disconnect the remote, which means, (unless you're an idiot and handle it roughly,) the only way to set it off is to do it manually. And whoever did it would be blown to smithereens." He got back down on his knees and searched through his bag until he found what he wanted. "It will take me a few minutes, but I can do it. How much time do I have?"

"Five minutes at the most," Hawk answered, glancing at his watch. He and SCO19 watched in silence as Cade carefully tinkered with the explosive. Several of the officers looked nervous, and jumped involuntarily every time Cade's tools made an unusually loud noise that echoed off the stone walls. Hawk remained impassive. Cade knew his stuff; he simply needed to do it as fast as was humanly possible.

~

Ian shifted his position for the hundredth time. He and the guys had agreed to communicate only when necessary, be that to alert the others that all was well for the next step, check in if they had gone past the allotted time, or warn the others in case of an emergency or a plan gone awry. Thus, he could only assume everything was going smoothly on Hawk's and Cade's end.

Ian didn't like assuming missions or people were okay. He wanted to know definitely, and as soon as possible. Hawk's voice came suddenly over his earpiece, causing him to jerk upright.

"We're all set. It couldn't be entirely disabled without detonating it, but Cade disconnected the mobile remote, so the Mallevilles have no power over it."

Ian nodded, his jaw set, a grim look in his eyes. "Good to hear. I'll let you know when it's over."

"Be careful, mate."

"I will." Ian switched the frequency over to Alex but said nothing. It wasn't time for the alarms just yet. He shifted his position yet again, feeling vaguely uneasy. Though he was confident in Alex's technological abilities, not to mention his acting, he still had cause for concern. There was a very real chance that someone would realize he wasn't the real Lachlan after all. Ian smiled wryly to himself. Both his plan and Damian's plan rested on the shoulders of one man. How ironic.

"Is it just me, or is it a mite stuffy in here?" Grant asked softly.

"A little, but it won't be for too much longer," Ian said. He, Grant, and half-a-dozen SCO19 officers were stuffed into a secret communication compartment inside the Palace. The Queen had a secret door that led from her apartments into the White Drawing Room, and there was just enough space between the two doors to accommodate several people.

The Mallevilles's plan to kidnap the Queen was actually quite simple, but dreadfully disrespectful. Disguised as flower delivery men, they were stowing themselves along with a driver they had bought off. They planned to take one of the large flower coolers into the Palace, which would brook no suspicion from the servants and people in charge. Then, they intended to make a bee-line for the White Drawing Room, get into the Queen's apartments via the secret door, stuff her in the cooler, and calmly walk out of the Palace and into the waiting flower delivery van.

This involved far less security guard corrupting than the Palace of Westminster, and relied more on ensuring the cameras and alarms were taken care of and monitored by those within their group. Ian almost chuckled as he imagined the looks on their faces when they opened the secret door and were greeted by SCO19.

It had taken a lot of persuading, and even some raised voices, to convince the Head of Security to let them do the job their way, and leave him and his security staff out of it. His staff couldn't be entirely trusted, whether he liked that fact or not, and nobody could know something was up. Playing the Mallevilles was like snake charming: possible to do, and incredibly dangerous, but make one wrong move and it was over.

Ian checked his watch, squinting at the brightness of the screen. Luminescent green numbers glowed back at him: 5:45 a.m. "They ought to be here any minute," he whispered. "Get ready."

Over his ear piece, Alex relayed excitedly, "They're coming, Cap. The truck pulled up, and they're on their way to the White Drawing Room now! Man, that's a big cooler..."

~

It didn't take very long for the three men to reach the White Drawing Room. Icabod took the lead, while Damian and Axel rolled a large cooler behind him, the word FLOWERS printed in bold letters on the side. Nobody really paid them any attention, and they entered the room without a single challenge.

"I told you this would be easy," Icabod muttered.

Damian said nothing. Of course the disguise part was easy. But the preparations for this very moment? Not so much.

The White Drawing Room was spectacular, but the men took little notice of the bright white walls gilded with gold, the massive gold and glass chandeliers, or the red and gold rug that covered the floor, let alone the elegant furniture. They were only interested with a mirror that stretched from the top of a large vanity up to the ceiling. The mirror and vanity were actually a hidden door that led into the tiny room where Ian and SCO19 waited. They, however, expected the space to be empty, allowing them to open the real door on the other side, letting them into the Queen's apartments.

Icabod took hold of the edge of the mirror and swung the hidden door open. Their expectations shattered, the three men stared at the officers in complete shock. Before they could make a move, SCO19 cocked their guns, and Grant stepped forward.

"Icabod Malleville, Damian Malleville, Axel Crane: you are all under arrest for numerous crimes against Her Majesty and the United Kingdom, not the least of which is breaching security at both the Palace of Westminster and Buckingham Palace, planning to blow up part of the Palace of Westminster, and for attempting to kidnap Her Royal Majesty, the Queen of England."

As Grant spoke, more SCO19, who had been hidden in nearby rooms, came pouring in behind the criminals. Icabod gnashed his teeth, but held up his hands. Resistance was not an option, due to all those guns trained on his back and chest. Grant attempted to begin explaining their rights, when an earsplitting screech drowned him out. Ian covered his ears and stifled a grin. The entire Palace echoed with alarms, and he could hear the

Queen's corgis howling in protest. In order to put the castle on high alert, Alex had been instructed to set them all off simultaneously. It was also the go sign for the SCO19 planted around the Palace to begin rounding up and temporarily replacing the Palace security guards.

"I told you we ought to have waited!" Damian screamed, heedless of the officers around him. "You ruined everything, you hear me? Everything! This is all your fault!" His eyes sparked viciously as he turned on his older brother.

Icabod back handed him with all his strength, causing the younger man to crumple to his knees. "My fault? I don't think so! You're the brains, you idiot!"

SCO19 separated them before they could go at it hammer and tongs. Axel attempted to rush one of the officers, but found his arms wrenched painfully behind his back before he even realized what was happening. Still in the compartment, Ian looked away from Axel's face. He could read lips, and was suddenly thankful for the blaring alarms that drowned out the man's string of obscenities.

"Okay, Tuck, I think everyone gets the idea," he yelled into his watch. "Shut 'em down."

Alex clawed at his ear. "Whoa, you don't have to rupture my eardrums!" Sliding his hands over the controls, he manually shut down all the alarms, returning the Palace to silence. Well, not exactly silence, since everyone was running around wondering just what the dickens was happening. And judging from the honking horns, backed up traffic, and hundreds of bystanders, he figured the populace was wondering the same thing. Grinning, he popped several jellybabies into his mouth. This would be a day neither he nor London would forget anytime soon.

~

As was to be imagined, Buckingham Palace was in uproar. Reporters swarmed the gates, demanding to know if a terrorist attack was being thwarted, or if fire had broken out in the Royals' bedchambers. Bystanders gawked at the amount of security personnel that flooded the place and refused to let anyone in or out. Ian, Grant, and the Head of Security found themselves at the center of the hubbub, trying to calm panicky servants, relay an explanation of the ruckus to Her Majesty, and of course deal with all the Mi5, Mi6, and special police agents who had absolutely no idea what had gone on or what was happening.

When the dust settled and Ian and his crew were allowed to return home, the sun was starting to sink on the horizon. Cade said goodnight to the guys in the driveway and headed to his place for some much-needed sleep. Upon entering the house, the rest of the guys found themselves surrounded by two bouncy little boys and bombarded by questions from Flynn. Lukas and Sean didn't know everything, but they understood enough to know that something important had happened in their dads' case, and wanted to hear the story.

"Tomorrow," Ian promised them. "We'll tell you the story tomorrow, okay? It's super late; you ought to be in bed."

Sean wrapped his arms around Ian and held on tight. "Awww, but I don't wanna go to bed. I ain't tired. Can't I stay up with you?"

Ian gave a short laugh. "I'm not staying up any longer than you are. I'm absolutely knackered."

"Why, Dad?" Sean demanded.

"'Cause he got up at two in the morning, that's why," Lukas answered. "Right, Dad?" and he peered inquisitively into Hawk's face.

Hawk nodded and tousled the little boy's hair. "Yeah, that's right. And you were crazy enough to get up then, too, and wave goodbye. Did you go back to sleep?"

"Yup." Lukas nodded vigorously. "And I almost missed waffles. Dad, did you know Flynn can make waffles? They're good, and he puts chocolate chips in 'em, like Mum used to. Can I have them tomorrow, too?"

"That depends entirely if Flynn wants to make them again," Hawk replied, stifling a yawn.

Lukas turned his big blue eyes pleadingly to Flynn. "Please?"

"Of course. I don't mind." Flynn turned to his uncle and held out his hands. "Hey, give me your gear, and I'll put it away. You look like you're about to fall asleep standing up."

Ian gave his nephew a tired smile. "I probably could if I stood in one place long enough."

"And then you'd fall over and crack your skull on the kitchen floor," Alex interjected, wrestling his equipment through the doorway. "Wouldn't that be a sight."

"Thank you, Alex, for that lovely image."

"Anytime."

Ian rolled his eyes and removed his vest and gun. "Thanks, Flynn. I'll see you in the morning."

How he made it up the stairs, Ian never knew. All the stress and pressure of the past few weeks, combined with lack of sleep and all the goings on of the day, crashed in on him at once, and he felt as though he could sleep for days. Opening the door to his room, he gave it a light shove with his foot to close it and collapsed on his back on the bed with a huge sigh. "What a day..."

Leslie came out of the wardrobe through the bathroom and gave him a sympathetic look. "You've got to be knackered."

"Completely." He forced himself to sit up. "I still can't believe it's over. Just like that. All those years of hard work and frustration and prayers and...bam. Done with. I think I ought to be more excited, but I suppose the reality hasn't sunk in just yet."

"I have a feeling it will sink in by the morning, after you've had a good night's rest, and then you'll be as giddy as a school boy." Leslie tightened the tie on her dressing gown and smiled at him.

"Probably." He loosened his necktie and was about to unbutton his shirt when he noticed his wife's face. Her smile was as wide as it could possibly be, her eyes danced in the low light, and her face seemed to glow with happiness. He figured she was as ecstatic about the culmination of the case as he would be, (after a good night's rest,) but there was something more to it, something he just couldn't put his finger on. "What?"

Leslie giggled softly. "I was going to tell you tomorrow, under more, oh, I don't know, fancy circumstances? But I can't wait! Unless, of course, you're too tired?"

"No, no, I want to know. Tell me what?" Ian raised an eyebrow as he stood up and laid his tie down on the dresser.

Leslie was unable to contain another giggle of excitement, and a little shiver went up and down her spine. "Ian, I'm pregnant."

Ian froze and whirled to face her. He blinked rapidly, not fully comprehending what she had said. "You're...you're...*what?*" He hadn't expected to hear her say those words again, and he wasn't entirely sure he'd heard her right.

"I'm pregnant," Leslie repeated, enjoying the look of utter and complete shock stamped on her husband's face.

They were both so engrossed with each other, neither of them heard Flynn come up the stairs and stop before their door, which was slightly ajar. Ian had left a few things inside his vest pockets, including some receipts, and since Flynn knew he hated clutter, he had refrained from putting them on his desk and thought he'd just ask him where he wanted them instead. Flynn raised his hand to knock, but caught sight of his uncle standing in front of his aunt, looking both stunned and delighted. He watched as Ian asked her, "Are you serious?"

Leslie looked blissfully happy as she nodded and said, "*Yes!*" Ian stared at her, a huge smile on his face, then suddenly pulled her to him and kissed her longer than usual. Slightly embarrassed at this display of emotion, Flynn dropped his eyes and quickly backed away. The desk would be just fine.

~

As was to be expected, the guys slept in the next morning. Leslie and Flynn set about making them a brunch for when they got up, and the little boys clamored to help. Flynn showed them how to make waffles, and at Sean's begging, Leslie allowed it to be their science experiment...even though it wasn't even school season. But what did the boys care? An experiment was an experiment, and if it was cool, then the time of year didn't matter.

Brunch was served around eleven, and by that time everyone was up and ready for the day. Well, mostly ready. Alex had been the last one up, and thus his hair was still damp from the shower and stuck all over the place. He also hadn't decided what he wanted to wear, and was sporting a wrinkled Avengers t-shirt. Not that his breakfast attire was anything new. Unless it was Sunday, or they had plans, Alex never put on what he was actually going to wear; he just threw on whatever was within reach. Breakfast was far more important than one's attire.

"I don't think I could have envisioned the case to end the way it did," Ian said as he helped himself to the Science Experiment, as the boys demanded it be called. He, Hawk, and Alex had given the others a very brief run-down of the chain of events, due to the little boy's presence. Both Leslie and Flynn knew they would get more details later.

"Me either," Hawk agreed. "And I'm so thankful God enabled us to protect the innocent and bring justice to the guilty, and especially for keeping us safe in the process." Handing a butter knife to Lukas, he continued: "I, for one, am thoroughly glad the Malleville case is wrapped up on our end, and I'm looking forward to a bit of respite."

"Yeah. It's been a wild ride these past few months!" Alex dumped a generous amount of syrup on his plate and glanced guiltily at Leslie. She wasn't looking at him, though, and he quickly spun his plate so as to keep it hidden.

"That looks like syrup soup, Uncle Alex," Sean whispered loudly.

Alex knit his brows and gave him an *are-you-serious* look. "Wow, ya think?"

Lukas stifled a giggle. "You're not supposed to say anything," he whispered back to Sean across the table.

"Oh. Whoops."

"Did you see the paper?" Flynn was saying. The syrup episode had gone virtually unnoticed by the rest of the occupants of the table. "It's all over the front page. Big, bold type: *Scotland Yard Strikes Again.*"

"Let me see that." Hawk picked it up and skimmed the article. "The press certainly got the facts the way we wanted them. No names, little info...looks good to me."

Alex reached out and snatched it away. "Bor-ring. Why, this guy has no idea how to write! This is flat, super flat. I could've written it better."

"The good news is the press didn't get sensitive details," Hawk broke in. "I personally don't want my name plastered all over Europe as the guy who caught the Mallevilles. They had a lot of influence, and I have a feeling several more little empires will come crashing down after this, and I don't want to be in the middle of it. The author did just fine, in my opinion."

Alex waved a hand impatiently. "Yeah, yeah, I'm not arguing with that. I'm saying his grammar and verbiage is severely wanting." He pointed viciously to a sentence and rattled off in a high voice, 'Striking six, the clock ran out of time for the Mallevilles.' Are you kidding me? That is just...no, just no. How does this guy even get paid?" Alex's rambling slowly faded to a light mutter, and finally vanished altogether as he silently corrected every grammar issue within the article.

A mutual look passed between Ian and Leslie, which did not go unnoticed by Hawk. "What?"

Ian's face broke into a huge smile. "Leslie and I have some more good news." He stopped, and glanced at his wife again.

Hawk instantly comprehended, and dropped his fork in surprise. "Are you serious?" he asked, echoing Ian's words from the night before.

"Huh? Serious about what? I'm missing something here." Alex broke off his internal rant about what actually constituted a dangling participle, and looked up from the newspaper.

Leslie laughed merrily and her eyes sparkled. "I thought I was having trouble with my allergies, but it turns out that's not the case. I'm pregnant!"

Instantly, the room was full of congratulations, exclamations of surprise and excitement, and even a few hugs. Sean and Lukas clamored to know if it was a girl or a boy, and Flynn grinned slightly to himself as he remembered what he'd witnessed the night previous; however, he wisely kept his mouth shut on that score. Alex almost fell out of his chair, and demanded to know how Hawk knew ahead of time. Hawk protested that he merely guessed it the minute Ian implied it.

"Come on, Mum, tell me what it is!" Sean begged.

"I don't know, Sean. It's too early to tell," Leslie explained.

"Why?" Lukas asked.

"Babies take a while to grow, Lukas dear, so you'll just have to wait a few months."

"Awww." Lukas looked very disappointed. "But we want to know *now*."

"Yeah, 'cause if it's a boy then that means he'll like LEGOs, and if it's a girl then we're in trouble," Sean agreed.

"Why in the world would you be in trouble?" Flynn asked.

"Because girls like dolls, not LEGOs!" Sean looked rather upset as he imagined his house strewn with baby dolls and pink ribbons.

"Not necessarily. My sis hated dolls, and she was more of a LEGO fanatic than I was," Alex piped up.

"Really?" Sean perked up at this. "Well, I guess if Luke and I teach her right, then it doesn't matter what it is." He smiled, thinking he must have said something very smart, as everyone at the table laughed.

After brunch, Flynn went upstairs to his room and checked his phone. Von had texted him a few minutes earlier, saying she'd heard about the Mallevilles on the news, begging him to give her a ring. He dialed her number and it hardly rang once before she answered.

"Hey Flynn."

"Hey, Von. So you heard the news, then?"

"I sure did. And I wanted to know if your uncle was involved in any way, him being a copper and all. Because, if he was, then you'd know more details than the press." He heard the rustle of a newspaper in the background. "This paper is horribly vague! And it has some serious grammar issues, but…"

Flynn could picture the cute little shrug of her shoulders as her sentence trailed off. "Regular coppers didn't do very much," he said, trying his best to skirt the issue without outright lying to her. "SCO19 did most of the work, you know. But hey, if my uncle gets some more details that weren't in the paper, and he's allowed to share them, I'll tell you first thing, okay?"

Von sighed. "Okay. But don't forget to ask him."

"I won't." The two chatted for a few more minutes before Flynn hung up and slipped the phone into his pocket. He glanced out the window and was pleased to see the sun was shining out amidst the clouds. Without a moment's hesitation, he opened his window, raised the screen, and leaned out to get a better view.

"I love it when the sun shines." Flynn looked over his shoulder to see his uncle leaning in the doorframe.

"Me too." He turned his gaze back outside. "I feel a little dazed," he added before he even realized what he was saying.

"And why is that?" Ian asked with some concern.

"I just..." Flynn shut the screen, fell into the window seat, and looked over at his uncle. "Less than a month ago, I finished school, graduated, packed, and flew here to live with you, where I proceeded to get shot, raid a headquarters, travel to Holy Island, re-raid the headquarters, and spend a nail-biting couple days at home while you take out one of the most dangerous gangs in the UK, and now it's suddenly all over and I find out my aunt is finally pregnant. I think it's perfectly normal for my brain to spin a bit, don't you?"

Ian chuckled and took a seat next to him. "Indubitably, my dear nephew. Though I'm—"

"Ah-ah-ah, if you apologize one more time..." Flynn raised a hand to stop his uncle from continuing.

Ian leaned back in the window seat. "My work is going to be rather dull without your shenanigans when you go off to university," he observed.

Flynn threw a small pillow at him. "That's several months away, so don't even think about it just yet. I know I'm not!" He rested his left foot on his right knee and sighed happily. "I'm really looking forward to the simulation training you're planning on giving me this summer. Oh yes, and the driving lessons."

Ian grinned. "Me too. And you know what? I think you're going to be an ace at it."

"Really? I hope so. I mean, I know I have a lot of stuff to learn, but—"

"You'll do just fine. And with those razor-sharp observation skills of yours, you'll become a valuable asset in no time." Ian winked at him.

"So, when do we start?" Flynn asked eagerly.

Ian held up a hand. "Whoa, let's give it at least a week, shall we? Things have been pretty crazy around here lately, and I think we all need a few days of relaxation." A thought seemed to hit him, and he raised an eyebrow. "Hey, I owe you a ride in the BMW, don't I?"

Flynn didn't think he could smile any wider, but apparently he could. "You sure do!"

"Let me see if Leslie needs anything, and if not, you up for a spin?"

"Are you even asking?"

Ian got up and hurried down to his room. Flynn went to the kitchen in anticipation of the drive and found Alex making a Ribena-and-Sprite-on-the-rocks, as he liked to call it. "Want one?" he asked, stirring the mixture with the back end of a long spoon.

"No thanks, not now. Uncle might take me out in the BMW." Flynn leaned on the counter.

"Ooh, niiiice. Do tell him to take a good CD, though, like Hawk's *Driving With The Top Down Medley*. Best hits ever for a sports car, custom made by him and Carliss." Alex sipped the foam off the top of his drink, wincing at the fizziness.

"No, we are *not* taking that CD," Ian said emphatically, coming in the kitchen. "You and Hawk can kill your eardrums, but not me. Ready, Flynn?"

"Oh yeah!" Flynn soon found himself in the passenger seat of his uncle's BMW, speeding down the highway with the windows rolled down. "God has been so good to us, Uncle," he said as the wind whipped through his hair.

"He most certainly has," Ian agreed.

"Sometimes I wonder what would have happened if He hadn't allowed certain things to be," Flynn continued. "But you know something? I'm perfectly content with life as it is. I really can't imagine it to be any better than it already has been."

"Even amidst the hardships?" Flynn nodded. "You're wise beyond your years," Ian said with a smile. "It takes a lot of people most of their lives to realize that hardships are a result of this fallen world, and you can either accept them, (since God allowed them into your life,) and move on, or live the rest of your life wishing for what might have been." He shook his head. "You've grown up so much, you know, and I'm incredibly proud of you."

Flynn ducked his head at the praise. "That means a lot," he said in a low tone. "And you know? Even though you're my uncle, you've really been the dad I never had." He turned to smile at his uncle, and was surprised to find Ian's eyes glistening, as though with unshed tears. Ian was about to say something, when Flynn's eyes shifted to the radio. "What the bloody dickens is *that*?" he cried, abruptly ruining the moment.

Ian turned the volume up to better hear what was playing. "Uhm, it's a CD of some famous opera pieces. That's something by Monteverdi, I think?"

Flynn covered his ears. "Even I have limits to what you term 'classical music.'"

"Aw, come on, that singer has an amazing vocal range," Ian argued.

"She's drowning while being strangled! If you don't shut that off, I'm jumping out." Flynn winced as the singer hit a particularly high note and pressed his hands tighter against his head. "You do know this ride was supposed to prove that your music is better than Hawk's, right?"

Ian made a face and rummaged in the CD compartment to find a different selection of music. "He's spoiled your ears." He glanced up at the rode, hit the cruise control, and looked down to make sure he could find what he was looking for. "Ah, here we go. Try this." Ian took out the opera disc and inserted something else.

As the sound of soft jazz filtered through the car, Flynn jerked his hands down from his ears and stared at the radio. "That's...that's...I *know* this music."

Ian placed the CD case in his nephew's lap. "*Jazz For A Lazy Day*. It was Jack's favorite."

Flynn looked at the case, leaned back in his seat, and closed his eyes. He couldn't remember the last time he'd heard that CD, but somehow he knew every note. Slowly, a smile slipped across his features. "You win, Uncle," he said. "Hawk's music is pretty dench, but this beats anything he can come up with any day of the week."

Ian grinned and poured on a little more speed. "My thoughts exactly, my dear nephew."

~~

Finis

~~

A Word From The Author

Obviously, all the characters in my story are entirely made up, save for the Queen herself. However, all the places I have used are, in fact, real. Even Ian's house is real, but I have refrained from mentioning the address as I do not own the house, and I have done some minor modifications to the blueprint. So, while the location is correct, the house does not exist exactly how it is described.

I have also used a smattering of British words throughout, since it makes more sense in my mind for British people to refer to things in their own way, and not like me, an American. (However, if you're reading this, I'm assuming you have already run into those words and know exactly what I'm talking about. If not, then why are you reading the back of the book first? Peeker.)

I got mixed views on this from my Beta readers — some said it made the story feel more British, and others said it was weird, since I'm an American living in, and publishing this book in, America. I opted to keep the words in, and have included a glossary in case you're left scratching your head over such things as "the boot," "hundreds and thousands," "dench," and so on. And if you happen to be British...well, here's hoping my research paid off and you're not laughing at me!

~

Glossary Of British Words

Ace – cool

Anorak – a nerd, braniac, more of an insult...

Barmy – crazy

Boot – trunk of a car

Chockablock – full to the brim

Crisps – potato chips

Dab hand – an expert at something

Dench – cool

Draughts – checkers, (the game)

Dressing gown – bathrobe

Flat – apartment

Flick knife – switchblade

Football – soccer

HMP – Her Majesty's Prison

Holiday – vacation

Hundreds and thousands – sprinkles

Jellybabies – jellybeans

Knackered – tired

Lorry – semi-truck

Number plate – license plate

Primary school – elementary school

Ring – call

Ring me a bell – call me

Spook – secret service agent, usually Mi5 or Mi6

Stock – inventory
Suss out – figure out
Ta – thanks/thank you
Trainers – tennis shoes
University – college
Wardrobe – closet
Whinging – whining

Acknowledgements

I want to thank, first of all, my dear parents for all they have done to encourage me in my writing. Dad, you got on me time and again to research things I didn't even know needed researching, kept me on track when I got distracted, helped me with the final edits, and always encouraged me to keep on writing and just get something published already! Mum, you listened to hours and hours worth of brainstorms and rants, and edited and edited until you and me were blue in the face – the entire process was a blast, and I am so indebted to you! As for my Beta readers, Leia, Zannah, Nao, and Mo: thank you for listening to me blab on and on about my story for years, (literally!) for answering all my random DM's and emails whenever I was stuck or frustrated or getting railroaded by my characters, and for all the helpful tips, edits, and ideas you gave me. To all of you mentioned here: I can never thank you enough. Without you, this would never have been possible. And finally, thank you to my Lord and Savior, Jesus Christ, for giving me the ability to write – may every book and story be for His glory!

About The Author

H.L. Roethle is a Christian author who has always had a passion for books. She has always loved reading stories, and began writing her own at a young age. Manuscripts – some finished, some not – began to pile up for over ten years until she finally decided to start publishing them. At the time of this publication, she lives in Kentucky with her family and little blue Betta, Finn. When she's not writing a book, (or two or three,) she's reading one...or two...or three...okay, make that a stack. Visit her website at www.hlroethlebooks.com.

67362911R00170

Made in the USA
Columbia, SC
25 July 2019